FLY BY NIGHT

A "Michelle Reagan" Novel
by
SCOTT SHINBERG

FLY BY NIGHT
Michelle Reagan – Book 3
Copyright © 2020 by Scott Shinberg

SECOND EDITION SOFTCOVER
ISBN: 1622537106
ISBN-13: 978-1-62253-710-5

Editor: Becky Stephens
Cover Artist: Briana Hertzog
Interior Designer: Lane Diamond

EVOLVED PUBLISHING™

www.EvolvedPub.com
Evolved Publishing LLC
Butler, Wisconsin, USA

Printed in Book Antiqua font.

BOOKS BY SCOTT SHINBERG

MICHELLE REAGAN
Book 1: *Confessions of Eden*
Book 2: *Directive One*
Book 3: *Fly by Night*
Book 4: *Sargon the Third*
Book 5: *A Shot in the Dark*
Book 6: *Kill Box*

DEDICATION

The core of the bad guys' plans in Fly by Night *came to me in a nightmare about a dozen years ago. I dreamt I was walking along a street in Vancouver, Canada, watching the terrorists' horrific attack unfold around me. I've never even been to Vancouver (at least as far as you know), so I have no idea why my subconscious picked that city, but the dream certainly made an impression on me. That night, I awoke suddenly and thought to myself, "Holy crap, that could actually happen, even today."*

It's only appropriate, then, for me to dedicate this novel to those who work so hard to prevent such attacks. Brave men and women risk their lives every day and night to keep terrorists out of our country in the first place, and, when that's not possible, they are our first responders who fly, drive, run, or crawl, into harm's way when the you-know-what hits the fan. To each and every one of them, thank you for everything you do.

Finally, to a firehouse captain and his team who let a half-dozen of us use their station's basement a long time ago, my thanks to you and your team of first responders. Thank you for both extending to us every courtesy and also not asking too many questions about all the electronics we trudged into your station and the antennas we stuck to the top of your building.

FLY BY NIGHT

A Michelle Reagan Novel
Book 3

SCOTT SHINBERG

Chapter 1

Mosul, Iraq

Michelle Reagan—CIA codename Eden—aimed the glow-in-the-dark Trijicon sights of her Sig Sauer pistol at the woman lying on the floor. Shadows flickered against the wall of the dark room as Michelle looked down, and said, "The farmer planted seven rows of corn."

Michelle did the calculations in her head—she had only two .45 caliber bullets remaining in her pistol. The woman in the soiled nightgown had only a few seconds to answer correctly. If she did not, Michelle would send both remaining rounds ripping into her target's chest before reloading and firing a third shot through the mop of stringy brown hair on the woman's head to end the mission decisively. Maybe not successfully, but certainly decisively.

The woman's faint voice answered Michelle slowly, drawing the words out as she searched through her cluttered mental filing cabinet for a memory from long ago. "Black crows ate all but three."

Michelle squinted at the thirty-something woman sprawled on an inch-thick mattress. Dark streaks ran across what had probably started as a white nightgown but looked green in the tint of Michelle's night vision goggles. Everything looks green in NVGs. The tactical operator from the CIA's Special Activities Center—the famed SAC—continued the challenge-response exchange with the woman in the sights of her silenced pistol. "His wife likes baking pies in the evening."

Anxious for a reply, Michelle shifted her weight from one foot to the other. The creak of a loose floorboard broke the eerie stillness of the house. At the sound, Michelle's eyes instinctively glanced toward the bedroom door. Everything sounds ominous at three o'clock in the morning when you're surrounded by a house full of corpses.

"But his son doesn't like boysenberry," the woman said resolutely. A thin smile formed on her lips.

Michelle tucked her pistol into the holster under her left shoulder, looked at her partner, Alex Ramirez, and said, "It's her. It's Bella Cirrone."

Alex nodded, agreeing that the CIA officer who went missing two years earlier had correctly completed the identification challenge.

Michelle reached under Bella's shoulders and lifted the frail woman to her feet. "We're Americans, Bella. We're Agency and here to rescue you. Come with us. We'll take you home."

"Ho-*ohme*?" the woman's faint voice repeated, cracking as she uttered the magic word. "Home?" she repeated more clearly.

"You bet. Baseball, apple pie, fireworks on the Fourth of July, and—my personal favorite—chocolate chip cookie dough ice cream. Here, lean on me and we'll get you to the SUV outside."

Bella put her hand on Michelle's shoulder. "I can... walk," the drowsy woman said, and proceeded to stumble as she tried to gain her footing in the dark.

"Okay," Michelle replied softly. She reached her left arm around Bella's waist as much to control as to guide the disoriented woman.

Alex led the way downstairs and out the front door. He scanned up and down the street using his NVGs to confirm it was devoid of pedestrians or anyone looking suspicious—not always the case, even at 3 a.m. in a city rocked by interminable violence for so many years. "Clear," he quietly advised his two companions.

He led the women to the SUV parked around the corner and started the engine while Michelle poured Bella's listless and emaciated frame into the back seat. Michelle climbed in and helped Bella secure the seat belt.

The thirty-minute ride to the US military base northeast of the city proved uneventful. Alex dimmed the SUV's headlights as they approached the guardhouse and showed his identification to the Kurdish Peshmerga soldiers protecting the base and its airfield.

Inside the compound, he parked the dust-caked vehicle outside a large green tent serving as the Air Operations Center. At a small metal table inside, two CIA helicopter pilots sat on folding metal chairs. The pilots who had flown Alex and Michelle up from the Army's Forward Operating Base at the Tal Afar airport—FOB Sykes—the previous afternoon peered over aeronautical charts of northwestern Iraq and sipped coffee as they planned their return flight. One pilot waved at Alex as the former Navy SEAL entered.

"Got our girl. Let's get going," he advised the chopper crew.

"Sierra Hotel!" the pilot replied. "Good job, from the looks of it." He slapped his co-pilot on the shoulder, and said, "Let's get this bird in the air."

The flight through unusually calm air lasted only forty-five minutes.

After touching down, Michelle led Bella to the female barracks where the rescued CIA case officer showered. Michelle paced the room and repeatedly looked at her watch while Bella stood in front of the bathroom mirror and attempted to brush a tangle of knots from the hair hanging over her left shoulder. After five minutes, she admitted defeat and changed into sweatpants and a plain gray t-shirt emblazoned with "US Army" in black letters across its front.

"The shower felt good," Bella said as she sat down on the edge of a cot with a bare mattress.

While the woman's words were positive, Michelle couldn't find an expression on her charge's face to match it. "I'll bet it did. Would you like something to eat?"

Bella shook her head. "No, my stomach's still not sitting right from the flight. You know the way helicopters vibrate, and... Well, I'm not much for flying. I'd just like to lie down for a bit."

Michelle set Bella up with clean linens, a pillow, and an olive-drab Army blanket on the bunk bed above her own. She gave her guest the sleep mask she'd saved from the commercial flight from Germany to Baghdad a week earlier.

Bella slept until after 10 a.m. Once dressed, she dutifully followed Michelle to the base's main dining hall for breakfast and then across the street to the medical clinic where an Army physician would give the newly returned CIA case officer from the Directorate of Operations a thorough physical. Two years of captivity in Iraq had taken its toll on the field officer. A shower and shampoo may have removed the superficial grime from Bella's pale skin, but Michelle fretted that she couldn't find anything resembling joy at being saved in the eyes of her new companion.

Michelle checked Bella into the clinic and smiled. Closing the door behind her on that late-November morning also successfully closed out her mission in Iraq.

She got a cup of coffee with one cream and one sugar at the dining hall and found her partner at a picnic table outside.

Alex was devouring a second helping of eggs over easy and a few pieces of turkey bacon that he felt were just as tasty as the real thing, but not nearly as artery-clogging. He held up a slice of faux-bacon and wagged it at Michelle. "Happy Thanksgiving."

Michelle sat down across the table and gingerly sipped her hot coffee. She put on her best John Wayne impression, and said, "Who-a, take 'er easy there, *Pilgrim*. Don't eat too much turkey before football this afternoon."

"You think they get the games via satellite over here?"

"Probably, it's the Army, not the Vatican, but how should I know?"

"*You* brought it up," Alex reminded her.

"Don't you men have some kind of innate football gene? Shouldn't you know these things just from the antennas on your Y-chromosomes, or something?"

"Wouldn't *that* be nice!" Alex said, and stuffed the entire strip of turkey bacon into his mouth.

Michelle shook her head. "*Men*. Why is eating your superpower?"

"Don't forget about leaving our clothes on the bedroom floor and dirty dishes in the sink. *Those* take practice."

"No wonder you're single."

"Hey, partner, I don't see a ring on your finger, either."

"That's different."

The pair relaxed in the morning sunlight for most of an hour, congratulated each other on another job well done, and debated whether they'd be able to catch a commercial flight to the States earlier than the one on which they were booked two days later.

A metallic clang reverberated from across the street as the medical clinic's door slammed open against the side of the pre-fab building. Bella Cirrone ran into the street barefoot, wearing—barely—a green hospital gown. She skidded to a halt in the middle of the dirt road and spun frantically as she looked around her unfamiliar surroundings. Her brown hair whipped from side to side as she searched up and down the street. She made a start to her left, then reconsidered, turned about, and rushed in the opposite direction.

"Shit," Michelle said under her breath.

"What the hell?" Alex added far louder.

Michelle jumped to her feet, knocking her empty coffee cup from the table in the process. She sprinted after Bella and caught the barefoot woman in a matter of seconds. Michelle pulled the woman's arm and brought her to a halt.

"Bella! What are you doing?"

The unruly patient twisted, pulled her arm from Michelle's grip, and started back down the street away from her rescuer.

Michelle grabbed the liberated case officer and wrapped her up in a bear hug. "What's going on, girl?"

The shivering woman bent her knees, dropped her center of gravity, and shook to loosen Michelle's grip. Two years in captivity hadn't dulled her muscle-memory of basic hand-to-hand combat tactics.

Michelle would have none of that. She reached under Bella's arms, wrapped her hands behind the shorter woman's head into a full nelson wrestling hold, and bent deeply at her knees. The maneuver dropped the pair to the ground in a controlled takedown. Michelle landed roughly on her backside and sat upright with Bella practically in her lap.

Bella's pale-green hospital gown flapped open in the back, and the emaciated woman's bare butt bounced on the dirt road. She came to a halt with a grunt, unable to move with Michelle's hands pressing forward on the back of her neck firmly enough to keep her immobile, but not hard enough to hurt too much.

"Okay, woman," Michelle said, exasperated, "*talk* to me!"

Bella remained silent for a few seconds and then started to sob and shake.

Two male medical orderlies pushed their way through the thickening crowd of soldiers.

Michelle looked up at the men sporting green scrubs, and asked, "You wouldn't happen to be missing something, would you? Or maybe some*one*?"

The shorter orderly raised an auto-injector in his hand, and said, "Sorry, ma'am. After I finished her lab work, the doctor was examining her, and she bolted out of the room. I can sedate her if necessary."

Michelle put her mouth close to Bella's ear, and quietly said, "Bella, you get to choose how you want to do this. It can go down in one of three ways. One. This nice gentleman with the big, scary needle can jab it into your thigh and you can sleep off your attitude problem. Two. I can put you into a wrist lock, and we'll walk back to the clinic like you owe me money, and I'm going to take this opportunity to collect it as the proverbial pound of flesh. Or three. You can remember how to be a lady, calmly walk with me to the clinic, and if you run again, so help me, I'll catch you and break your right kneecap. After that, you'll be *begging* for the sedative. I'm down for whatever. It's your choice, my friend. What do you say?"

Bella choked back another sob. "I'm sorry. I got... scared."

Michelle comforted the panicked woman. "I get it. I *do*. I might have reacted the same way. But now we're going to go back to the clinic and take our medicine like big girls, right?"

Bella paused and then agreed. "Okay. I'll go with you."

"Option two or three?"

Bella tried to turn her head to see if Michelle was joking or not, but the gaunt woman was being held too tightly to turn her head far enough to make eye contact with Michelle. After a short pause, she simply said, "Three."

Michelle released Bella, and they stood up. Michelle pulled the rear-opening hospital gown closed around Bella's dirt-caked bottom. The two women returned with the orderlies to the clinic at a slow but steady pace.

Two male doctors stood in the entryway and watched the foursome walk into the reception area. Michelle stopped and gestured for Bella to go with the medical team.

Bella turned, and the drawn look on her face surprised Michelle. "Would you come in with me?"

Michelle protested. "This is not my area of expertise, I—"

"*Please*?" the scared CIA officer pleaded.

Michelle dipped her head in resignation. "*Fi-ine*, but I'm going to miss my spa appointment for a mani-pedi."

Bella furrowed her eyebrows, and asked, "They have a spa here on base?"

Michelle shook her head. "No, you id—*umm*—silly girl. I was joking. Never mind. Lead the way."

The shorter of the two orderlies led the women into an examining room. Michelle plopped herself down in the chair next to a countertop stacked high with medical supplies.

White paper crackled as Bella climbed onto the dark blue examining table. She brushed dirt from her bottom, then folded her arms around herself as the doctor and an orderly entered the small room.

The doctor greeted Michelle. She tried to figure out by his accent if he was from Brooklyn or the Bronx. Sometimes she had a difficult time differentiating the two.

The doctor pulled a rolling stool from under the counter, sat down, and addressed Bella. "It's perfectly fine if you want your friend to be here as a chaperone during your exam. I just need your permission to discuss your medical condition with someone who's not a family member or in your chain of command."

Bella nodded.

"Good," he replied, and turned toward Michelle. "How do you know Bella?"

"I was on the rescue team that recovered her last night."

"Ah, I see," he said. "Maybe you can shed some light on the living conditions you observed there."

"I'll tell you what I can," Michelle said noncommittally.

The doctor flipped open a metal clipboard and reviewed Bella's lab results. "Bella, your tox screen came back negative, which is good, but you have a severe vitamin deficiency. That's not surprising considering how malnourished you are. I rarely have to tell people to *gain* weight, but you should add a lot of leafy greens and protein to your diet—poultry and fish mostly, several times a day. Some red meat is fine, on occasion, just not too much. I'll prescribe some multivitamins and iron supplements for you to take with you. Finally, Bella, you have a slightly elevated white blood cell count, which means you may be fighting a low-grade infection. That's not too serious, and, before you leave, I'll give you a blister pack with a full regimen of Azithromycin. Make sure you finish all the antibiotics over the next five days."

Bella shrugged.

"Your X-rays show mixed results. At some point, you had two fractured ribs which left some scarring when they healed improperly. It must have happened quite a while ago. I'm guessing you didn't get your rib cage wrapped when you were injured, did you?"

Bella shook her head but didn't elaborate.

"Well, there's nothing we can do about that, now, and they shouldn't bother you in the future unless you reinjure the same ribs. Do they hurt anymore?"

Bella shook her head again.

"All right," the doctor said as he closed the file and set it on the counter. "That's the good news. Now for the bad part, Bella. I need you to tell me what happened to you."

Bella sat silently.

"I know it was bad, but I can't help you unless you can give me some specifics."

Bella didn't reply.

Michelle looked back and forth between patient and doctor, unsure what the two of them knew but she was being kept out of.

"Bella, you've been subjected to repeated violence, that much is obvious. I know it's hard to talk about, but for me to be able to help you, I need to understand what you went through during the two years you were in captivity."

Bella dropped her eyes and stared at the floor.

The doctor looked at Michelle. "Did you... I'm sorry, I didn't get your name."

"Michelle."

"Michelle, what can you tell me about the conditions in which you found her? Who else was living there?"

"We rescued her from a small single-family house on the eastern outskirts of Mosul. I'd call it middle-class by Iraqi standards. The head of the household was a middle-aged male—the husband. He had two wives and one teenage boy in the house with him. The pre-mission briefing said he had two older children, but neither was home at the time. We found Bella asleep on top of some makeshift bedding on the second floor in a very small room barely larger than a walk-in closet. The bed had no frame and was more, I'd say, *padding* than a true mattress."

"Bella," the doctor asked, "was it the husband?"

Bella stared at the floor for a moment, then covered her face with her hands.

"Or maybe the teenager?"

Bella dropped her hands, shoved them between her knees, and shook her head violently.

"No," the doctor asked, "it *was* the father, then, wasn't it?"

She nodded reluctantly, and teardrops stained the front of her light-green gown creating dark spots on her thighs.

"Bella," the doctor said holding his hand together as if praying, "repeated and violent sexual assault—"

Michelle shivered. *Oh, hell.*

"—is significant trauma. We need to treat both your physical symptoms as well as your emotional injuries."

Bella continued to cry silently.

Michelle asked the doctor, "Besides her ribs, does she have other physical injuries?"

The doctor answered, "I'm going to recommend that when she gets home, she receives cranial scans to diagnose any traumatic brain injuries she may have suffered from any of the beatings she received. Her symptoms are inconclusive for a concussion, so I don't think she has one at present, although she might have had one earlier in the year. But...." He paused and took a deep breath before continuing. "That's not what concerns me the most. What worries me was her forceful reaction to the physical exam I was conducting. That's what's foremost in my mind. She has residual bruising of the genitals and upper thighs which are common in rape cases. What's not common is that when I just barely started to probe around her rectum, the sphincter relaxed immediately, opening completely."

Bella convulsed and twisted from side to side. Michelle feared she might bolt from the table again, but Bella stayed seated.

The doctor paused and let her recover her composure. He looked at Michelle and continued. "That's when she shot up from the table, pushed me aside, and ran out the door. I've never personally seen that physical manifestation before, but I've read about cases of severe child abuse where it happens. Essentially, over an extended period of months, the victim develops a conditioned response to limit the pain caused by repeated violent assaults."

Michelle slowly shook her head. "I can only imagine the horror...." She turned and looked at the woman on the table, and said, "Bella, he can't hurt you anymore. I know that doesn't magically make things better all of a sudden, but from this moment forward, things are going to get back on the right track. No one can hurt you anymore, and now you can start the healing process. Okay?"

Bella remained silent.

"Bella," the doctor asked, "I need to finish your physical exam, now. I understand it's uncomfortable, but I need your cooperation for a few more minutes, all right? Will you let me examine you?"

Bella didn't say a word.

"Bella, I really need to examine you for residual effects and to identify any other conditions I may not have found, yet. Unfortunately, there are no female doctors on rotation here this month, but if you want, I can call in a female nurse."

Bella still said nothing.

"Bella," the doctor tried again, "I—"

Without a word, Bella extended her hand and pointed at Michelle.

"Of course," Michelle said, "I'll stay right here. Would you like me to hold your hand or something?"

Bella nodded. She extended her arm toward Michelle and allowed the doctor to lay her back on the table.

Michelle gently gripped Bella's hand and stroked it slowly.

The doctor probed and prodded the distressed woman, and Bella squeezed Michelle's hand when things got uncomfortable.

The women switched hands as the doctor rolled Bella over and continued the exam. When he finished, Bella sat up and rubbed her eyes.

The doctor pulled his latex gloves off, tossed them into a trashcan, and finished jotting notes into Bella's medical chart. He looked at Michelle and said, "When you get her home, I'm recommending both a full psychiatric consult as well as long-term psychological counseling. You should —"

"*Whoa*, doc," Michelle said, raising her hands, "I've done my part on this mission. I got her out of that hellhole. I don't collect strays or take them home with me. Another team is going to arrive from Baghdad this afternoon to take her home."

"I see, but someone's going to have to look after her, and it will help for it to be a familiar face."

"I'm sure she'll get a full medical workup back home, and —"

"Michelle," Bella said with a start, "please... *please* don't leave me. I'm not... I can't... I don't... I'm just not ready to face the world. Not yet. I need... I don't know... time. You're the only friend I have right now. You're the only one who understands what happened to me. I can't face my family. Not now. Not... not yet." She looked at Michelle with drawn eyes and a pout that could melt an iceberg. "*Please?*"

Michelle raced her eyes around the room looking for something — anything — to latch onto as an excuse to say no. She rolled her shoulders back and opened her mouth but couldn't utter a word. She looked at Bella and felt a knot tighten deep inside her stomach. Michelle lifted her palms face-up and shrugged. "Okay, I'll get you to the Farm and stay for a day or two... For a couple of days at least, okay? I don't know what's going to happen after that, but at least you'll be safe and in familiar surroundings. All right?"

Bella's head barely moved as she nodded.

The doctor excused himself, and Michelle helped Bella dress.

The healthy CIA officer looked at her companion's ribs as they pushed outward through her pale, withered torso. Michelle shook her head, and said, "Let's go get you some lunch."

Chapter 2

CIA Training Center "The Farm," Central Virginia

Michelle Reagan entered the Chief of Base's conference room in the Farm's headquarters building and realized she was the last to arrive. Ervin Schal, the senior executive in charge of the sprawling training campus sat at the head of the rectangular oak table and asked Michelle to shut the door behind her.

A forty-something, straw-blonde woman in a white top and ankle-length floral skirt approached Michelle and extended her hand. "Caroline van der Pol. Counterintelligence Mission Center."

Michelle extended her hand to the woman who had more of an athletic build than one she'd call statuesque. "Michelle Reagan, Special Activities Center."

A short, gray-haired woman standing across the table from the chair Michelle selected waved to the newcomer and introduced herself. "I'm Dr. Ellyn Stone, Office of Medical Services Psychology team."

The older, pudgy, balding man sitting next to Erv Schal stood and shook Michelle's hand. "I'm Nino Balducci. Bella worked for me at the time of her disappearance. I was the Chief of Station in Baghdad when that unfortunate incident occurred. I work out of headquarters, now, and still do some field consulting here and there. I understand we have *you* to thank for getting our Bella back safely."

Michelle shook his hand and pointed a pink-painted finger at him. "I have about a million questions for *you*."

Caroline van der Pol took her seat and added, "As do I, Nino."

Dr. Stone took her seat and started the conversation. "I have at least that many for each of you. I have two responsibilities here and understand full well that each of you has your own interests and needs in this case. I hope we can pool our resources and help each other fill in as many of the blanks as possible. First off, I need to assess Isabelle Cirrone's current mental state, and second, I need to devise a treatment plan. Eventually, I will make a recommendation as to whether or not she should be retained as an Agency employee, be released from service with a disability package, or be employed part-time in some capacity."

Caroline van der Pol opened a leather folio in front of her, clicked her ballpoint pen open, and laid it on the exposed notepad. "I conducted the field investigation in Iraq two years ago when Bella disappeared. Now that she's returned, I'm leading the follow-up inquiry."

Nino Balducci said, "Good to see you again, Ms. van der Pol. I'm glad it's under better circumstances this time."

Michelle smirked inwardly. She had no doubt that a below-average-looking man like Balducci would remember a blonde bombshell like Caroline. A man like him can walk unnoticed through any room. He's someone no one even *wants* to pay attention to, a quality that made him such a successful case officer and ultimately promoted into the senior executive ranks as Chief of Station in one of the CIA's highest-priority field postings on the planet. Caroline van der Pol, on the other hand, practically glowed in the dark. Her naturally bright hair, radiant face, and figure of an aerobics instructor would make it impossible for her to hide from a surveillance team in a crowded city in the middle of the night during a blizzard—especially if any of her pursuers were male. They'd be able to track her with their eyes closed, using nothing but the scent of her pheromones.

Caroline smiled broadly, and said, "Glad to see you again, too, Nino. Now, Michelle, I'd like to understand more about the rescue effort and its aftermath. When I first got word of Bella's recovery, I immediately reread the incident report and my notes from two years ago. Then, yesterday, I looked for the after-action report from your team's mission in Mosul, but I couldn't find one. How did you know where to look for her in the first place?"

After-action report, Michelle thought. *Yeah, like we ever write those on our team! This woman is exactly who we work so hard to keep from knowing we even exist.* "It was the US Army that spotted her in Mosul, so they get all the credit. The body camera worn by a patrolling solider caught Bella on video one day walking down the street with the two other women who lived in the house. Based on what they were carrying, it looked like they were coming back from the market. The solider wearing the camera had no idea who Bella was, and, as I understand it, it wasn't until his video feed was analyzed a week or so later that facial recognition software reported a probable match. The Army was not out looking for her. It was just random good luck."

Nino jumped in. "Was Baghdad Station alerted?"

Michelle shrugged. "I don't know. That's above my paygrade. I'm sure Caroline can send a cable to ask."

"Yes," the counterintelligence officer agreed, "I will. So, Michelle, why were you in particular sent in all the way from stateside to Mosul, Iraq, to perform a rescue that US forces already in-country could have performed just as easily?"

Michelle's team lead, Michael, had prepared her for this question with an answer that was completely honest, yet left the truth out entirely. "The SAC got tasked instead of military special forces because the man holding Bella captive had a minor connection to ISIS but wasn't a high-value target or considered of much interest for intelligence purposes. Complicating the matter was that he is—or, rather, was—a second cousin of the chief of police in Mosul. That presented a potential political problem and risked a reduction in the chief's future cooperation on counterterrorism operations if he heard or suspected that the US military conducted an operation against his family. My team leaves a very small footprint with no visible ties to the US government."

"Why were *you* in particular on the mission?"

Michelle smiled at Caroline. "I have small feet."

"Your footprint was to leave four dead civilians?"

Michelle remained stoic. *If Bella had failed the authentication challenge, it would have been five.* "Like I said, there was no attribution to the US government."

"Did you bring back any intel? Computers? Cell phones? Anything like that?" Caroline asked.

"No, I didn't see any computers. As for cell phones, well, that just wasn't at the top of my list of things to recover. With such a small team, we don't have enough people to watch our backs while we root through the house to search for hidden treasure. I realize it can be valuable, but we're simply not able to do that. We get in, we get out, and we get drunk." Michelle grinned, and continued, "Eventually, I mean. Not right away, of course."

Dr. Stone interrupted the women's sparring. "Michelle, the Army doctor attributed Bella's conditions to years of repeated, violent sexual abuse. Has she provided any details about that to you?"

Michelle shook her head. "No, not really. It's clear that Achmed—the man of the house in which we found Bella—kept her as a sex slave and repeatedly beat the tar out of her to keep her in line and too scared to escape. She's been so introverted since her recovery that I've been afraid of pushing the wrong button and setting her off again. I just wanted to get her back here to you. Getting information out of her has not been on my agenda. Truly, I wish you all the best in diagnosing and treating her. I certainly hope she recovers fully. There's something inside her noggin keeping her from opening up. Sometimes, I'm convinced she wants to talk about it, but other times, she just stares off into the distance."

"That," Dr. Stone said, "is classic post-traumatic stress disorder. PTSD is treatable, sometimes with drugs and sometimes with other methods of therapy. By the way, where is Bella now?"

Michelle hooked her thumb over her shoulder. "I sent her to take a beginner's yoga class at the gym, walk two miles around the track, and then shower before I meet her for lunch. I figured that calm activities were probably best for her to start out with."

"Yes," the doctor confirmed, "that's a great start. As you continue to engage with her and aide in her recovery—"

"*Whoa*, doc," Michelle said cutting in. "My job was just to get her out of Mosul and then home safely. I've done my part. I told Bella I'd stay for a day or two, and I have. My time's up after dinner tonight. Then I drive—"

"Michelle," Ellyn Stone interjected, "Bella needs a friendly face for continuity and to have someone she can trust and work with as she struggles through the beginning stages of her recovery. Over the next few weeks, she—"

"Whoa, again, doc. That's not really my thing. I'm far better at taking people apart than I am at putting them back together."

"Michelle," Dr. Stone said in a soft voice, taking an alternate tack, "Bella is one of *us*. We need to pull together to support her, and—"

"Oh, hell," Michelle said to the medical professional, "you've spent far too much time inside the heads of case officers. Or maybe they get their guilt-trip techniques from you, I don't know. But I *do* know that I'm not the right woman for this particular job."

"Actually," Caroline van der Pol said, "woman or not, I think you're the *only* person for the job. You have Bella's trust, you understand her mental state better than anyone else in the world, it sounds like she genuinely likes you, and, frankly, we've got no one else to turn to. We're not DOD. We don't have an entire organization dedicated to treating returned prisoners of war. It just doesn't happen to CIA officers often enough, thank God, so it ends up falling to those closest to the person to shoulder that burden."

Michelle sunk back into the chair, deflated. She just wanted to get home to her boyfriend and put this mission behind her. She gestured to van der Pol. "So, *you* want me to gain her trust to find out if she poses any threat to the Agency or might have been turned into a mole while in captivity." She gestured to Stone, and said, "and *you* want me to become her therapist and give her a shoulder to cry on until her mental dam breaks and who-knows-what floods out."

Michelle looked at the head of the table and pointed at the chief of base. "And you, Erv, what's your angle?"

Erv Schal smiled, and said, "Me? I have no angle, Michelle. I'm happy to make the full resources of the center available to all of you — that's what we do here, whether it's for training or conferences or, well, whatever *this* is. I'm the host with the most. You and Bella are welcome to avail yourselves of the extensive facilities we have here while Dr. Stone from Medical and Ms. van der Pol from the CIMC do what they need to do. I hope you and Bella are finding that the quarters we've provided are to your satisfaction."

"Yes," Michelle replied, "thank you. Giving us a whole house to use was quite generous. The temporary family quarters are perfect. I let Bella settle into the master bedroom figuring she'd have more space and would be here longer. I'm not planning on staying. I've already packed my sh—*errr*—stuff so I can drive home tonight."

Ellyn Stone shook her head. "I really hope you change your mind, Michelle. At the moment, you're the only person Bella has any kind of connection with. I hope you can see that and will agree that investing a couple of weeks out of your career to help a fellow officer at what I'm sure is one of, if not *the,* most difficult times of her life would be a kindness that—"

Michelle threw up her hands. "Oh, that's laying it on a bit thick, don't you think, doc? *Fi-ine,* I'll stay for a week, but I won't commit to more than that. I—"

"A week is a good start," Dr. Stone said, smiling at having won the argument to the benefit of her patient.

Michelle gestured toward Nino Balducci. "Well, Nino, I guess I'm sticking around for a while to rummage through Bella's noggin for the good doctor. I need to talk to you to find out more about the Bella you knew before she disappeared."

The former chief of station smiled at the attractive brunette, and said, "It would be my pleasure, Michelle."

Chapter 3

The Farm, Central Virginia

That afternoon, Michelle Reagan led Bella Cirrone out of the dining hall and along the tree-lined street. Michelle gestured to a metal bench under the bare branches of a mature dogwood, and the women stopped to sit and talk.

Bella pulled her scarf tighter against a chilly November breeze and tucked it into the neckline of the new winter jacket she purchased the evening before. She pointed to one of the buildings beyond a stand of green Virginia Pines still carrying their needles. "They've renovated that dorm since the last time I was here."

Michelle squinted in the afternoon sunlight and followed Bella's finger in the distance. "Yeah, there's been a lot of construction here since I came through, way back when. The meals have gotten a lot better in the last year since they changed out the food service contractor. That's been a nice change from the same ol' same ol'."

"I'll bet. You come here for training a lot?"

"Ohhh, *yeah*. I know this place like the back of my hand." Michelle pointed as she talked. "Dining hall and dorms, of course. Firing ranges, driving course and airfield. I hang out in the Cantina a lot and visit the infirmary, well... way too much."

Bella snickered. "We didn't go to the Cantina during my training here. We'd just drink in the Student Recreation Building."

Michelle nodded. "Yeah, the rest of us mostly leave the SRB for the case officer trainees to use so you can get away from the rest of us and decompress after all the mind games they put you though."

"Yeah, *tell* me about it. So, you didn't go through that class?"

Michelle shook her head. "No, I'm not in the intelligence-collection business. I went through the Operations Basic Class, advanced counter-surveillance training, and then a bunch of specialized tradecraft classes like lockpicking, alarm defeat, advanced disguises, specialty firearms, close-quarters combat, and so on. Making dead drops out of paper-mache isn't for me."

Bella smiled, recalling her six months of intense training at the Farm years earlier. "When I was here, I made mine out of a thin aluminum tube shaped like a spike. I'd step on it to push it into the ground and put a lump of brown clay on top to make it disappear into the dirt. But I guess dead drops aren't your thing. You just make *people* dead."

Michelle didn't take the bait and chose to sit silently.

"I'm sorry," Bella said. "You and Alex pulled me out of Achmed's house quickly, but I saw his body through the doorway. Did you kill him or did Alex?"

Michelle looked directly into Bella's eyes, and asked, "Are you upset that he's dead?"

"Are you going to answer all my questions with questions?"

Michelle sat up straighter, crossed her legs, and pulled the neck of her jacket closed. "No, I'm not here to spar with you. If you want to do that, we can go to the gym. I'm just not used to talking to people outside my team about these things. Sorry, it's a defense mechanism more than anything. Alex did."

"And his wives and—"

Michelle interrupted Bella. "I don't think you really want to have those images in your head, do you? There's enough up there that's unsettled as it is."

"I may still be malnourished, but I'm not insane like that shrink thinks."

"I see you've met Dr. Stone. No, you're not crazy, but you are still healing."

"I can handle myself."

"Glad to hear it," Michelle said with a put-on smile. "Now that you're all better, would you like to call your parents and tell them you're safe and sound?"

Bella crossed her arms and stewed in her seat.

"You're *not* crazy, Bella, and your injuries—both physical and emotional—will heal in time. To my simplistic way of thinking about it, you're like a pipe that's partially blocked. You've opened up more to me in the last day or two than in the week since we rescued you, but there's still something gumming up your noodle-works upstairs."

"So, you're saying that I'm not crazy, just emotionally constipated?"

Michelle bobbed her head forward slightly. "You said it, not me. So, when you feel like talking, I'm here for you."

Bella looked off into the distance as the sound of a propeller aircraft flying overhead grew louder.

Michelle gently laid her hand on Bella's shoulder. "Bella, I'm not here *because* of you, I'm here *for* you. I'm here because you asked me to stay with you. I'm happy to do that—to get you readjusted and back on your own two feet. You're certainly making progress. At least you're not screaming out in the night from nightmares. I used to have nightmares."

"No, I'm sleeping pretty well, but maybe that's because of the pills the Army doc gave me."

Michelle shrugged, stood up, and said, "I don't know, but it's a blessing that you're back at all, so don't look a gift horse in the mouth. Why don't we walk over to the SRB and see if anything's going on this afternoon? Dr. Stone said it might be good for you to see some of the places that bring back good memories, so let's start there."

Bella sat still. "It's way too early for the bar to be open. And are you going to do everything Ellyn Stone tells you to do?"

Michelle shook her head. "No, but if you don't want to see what's changed in the SRB," she spun on her heel and pointed toward an area of the campus few went to, "we can always go check out the interrogation training building and see what memories *that* brings back."

Bella popped to her feet and stepped forward. "The SRB sounds like a *lovely* idea, Michelle! I hope they still have the pool table. Lead the way."

***

Michelle and Bella spent the next few days walking and talking, eating and working out. Michelle let Bella choose the topics of conversation and supported her without digging into the most sensitive areas.

One morning, Michelle took Bella off-base to a hair salon to color away the few strands of gray that contrasted her naturally dark brown hair. After that, the two spent the afternoon conducting some much-needed retail therapy at the local outlet mall.

CIA's human resources department straightened out Bella's personnel and payroll records for the two years of her captivity. Bella received retroactive credit for accrued vacation time, sick leave, a small civil service "Step Increase" pay bump, and full back pay. She did a double take when she looked at the six-figure check the HR rep handed her.

Michelle took her out shopping again the following day.

That evening, the women shared a bottle of wine in the living room of their house and talked until after midnight. Before turning in for the night, Michelle suggested they look at movie listings the next day and head into town to see whatever chick flick might be playing.

Michelle awakened to an ear-splitting shriek. The red digits on the digital clock on the dresser glowed 1:59 a.m. She scrambled out of her bed, threw the door open, and ran toward the source of the screams — the master bedroom.

Michelle flung the door open, jumped into the queen-sized bed, and wrapped Bella in a comforting hug. "I'm here, Bella, you're safe. I'm here for you."

Bella shook in Michelle's arms and buried her face in the bed sheets. Michelle gently rocked and stroked Bella while wails of pain pierced Michelle's ears.

"It's okay, Bella. I'm here for you. You're safe. No one can hurt you anymore. Not now. I've got you."

Bella cried and shivered.

Michelle checked the clock on the nightstand periodically and was repeatedly surprised at how long it can take for five minutes to pass when you're sitting in the dark.

As the minutes passed, the volume of Bella's cries diminished. When she spoke through gentle sobs, her words were barely audible. "I *broke*."

"It's okay, Bella. Everyone does, eventually. You're only human. We're all taught in training that it's inevitable. You held out for as long as you could before breaking cover."

Bella shook her head. Her hair tickled Michelle's chin. "No, not that."

"No? Then what?"

"I *broke*."

"It's okay, Bella, no one expects you to maintain your cover story forev — "

"No, he *raped* me."

"I know. That was horrible. No woman should ever have that happen to her even once, much less so many times."

"Wasif would read me poetry in Arabic like it was foreplay for him, and then he would...."

"You don't have to say it, but I thought his name was Achmed?"

Bella shook her head again and wiped her tears into the bedsheets. "My cover job is with the Federal Aviation Administration. I was doing an inspection at the Mosul Airport when six men in a van kidnapped me in broad daylight, right in the middle of the airport's parking lot. After that, they kept me blindfolded the whole day. The next day, they gave me to Wasif to be his sex slave. Every night, he'd read me poetry, then force himself on me. I fought back—"

"I'll *bet* you did."

"—and he...." Bella shivered and spoke through renewed sobbing. "He beat me until I couldn't fight him off anymore. He's so tall and strong." Her sobs grew louder in Michelle's ear.

Michelle hugged Bella tightly and let her continue at her own pace.

"He came to my room every night. He kept my hand chained to a metal anchor driven into a large stone in the wall of his old house. The handcuff didn't even have a key or lock—just a metal pin he hammered into it to keep it on my wrist. It was like something out of a medieval dungeon."

"That's terrible. It's inhuman."

"He did the same thing to me every night for weeks. He'd sit in on old wooden chair in the corner of my room, read from the same book, and...."

"You don't have to say it. I understand. There are no words."

"He'd put the book down on the chair and walk across the room to me." Bella curled into a ball in Michelle's arms and pulled the bedsheet up under her chin. "I knew it was coming, and he was going to do it to me again. Every night, I watched him read to me, get undressed, and then walk across the room the same way he always did. Night after night, he walked across the floor slowly, and I got so scared. I cowered against the cold wall because I knew what was coming—what was going to happen—and all I could do was watch his bare feet walking toward me. The same thing every time. Every night."

"Oh, *Bella*."

"Wasif pulled at my dress and yanked it up. He'd torn away my panties the first night. Those were long gone." Bella shook violently. "He beat me until I couldn't defend myself, and then he forced himself on me. Night after night after night after night."

Michelle clutched the shaking woman.

"He did the same thing the same way every time. He read poetry. He walked over to me. He beat me, and he raped me."

Bella's cries rose to a wail, echoing through the quiet of the night, and stopped suddenly. She looked Michelle in the eye and spoke with surprising clarity. "Then, I broke."

Michelle didn't understand what Bella meant, but didn't want to interrupt her flow.

When Bella didn't continue, Michelle asked simply, "How did you break?"

Bella pulled the sheet over her face and spoke through the paper-thin cotton barrier. She could barely get the words out. "I sto-opped fi-ighting *ba-ack*."

Michelle stroked Bella's arm through the sheet and sat silently.

"I'm so ashamed, I can't even...."

When Bella rubbed her face to wipe away the tears, Michelle watched the sheet move as if a ghost had curled up underneath it.

Bella spoke softly. "One day, after weeks or maybe a month—I don't know—I stopped fighting back. The beatings hurt more than the sex. He was surprised that first time, and I was afraid he'd beat me just... because. But he didn't. From then on, I'd just look at the wall the whole time he was on top of me and wish the heavy stones would come crumbling down and crush him. Crush us both."

"Oh, Bella. I'm so sorry."

Michelle hugged Bella and stroked her shoulder. After a minute, she asked, "Is that how your ribs got broken? His beatings?"

Bella shook her head. "No."

Bella quivered briefly, and Michelle could have sworn it was a from a laugh and not a cry.

"Even though he beat me so often early on, it was his wife, Noor, who broke them when she kicked me."

"Jeez, you were getting it from all ends, weren't you?"

Bella nodded, and said, "Literally."

Michelle's hand shot up to her mouth as she realized her gaff. "Oh, hell, I'm sorry Bella. I didn't mean to make light of what you had to endure."

Bella emerged from the sheet, sat up next to Michelle, and leaned back against the headboard. She pulled the top sheet up, gathered it in both hands under her chin, and said, "It's okay. You were with me at the Army clinic and heard everything, anyway. I don't think I could have admitted it out loud. This way, I—"

"You don't have to. I'm *sooo* sorry for being an insensitive bitch."

"No, you're not. It's not like the wives over there like it, either. They have to care for the women their husbands are screwing right in their own homes. Wasif justified it as a religious duty and said it's permitted because I wasn't Muslim. They can't keep fellow Muslims as slaves—just us heathens. One day while I was sleeping, Noor kicked me in the ribs. She always behaved really oddly. Some days, she'd walk by my door and spit at me. Other times, she'd stand in the doorway and talk and talk and talk. I'd just listen. I never really figured her out. Maybe she didn't have any friends. I don't know."

"Who would *want* to be friends with a woman like that? I'm sure she didn't dare do anything against her husband, though, or he would have beaten her, too. You were simply an easy target for her."

"Yeah, I got the feeling that she really loved him, anyway. But me? Not so much. He was a retired Iraqi Air Force colonel—a fighter pilot."

"Really?"

"Yeah, my Arabic wasn't as good back then, but I got the message clearly that their son had also been an air force pilot and American forces killed him during the invasion back in 2003. He was their only son, so—"

"Okay, yeah, I get the picture. She also blamed you for being American and taking her son away from her. So, if that was Wasif, then who was Achmed?"

Bella nodded. "After about six months, Wasif al-Bakkar and his wife Noor were getting ready to move somewhere. I heard them making plans, but never found out where they went. Wasif sold me to Achmed Hasan, and it started all over again."

"Oh, man."

"I fought back against Achmed maybe three times before giving up hope again. I—"

"You don't have to explain."

"Well, things just continued that way for, I guess, the next year and a half. I don't know. I lost track of time. I just tried to make it through each day, one at a time. I *did* almost escape once when they left me alone, but the next-door neighbor tackled me in the street."

Michelle smiled. "There seemed to be a lot of that—tackling you in the street, I mean—going on in Iraq, wasn't there?"

Bella elbowed Michelle gently in the ribs. "Achmed not only beat the shit out of me that afternoon, but beat his second wife, Aveen, right in front of me because she left me alone."

"After hearing all this, I wish I *had* been the one to shoot the bastard."

"I'm not a violent person, Michelle, but shooting was too good for him. It was over way too quickly."

"Bella, I'm not someone who likes causing other people pain, but in this case, I would have gladly made an exception for him."

"Me too."

"I do have one question, though. When the Army unit patrolling that area of Mosul videotaped you, you weren't restrained. No handcuffs or anything. In the video clip I saw, you and a woman younger than you were walking down the street carrying baskets. Had you gone shopping?"

Bella nodded. "That was only the third time they'd let me out of the house. Both of Achmed's wives were with me each time, but maybe you didn't know what the other woman looked like. Part of me wanted to run away again, but I didn't know the area well enough, and it was broad daylight. I wouldn't have gotten far, and Achmed made it clear that anything I did wrong... well... he'd also take it out on Aveen. I didn't want her to suffer on my account. Noor, on the other hand, I would have gladly fed to a pack of rabid, starving dogs. But Aveen was always nice to me. It seems stupid, now, that I could care about her at all, but the beatings were...."

"It's not stupid at all, Bella. The kind of behavioral conditioning you were subject to is intense. It's taken you weeks just to be able to acknowledge what happened. I never knew nightmares could be so cathartic."

Bella chuckled. "Actually, tonight I was dreaming of something that happened to me at Yale." Bella pointed to Michelle's t-shirt, and asked, "Did you go to Columbia University? In New York City?"

Michelle smiled. "No, my boyfriend graduated from there. I never went to college. I just wear his t-shirt when we're not together because I imagine I can still smell him when I do. It's mostly in my head, but I like to think it's how we can be still together even when we're hundreds of miles apart."

"That's sweet." Bella leaned in and sniffed at Michelle's shirt. "I'm thinking... Chanel Number Five."

"That would definitely be *me*, not him."

Both women laughed.

"So?" Michelle raised an eyebrow at Bella, and asked, "Yale?"

"Oh, right. My senior year I was at this frat party, and a guy I kinda liked was walking around the living room drunk, wearing this hideous clown mask. In my dream, I walked up to him to give him a kiss, but when I pulled the mask up, it was Achmed's face. I stumbled backward and screamed—"

"Yeah, I heard. I think the whole neighborhood heard."

"I'm sorry. I—"

"*No*, Bella, there's no need to apologize. You never did anything wrong. It's important that you remember that. Nothing that happened to you was your fault."

The women sat against the headboard for a minute without speaking.

Bella yawned first. "I think the adrenaline has worn off. I didn't take a sleeping pill tonight, but the wine is still doing its thing."

Michelle slipped out of the bed. "Let's sleep in tomorrow, and then we'll look at what movies are playing after lunch. We can skip anything that looks like it has clowns in it."

Bella smiled at Michelle and waved goodnight.

Chapter 4

The Farm, Central Virginia

The next day, rain kept Bella and Michelle from enjoying the rustic vistas of the CIA's training center. They sat in the dining hall lazily eating lunch while thumbing through movie listings. Neither felt inspired by any of the films playing that week.

Bella finished reading the listings on Michelle's cell phone for the fourth time and laid it on the table with a groan. "I'll pass. Werewolves really aren't my thing."

"Mine, neither," Michelle agreed. "I prefer my men with much less hair."

Bella smiled.

"You know, after last night, I was thinking...."

The smile melted from Bella's face.

"Movies are fine and all, but we're really not restricted to staying in the local area."

Bella's eyes narrowed to slits.

"According to Dr. Stone, I'm supposed to have you spend time in familiar settings that make you comfortable. We don't have to stay on base. I mean, it's convenient since the food and lodging are paid for by Uncle Sam, and we don't have to worry about our cover stories, right? But, what would you say to a couple of nights away?"

"What did you have in mind?"

"Last night, you mentioned your time at Yale. How about spending a night in New Haven? Instead of me dragging you around the Farm, we'll change it up and *you* can play tour guide. You can show me around your old stomping ground."

Bella perked up. "Walking around campus and reminiscing could be fun for a day. There's also a wonderful art gallery there. We might stick out a bit in the local bars in the evening, but, well, sure, why not. I think it'll be fun."

"And," Michelle added as Bella cocked her head, "instead of seeing a movie around here, what if — on the way up north — we spent a couple of nights in New York City, saw some sights there, and caught a play?"

"Can we *do* that? What about my daily sessions with Dr. Stone?"

Michelle shrugged. "Why *shouldn't* we be able to do it? And I'm sure we can rearrange your schedule with her. You're not a prisoner here. You've done your time in irons, so this is an opportunity for you to reconnect with some good ol' Americana. We've just about tapped out suburban Virginia, so why don't we take it up a notch or twelve and try the Big Apple on for size?"

Bella's eyes brightened as she considered the possibility. "It's still a few weeks until the ball drops, but I've never been to the Ground Zero memorial. If we're going all the way to Manhattan, it seems appropriate to pay our respects."

Michelle nodded her agreement. "And, since there are no rom-coms showing at the theaters around here right now, how about instead we pick out a musical on Broadway? I'm sure there's some kind of impossible love story about two star-crossed kids from different sides of the tracks whose parents want to keep them apart, but their hearts find a way to bring true love together against all odds."

Bella chuckled. "Isn't that the plot of *every* musical?"

"Pretty much," Michelle said with a grin. "Maybe for my next career I'll become a playwright. Coming up with catchy song lyrics is probably much harder than writing cheesy dialog. But, if you ask me, I think you're ready for a night out on the town, and we'd both enjoy an evening in ruby-red lipstick, three-inch heels, and skirts with aggressive hemlines."

Bella's face lit up. "I have to say, Michelle, I *do* like the way you think. Okay, I'm in."

"Great," Michelle said, "I'll make a reservation for somewhere in the Times Square area, so we'll be within walking distance of the theater district. Where should we stay near Yale?"

Bella rattled off the names of three hotels near her alma matter, and the women refined their travels plans.

Michelle enjoyed seeing Bella's face sparkle. The combination of the previous night's catharsis and the prospect of a girls' trip to the city that never sleeps sparked her in a way Michelle hadn't seen during the three weeks since the rescue.

***

The next day, Michelle and Bella stopped at CIA headquarters in McLean, Virginia, on their way north. Michelle led Bella to the basement gym in the Original Headquarters Building to work out and shower before lunch while Michelle ran a couple of errands in the building.

Her first stop was in her boyfriend's office. Dr. Steven Krauss, an executive in the Directorate of Analysis, frowned at the computer on his desk and stabbed his index finger at the button on the mouse. His face lit up as Michelle rounded the corner and stepped through the doorway.

"Hey there! Look who it is," he said with an ear-to-ear grin, and pushed his chair back from the computer. "Are you here to see me," he pointed to the small suitcase in the corner as he rose from his chair, "or did you just have separation anxiety from your fancy clothes?"

Michelle sidled up to her love and kissed him firmly.

Steve slowly stroked Michelle's back and lingered in the kiss, stopping only when he needed to breathe. "It felt weird, you know, *me* packing your clothes. Everything was right where you said it would be, though. Do you have your entire wardrobe memorized? Anyway, I think the only other time I've done that is when I picked you up from a hospital, and I had to root through your dresser for sweats. Glad that this time it was for something more fun than getting you to physical therapy."

Michelle held Steve fast, and looked up at him. "Thank you. I appreciate you helping me out. But what, you don't like touching my clothes?"

"It's not that I mind," Steve said, and grinned, "but I enjoy it far more when you're in them. Or," he whispered, "getting *out* of them."

"Ooh, I do like the sound of that. But don't worry, I'll be home in a couple of days, and this'll all be behind me. Once my new sidekick and I are done with our little field trip and arrive back at the Farm, I'll turn Bella over to Medical once and for all. After that, I'll be home before you know it."

"Great," Steve said, "and have you decided about that other thing?"

"Yeah, I've had a lot of time to think about it. I *will* go with you to your aunt and uncle's house in Queens. It'll be fine."

"My mother can be a nudge, but it'll just be for a few days around New Year's for my aunt and uncle's anniversary party. Are you sure?"

"Oh," Michelle said, "it's fine. Your mom's just so predictable in the way she treats me sometimes."

"I'm sorry about that. She had my whole life planned out in her mind, then you snuck up on me."

Michelle smiled, and whispered, "Yeah, that *is* kinda what I do to people, isn't it?"

Chapter 5

New York City

Michelle and Bella arrived at Penn Station on Amtrak's afternoon Acela run from D.C.'s Union Station. Their taxi bobbed and weaved through traffic for the fifteen-block trip to the Marriott Marquis in Times Square. Twice during the ride to midtown, Bella—still considered underweight by Dr. Stone—was practically thrown across the aged Chevrolet Caprice's back seat and into Michelle's lap.

The women checked into the Marriott and hurried upstairs to freshen up. The adjoining rooms Michelle requested provided both proximity and privacy for their two-night stay.

At Bella's request, the first order of business after dropping off their bags was to catch a cab for a trip to the National September 11 Memorial & Museum. To keep Bella from being bounced around in the back again, Michelle made it a point to tell the driver they were not in a hurry.

The taxi let them off on Liberty Street on the south side of the plaza, and they crossed the street onto hallowed ground. The women walked slowly around the pair of sunken, city-block-sized squares—matching voids memorializing where the Twin Towers once so majestically stood. Inside each immense pit, water falls endlessly into the depths left forever empty by the two destroyed skyscrapers. The water flowing in unbroken sheets mesmerized Bella. Michelle had to gently nudge her elbow to rouse her from her trance.

The women walked in a figure eight around the two squares. From time to time, they paused to read a few of the nearly three thousand engraved names honoring those who lost their lives on the day America will never forget. Neither said much on their taxi ride back to Midtown.

After an early dinner, they shared a bottle of white wine in the hotel's forty-eighth-floor revolving bar. The panoramic view of twinkling lights across Manhattan's skyline enthralled Bella. Michelle delighted at seeing her charge's face so animated after three long weeks of a slow and trying recovery. Bella remarked at being glad the bar rotated slowly since going two years in Iraq without a drink was leading her along the path to a full-on buzz far faster than she would have experienced in the past.

They slept in until mid-morning. Michelle insisted they use the hotel gym to not totally disrupt their established routine. Michelle ran on the treadmill for a half hour while Bella stretched on a mat and practiced a few of the yoga poses she'd been learning at the Farm's Wellness Center. Michelle beamed seeing Bella getting the hang of the Devotional Warrior pose without falling over when she leaned forward and stretched her arms back and up. She also enjoyed seeing that Bella's ribs were not showing through her t-shirt as prominently as they did just a few short weeks earlier.

Outside the hotel, the women walked north toward the restaurant recommended by the hotel's concierge. They couldn't help but stare at the famous Naked Cowboy strumming his guitar and singing as he stood in the open air wearing just his tighty-whities and cowboy boots on Broadway's concrete median.

With a pained look on her face, Bella remarked, "How can he stand out here for so long in this cold wearing just his briefs and a guitar strap? It's not snowing yet, but, *brrrr*. How can his you-know-what *not* freeze off?"

Michelle laughed and agreed, "I'm with you. No thanks." She glanced at the man as he swung his guitar to the side. "Well, looking at him closely, you know, maybe he's got one of those hand warmers people take to football games stuffed, *umm*, down there?"

They both giggled.

After brunch at Junior's—a Times Square staple for its electric-orange décor and large breakfast dishes—they meandered aimlessly around the shops and theaters along Broadway. They passed the century-old Winter Garden Theatre and remarked that neither of them had heard of the play advertised on the framed playbill. Further along, Bella stopped into the Duane Reade drugstore to buy a different shade of lipstick than she'd brought with her from Virginia.

They returned to the hotel and changed into their outfits for the matinee performance. After appraising and complimenting each other, they walked across the street and one block up to the Palace Theater. While still a few weeks before the holidays and not quite prime tourist season, the show was almost sold out.

The two undercover CIA officers laughed at the double-entendre-laced comedy of the first act as the play's young would-be lovers met and were then torn away from each other by unsympathetic immigrant parents steeped in the cultures of their native lands. During the play's raucous final number, the women clapped and sang along with the rest of the audience as they rooted for the teenage lovebirds to cross the barriers of culture and language to finally let their hearts sing in unison and bring their reluctant families together in the end.

The audience trickled out of the theater smiling, saying how much they enjoyed the show. Michelle and Bella carefully navigated the narrow, carpeted aisles and oddly sized stairways in high heels. As they stepped into the dimming light of the brisk afternoon, the growing crowds of Midtown Manhattan's biggest tourist attraction flowed around them. The women laughed and smiled as they strolled back along 7th Avenue toward the Marriott, alternating as they sung verses of the show's recurring signature song.

After crossing one street and turning right to cross the next, Michelle stopped behind the waiting crowd and shivered. She pulled the collar of her jacket closed and held it tightly as a frigid gust of wind swirled around them.

The pedestrian crosswalk signal glowed its orange "Don't Walk" warning, and Michelle paced in place as they waited. She looked at Bella, stomped her feet, and softly said, "I hope the traffic light changes soon. I need to pee."

When the cross-traffic stopped and the signals in all four directions glowed red, Bella pointed at the corner gift shop a dozen feet behind them, and said, "Why don't you go on ahead to the bar in the Marriott, and I'll meet you upstairs. We're leaving tomorrow, and I want to buy an 'I love New York' t-shirt and maybe a Statue of Liberty figurine. I'll catch up with you in the Broadway Lounge. Order me a glass of chardonnay, all right?"

Michelle nodded and surged forward as soon as the light changed.

The bright lights and turquoise carpet of the eighth-floor lounge shone like a beacon to Michelle. She hurried past the hostess stand while asking directions to the ladies' room without stopping. The stick-figure blonde in a slinky black dress pointed silently toward the corner of the room, adjacent to the bar.

Minutes later, a refreshed and relieved Michelle sat facing the floor-to-ceiling windows of the bar and looked down seventy-five feet onto the million-dollar-per-square-foot plaza below. She ordered two glasses of wine from an upstate New York vineyard near the Finger Lakes.

As she waited for the two glasses of chardonnay she'd ordered for her and Bella, she looked at the gawdy display of Times Square arrayed in front of her. The garish neon signs up and down the street—from a teen-girl-focused clothing store on her right, to the electronics and gifts shop Bella ducked into on her left—blinked with no perceptible pattern.

That evening, besides Michelle, only four patrons occupied the bar. Three weeks later, revelers would pay five thousand dollars per ticket to stand shoulder-to-shoulder to watch the world's most famous crystal ball drop as the East Coast rang in the New Year.

Michelle leaned forward and squinted through the window. She watched Bella emerge from the corner shop with a white plastic bag in hand. Michelle waved, even though she knew it would be impossible for Bella to see her through the hotel's bright exterior lights and the bar's dark-tinted glass.

On the corner, Bella waited for the traffic light to change and the iconic white pedestrian stick figure to signal it was safe to cross the street.

Michelle leaned back in her padded chair as the waitress placed two glasses on the small circular table in front of her. She signed the tab to her room and enjoyed being able to expense her travel charges to the Agency. Since this was part of Bella's recovery, she decided—for Bella's well-being, of course—that Uncle Sam would spring for a couple of glasses of white wine.

Bella's lunge on the sidewalk across the street caught Michelle by surprise. Bella back-peddled a half-dozen steps and teetered on her high heels. She fell backward into the thick plateglass window of the corner store as a tall man in a long, white Arabic thobe and puffy white winter coat grabbed for the CIA officer. She stumbled and regained her balance as the man seized her arm and yanked her away from the gift shop.

Michelle jumped to her feet, and yelled, "Bella!" out of instinct, not expecting the woman struggling on the street below to hear or acknowledge her name. The waitress spun and looked at Michelle quizzically.

Michelle sprinted from the bar and through the hotel's main lobby—a strange feature for the eighth floor of a hotel, but nothing about the showpiece of Times Square was normal. Her high heels clacked like a train barreling down the tracks as she raced across the marble floor. She glanced at the elevators, decided against risking that some insolent child hasn't pressed every button on his way up, and made a beeline for the escalator. She ran and U-turned down three escalators taking steps two at a time at the risk of breaking a heel or an ankle.

She flew out of the hotel's massive front entrance into a chill wind and bolted across the valet parking arrival lanes. She dashed past guests in black tie arriving for a dinner hosted by one of the city's large financial firms, and skid to a halt at the curb.

Across the street, she watched a tall man half-drag, half-push Bella through the side door of a windowless white van double parked alongside the gift shop.

Michelle darted into traffic on Broadway, barely glancing at the oncoming cars. A horn blared in her ear. She skittered to a halt as a yellow taxi swerved to miss her as it continued its way down the wide boulevard without stopping.

Michelle weaved her way through cross-traffic and jumped onto the concrete median. She caught sight of the white van's red taillights as its tires screeched. She squinted at the black-and-orange license plate, glimpsing fragments between passing taxis, limos and delivery trucks as the van jerked forward and accelerated away from her on West 46th Street.

When the traffic light turned red and the white pedestrian signal appeared, Michelle lunged forward to cross the street and bounced off the driver's door of a blue Camry that ran the red light.

Michelle flew backward and landed on her side, grunting, "*Oomph.*" She struggled to her feet amid the stares of colorfully clad pedestrians bundled up against the early evening cold. She ran her hands along her blouse and looked at the ground around her. The spaghetti strap of her purse had snapped, and the small black bag lay on the sidewalk a few feet away. The CIA officer regained her footing, retrieved her purse, and, this time, looked both ways before hustling across the 7th Avenue side of Times Square.

She pushed her way through a gaggle of tourists clogging the corner as they waited to cross one of New York City's busiest arteries. She darted down the street after the white van that had already disappeared from view. She jumped onto the hood of a black Chrysler 300 parked along the street and scanned the horizon for anything that resembled a van—color be damned. The traffic light behind her glowed red, so only a few vehicles were visible along the long block in front of her. Taxis and sedans swerved to avoid two double-parked FedEx trucks along the street, but the white van and its precious cargo were long gone.

Michelle balanced on the hood of the car and peered down the street until a steady stream of curses pierced her intense focus. The owner of the car on which she stood spewed invectives at her in a way only a native New Yorker can, proving for everyone within earshot the remarkable versatility of the English language, in general, and a certain four-letter word in particular. He swiped at Michelle's legs and, if not for the fact that she wore a miniskirt, she might have buried the toe of her dress shoe in his nose.

Instead, she dismounted his car and walked back toward the corner to escape his wrath and plan her next move. She approached passers-by and asked — indeed pleaded — to know if any had seen the van or the woman forced into it. She confronted a couple wearing matching scarlet Rutgers University sweatshirts and holding each other tightly. They gave her cross looks but said nothing.

Michelle hurried a dozen yards down the block and accosted a small church group singing an energetic rendition of "Let it Snow." She demanded to know if they had seen anything or could describe the man who took Bella. For her efforts, Michelle was pushed by a middle-aged woman in a red parka who continued singing and turned away from the crazy woman with no jacket and whose breath smelled like wine.

Michelle backtracked and frowned that of the eight million people in New York City, she couldn't find even one who saw the abduction — or would at least admit to it.

A cold breeze whipped through the thin material of Michelle's blouse. She wrapped her arms around herself and rubbed vigorously. Her purse dangled from the broken leather strap she clutched in her fist, and the small bag bounced against her side. Slowly, she walked back to the corner, looked around, and realized she'd left her jacket on the back of her chair in the Marriott's bar.

Michelle pulled her cell phone from her purse and unlocked it with her thumbprint. She tapped the icon for CIA's secure voice app and hovered her index finger above the speed-dial label for the Agency's twenty-four-hour Security Operations Center. She had to call the SOC, but what would she say? That she'd lost the woman she'd saved not even a month before? That Bella got kidnapped *again*? Who would believe her? Michelle didn't even know what to think of it herself.

She waved her thumb over the circular, white-and-blue icon and thought through the specifics of what she'd report. She looked back at the Marriott, let her eyes climb the glass side of the tall building, and slowly lowered the phone to her side. She decided to make the call from her quiet room instead of the noisy street where the church group was finishing their hope for a White Christmas.

Inside the hotel, Michelle retrieved her jacket from the eighth-floor bar. She turned in place and found the waitress hurrying to serve the growing crowd gathering to enjoy their crow's nest view of the street scene below. Michelle handed her a twenty-dollar tip, and the waitress thanked the woman she had silently cursed just minutes before.

In her room, Michelle called the CIA watch desk and made her report. As expected, they advised her to stay by her phone and wait for instructions. She followed that call with one to her team lead, Michael, and told him what happened. He offered his full support, and Michelle said she'd call or text him if she needed anything.

When her phone rang, Michelle answered and did a double-take when she recognized the voice on the other end of the phone — Caroline van der Pol.

Michelle paced barefoot around her bed as she recounted the previous twenty-four hours for the counterintelligence investigator. Caroline listed intently, interrupting twice to ask for additional details.

When Michelle finished her explanation, she stared out the window and listened to silence from the other end. "Are you still there?"

"Yes," van der Pol answered, "I'm just trying to figure out how to explain this to my branch chief when I call him after we hang up. I don't know what he's going to think — or what anyone in the Company is going to think — when they hear that the same officer was kidnapped twice in two years. On two different continents. I — "

"Yeah, I'm with you."

"You said you were drinking wine, so I have to ask, but — "

"No, I said I'd *ordered* two glasses of wine. I only took one sip of mine. Both glasses were still on the table when I ran out of the bar. I even forgot to grab my jacket when I left. I went back for it later and got it from the bartender who'd already put it into their Lost and Found pile in the back. The wine was long gone, unfortunately. That's when I realized how much I needed it. But, no, I wasn't drinking before that, and neither was Bella."

"All right, fair enough. Did you report this to the police in New York?"

"No, I did not. I couldn't think of what to tell them. She and I are both undercover employees with completely different cover stories. She's FAA, and I have a non-official, commercial cover. I don't even know how well Bella is backstopped anymore. I have no way to explain to NYPD how she and I would even know each other. I — "

"That's okay, Michelle, that's all right. We'll handle that from the Counterintelligence Mission Center. CIMC has law enforcement contacts with cleared reps from all the major departments. If that's the way we decide to go, we'll handle the initial report to the police and put you in touch with the right point of contact. I'll call you back once I talk to my boss and we figure out what the next steps are going to be. Stay by your cell phone and keep it charged. I have a feeling this is going to be a long night for both of us."

After hanging up, Michelle changed out of her dress and into a pair of black slacks with the shirt she planned to wear to Yale the following day. She plugged her cell phone in on the nightstand and paced the room from the window to the door and back again. Memories of everything that happened to her and Bella since leaving the theater raced through her mind. Nothing she recalled seemed out of the ordinary.

She mentally retraced her steps from the hotel to the theater and back again with a focus on identifying anything or anyone out of the ordinary. Were they followed? Could she recall seeing anyone before the show who also showed up elsewhere afterward? Had anyone looked at the women strangely?

Nothing jumped out at her. Nothing seemed out of the ordinary.

Her cell phone pulsated on the night table and gave a rapid *bee-dee-dee-bleep* from the ringtone assigned to the secure voice app.

Caroline's voice came through crystal clear. "We're flying up tonight. Meet us at midnight at the Agency's National Resources Division office in Manhattan. We'll meet in NR's main conference room."

Michelle memorized the address and door-access PIN code as Caroline recited it.

After ending the call, Michelle looked at her watch. *Three hours to go. I wonder who 'we' will turn out to be?*

***

Michelle changed taxis twice on her way to the meeting, first after ducking through the shopping mall in Columbus Circle and then after walking a roundabout route through the South Street Seaport area of lower Manhattan. She wasn't prepared to execute a full surveillance detection route but kept her eyes open on the mini-SDR she concocted. She didn't detect any surveillance and entered the NR Division's undercover office in the Financial District with five minutes to spare.

Chapter 6

Financial District, New York City

The National Resources Division's conference room looked exactly like any other conference room on Wall Street. Plush brown leather chairs surrounded a well-polished mahogany table with a dual-screen video-teleconferencing setup hanging on the front wall. Only the three-foot-tall CIA logo hanging on the rear wall would look out of place in any of the thousands of investment bank or Fortune 500 offices within walking distance.

As Michelle entered the room, the middle-aged man with neatly combed, sandy-colored hair sitting at the head of the table rose to introduce himself. "Jordan Hastings, Chief of Station."

"Michelle Reagan," she said, and waved politely. "Peon."

Hastings chuckled. "Not when you're in my station you're not. Here you're my guest, so please make yourself at home."

Michelle thanked him and took a seat in the middle of the table.

A minute later, the conference room door swung open, and Caroline van der Pol stepped in. She thanked an unseen man holding the door open behind her. A taller, lanky woman with close-cropped graying hair strode into the room after Caroline. Michelle saw that the older woman wore one of her characteristically drab, light-brown pant suits. Two men followed the women into the conference room and the door slowly closed.

Michelle rose to greet the newcomers.

"Good evening, Michelle," the short-haired woman said.

"Hello, Dagmar." Michelle shook hands with Dagmar Bhoti, the chief of CIA's Counterintelligence Mission Center. Bhoti had once described herself to Michelle as the agency's chief "mole whacker."

Caroline's eyes narrowed. "You two know each other?"

Dagmar nodded. "We've had occasion to meet here and there at Langley."

The man standing behind Bhoti extended his hand to Michelle.

Dagmar made the introduction. "Michelle, do you remember Phil Thompson?"

Phil shook Michelle's hand, and said, "From Bermuda."

Michelle nodded. "Of course. With the FBI guy, Craig, *umm....*" Michelle remembered Assistant Special Agent in Charge Craig Marx's last name perfectly well but wanted to let Phil look good in front of his boss.

"Marx."

Michelle pointed a pink-painted finger at him. "Right, that's it."

Caroline pointed at Phil, and said to Michelle, "Phil's the branch chief I mentioned to you on the phone."

"*Ahh,* that makes sense." Michelle looked at the other man who'd entered the room but not yet introduced himself. "And you are?"

"Bob McMillian." He pointed to Jordan Hastings. "I work for him here in the city."

"Well," Jordan said to Dagmar, "this is exactly what I always imagined you folks in the CIMC do all day: point fingers at one another." He smiled to let everyone know he meant no harm by his joke.

A few polite smiles crossed the faces of his guests. No matter how frequently officers from the CIMC hear "friendly" comments like Hastings', sometimes the truth still stings.

"I'm just kidding," Hastings said. "Please, take a seat and let me know how I and my station can help you at this late hour of the night."

For the group's benefit, Michelle repeated the story she had related to Caroline by phone earlier that evening.

When she finished, Hastings asked the first question. "How did you come to know Isabelle Cirrone?"

"I was on the tactical team that rescued Bella in Mosul."

"You're Special Activities Center, then?"

Michelle nodded. "SAC Ground Branch."

Hastings thought about that for a second. "I must not have noticed your knuckles dragging on the ground behind you earlier when you entered."

Michelle grinned politely. The intra-agency rivalries between CIA offices frequently led others to call SAC's Ground Branch paramilitary officers thugs or Neanderthals. Most often, though, people only dared to say such things behind their backs. Most paramilitary officers did have former military training and many of those in Special Forces. Michelle, though, had a far different role than anyone else in the Ground Brach, save Alex. "Well, I've been told I clean up well."

Dagmar got the conversation back on track. "You have to admit, Michelle, it's highly unusual for anyone to be kidnapped twice. It's never happened to anyone else in Agency history. That's why I flew up here tonight. This situation, if it is as it appears, raises a myriad of questions. The story strains the bounds of credibility."

Michelle nodded. "By *the* story, you mean *my* story. Yes, I know, and if I hadn't been along for the whole adventure over the past month, I don't know that I'd believe me, either. You and I have had dealings before, Dagmar, and I think you know I'm not really the 'catch and release' kind of girl. I prefer a more concrete finale, even if not everyone gets their 'happily ever after' ending."

None of the others at the table knew quite how to take Michelle's unusual comment, but Dagmar understood her perfectly. While Michelle preferred to describe her job using the military's term, operator, the rest of the world would refer to her and her partner as assassins. Michelle disliked that word and Dagmar would never dare utter it to her face.

Bob McMillian waded into the fray with an offer. "My branch handles all local liaison activities with the FBI, NYPD, and other law enforcement agencies. I have analysts and operations officers working on the Joint Terrorism Task Force, the JTTF, here in New York. Because of Times Square's historical attractiveness to criminals and terrorists, there are now so many video cameras in the area—especially with New Year's approaching—there's no *way* something like Michelle described wasn't caught on tape. I can have my folks request everything from the JTTF and have a dozen video clips and best available stills sent over first thing in the morning, if you'd like."

Phil Thompson thanked him and asked for copies of everything he could gather.

Thompson glanced from the chief of station to Caroline van der Pol and back. "Jordan, Caroline will be leading the field investigation for the CIMC. She'll be our primary go-between for Bob and his team. I'd appreciate it if you can make working space and secure communications available for her in this office."

Jordan Hastings nodded enthusiastically and gestured to Bob McMillian. "Of course, *mi casa es su casa*. Bob will provide liaison between us, Ms. van der Pol, the FBI and NYPD. He can request the videos based on what you've already told us of the timing of the event and which corner it happened on. However, if you want to make a formal report of a kidnapping and ask the police to try to find our wayward officer, you should be prepared to provide a few recent photographs and some personal details of her, consistent with her cover. Also, since all personnel on the JTTF have Top Secret security clearances, it's not a problem telling them that Bella is a UC Agency officer, if you choose to share that particular tidbit."

Caroline said, "I can provide the photos and cover-consistent background info for her supposed employment by the Federal Aviation Administration, but let's wait until we see what the videos show in the morning, okay?"

Everyone agreed.

Michelle stewed in her seat. She couldn't decide whether she'd end up looking like a hero for her dash across busy city streets, or a chump for losing a woman who wasn't even trying to get away. She feared that once the videos arrived and she had to watch it all play out again and again on the conference room's big-screen TV, the next day would be a real shit show for her.

Chapter 7

Times Square, New York City

Michelle awoke shortly after eight and worked out in the hotel gym before eating breakfast. She dressed in her last set of clean clothes and studied herself in the bathroom mirror.

"Well, kiddo, when the going gets tough, the tough go shopping."

She took a taxi to Macy's flagship store on 34th Street and stocked up on the essentials she expected to need over the next few days.

After another taxi ride downtown, Michelle lugged an overstuffed shopping bag into the National Resources Division's conference room. She settled into the same chair she'd occupied the night before and waved politely as Bob McMillian and Phil Thompson entered.

Bob pointed to her shopping bag, and said, "You're either two months early or three months late for fashion week."

Michelle shook her head. "Too rich for my blood. On a government salary, Macy's is more my speed."

Phil billowed his gray suit jacket out, and said, "You and me both."

Once the rest of the group arrived, Bob McMillian played surveillance videos and clicked through the slideshow of still photos from Times Square he'd received from the JTTF. For close to an hour, the gathered team replayed and reanalyzed photographic documentation of Isabelle Cirrone's abduction from a dozen angles.

Bob McMillian ended the presentation with a closeup of the white van's orange-and-black New York State license plate. The JTTF analysts had provided the CIA with DMV records on the van's owner and utility records for the apartment listed as his residence.

Bob McMillian thumbed through the file on the table in front of him, and said, "The van is registered to one Wasif Ali at an address in lower Manhattan. The electric and telephone utilities are registered in the name of a woman with the same last name, so I'm assuming it's his wife. Her name is...."

A chill ran down Michelle's spine, and goosebumps rose on her forearms. "Noor," she added. "It means *light* in Arabic."

Simultaneously, four heads around the conference table snapped in her direction.

McMillian traced his finger down the page and stabbed at the file. "Noor, that's right. How—"

"Bella told me," Michelle said, "but she called him Wasif al-Bakkar. He was the first, umm... I don't know how to say this. He was her first *owner*, I guess. I don't like the term, so maybe first *captor* works better. Noor's the one who broke Bella's ribs one night by kicking her while she slept. The wives over there don't really like their husbands' sex slaves, but in that culture, wives have no say over much of anything beyond what's for dinner."

Dagmar asked, "When did Bella tell you all this?"

"A couple of nights ago at the Farm. Early one morning, she woke up around 2 a.m. screaming her head off. I ran into her room not sure what was going on and, after a lot of crying, we had a long talk. I gave my notes to Dr. Stone."

Caroline van der Pol rifled through her file, and said, "Ali is not the name in Dr. Stone's report."

"No," Michelle answered, "Bella used the name al-Bakkar, but how many Wasifs married to Noors can there be? So, when Bob said the van is registered to a Wasif Ali, it's not much of a leap to think it's the same Wasif and Noor. I'd bet dollars to doughnuts that Wasif's name is Wasif Ali al-Bakkar. In his culture, the al-Bakkar part is more of a tribal affiliation than a last name. His father's first name was probably Ali, so when they came over here, he used that as a family name. Saddam Hussein's full name was Saddam Hussein something-something al-Tikriti because he was from the city of Tikrit, but no one over here ever referred to him by that name. I figure Wasif's full name is along the lines of Wasif Ali something-something al-Bakkar."

Dagmar Bhoti looked across the table. "Bob, does the JTTF have a file on either Wasif or Noor Ali?"

Bob scanned through the file, and said, "No. The analyst's notes say that neither of them is on any watch list." He rifled through a few sheets of paper and mumbled as he read. "Not on the No-Fly list. No NYPD file, and he doesn't come up in any FBI investigation, either. He has a valid city business license as a consumer electronics reseller and has that one vehicle—the white van—registered to him. He does have one outstanding parking ticket. All in all, if he's a bad guy, he's flying under the radar."

"Electronics reseller?" Caroline asked. "Go back to one of the videos from Times Square."

Bob McMillian queued a wide-angle video of Bella taken by a camera across the street.

"There," the counterintelligence investigator said as she tucked a lock of blonde hair behind her left ear and pointed to the screen. "The sign over the corner gift shop says they also sell electronics. Maybe Wasif's one of their suppliers?"

Phil Thompson crossed his arms. "That's too many coincidences for me, and I don't believe in coincidences. First, Wasif just happens to live in the first city Isabelle Cirrone goes to once she's away from the Farm. Second, Bella stays the night in a hotel across the street from a business Wasif just happens to supply. Third, Bella happens to be alone outside that store, and fourth, at that exact moment, Wasif just happens to drive up in his van and kidnaps her."

Caroline agreed. "I don't buy it either."

"Michelle," Dagmar Bhoti asked, "how often did you let Bella out of your sight here in New York?"

"Not often," Michelle said. "We have adjoining rooms at the hotel. I wanted to have easy access to her in case she had another nightmare. We always went out to restaurants together. We went to the 9/11 Memorial together yesterday and the play last night. We rode in taxis together, and we used the hotel gym together. If she wanted to get away, though, she could easily have left anytime I was in the shower or in the middle of the night, but I never got the sense that she ever left her room without me."

"So," Bob McMillian asked, "how did she end up alone at the electronics store?"

"Bella told me she wanted to buy some souvenirs, and I said I had to use the bathroom. I went to the hotel bar by myself while she shopped. I had to go pretty bad."

"Just out of curiosity," Bob asked, "who said what first?"

Michelle's brow furrowed. "Excuse me?"

"I mean," Bob added, "was she the first to say she wanted to go shopping and then you responded by saying you had to find a restroom?"

Michelle thought for a moment. "I think I said I had to pee, first. I was probably stomping my feet the whole time we waited across the street for the traffic light to change. It was cold out, and I really had to go. After we got across the first street and started waiting for the light to change on the cross-street, she said she wanted to buy a t-shirt and a statuette of the Statue of Liberty. You know, one of those—"

"Yeah," Bob said, "those tchotchkes are sold in every gift shop in town. Michelle, that makes me wonder something. I'm going to ask you to play along with me here for a moment, if you will, and let me walk you through the chain of events leading up to this point. Let's start back at the Farm. Why did you decide to come to New York City in the first place? Whose idea was that?"

Michelle crossed her legs and pulled her chair closer to the conference table. "Mine. Dr. Stone, the agency psychologist evaluating and treating Bella asked me to take Bella around the Farm and the local area to have her experience some familiar and comfortable sights. During one of our talks, Bella mentioned she went to Yale. Later, I suggested instead of us just wandering around the Farm and the local mall, we take a field trip to New Haven, and she could show me around her old haunts. Earlier this week, we looked for a movie or something to do besides work out at the gym and go shopping—not that either of us complained about either of those. Anyway, I suggested that on our way to New Haven, we should stop in New York and see a play instead of a movie."

"So, *you* were the first to mention New York?"

"Yes," Michelle said, and then thought about it again. "Well, *sort* of."

Jordan Hastings, the Chief of Station, said, "Would you care to elaborate?"

"Yeah," Michelle answered, "okay. What happened was that Bella had a nightmare and screamed her head off in the middle of the night. I ran into her room to see what was going on. I was wearing an old Columbia University t-shirt I always sleep in, and she commented on it. Well, more specifically, she asked if I went there. I said 'no,' and then we got to talking about where she went to school, Yale."

Bob McMillian peered intently at Michelle. "Columbia is pretty far uptown, north of Central Park. Times Square is south of the park. Do you remember who first mentioned Times Square?"

Michelle stared at a smudge on the conference table in front of her and focused on recalling her conversation with Bella. "*I* definitely mentioned Times Square by name first. But earlier, Bella made a comment about visiting Manhattan but it being too early to see the ball drop. Or... the ball wouldn't drop for another few weeks. Or something like that. Why does any of that matter?"

"Maybe it does, and maybe it's nothing," COS Hastings said.

"But," his branch chief, Bob McMillian, added, "it seems like everything you suggested the two of you do was not an original thought. I mean, one way or another, you were reacting to something Bella said earlier."

Caroline van der Pol asked the career case officer, "So, Bob, are you suggesting that Bella influenced Michelle by planting suggestions into their conversations?"

"Maybe. Michelle *wore* the t-shirt, but Bella made a point of *mentioning* it. That brought New York City into the conversation. It's obvious that New York is on the way from Virginia to Connecticut, so a stop here whether to see a movie or a play could feel like a natural extension of the conversation and not raise suspicions. Then, Bella puts a hint about the ball dropping into play and, without mentioning it by name, *implies* the location of Times Square, because everyone knows that's where the most famous ball in the world drops during the country's biggest New Year's Eve celebration. Bella didn't have to connect those dots for Michelle. They're common knowledge and, again, the conversation continues to feel perfectly natural."

"Are you suggesting," Caroline asked pointedly, "that Bella intentionally manipulated the conversation—"

"And manipulated *me*?" Michelle asked, not sure if she should be getting angry or not.

Caroline continued, ignoring Michelle's interruption. "—so they'd not just visit New York, but specifically stay overnight in Times Square?"

McMillian shrugged. "I don't know, but it's a possibility. Isabelle Cirrone is a trained case officer. That's what we do—manipulate conversations."

"And people," Michelle added.

"And people," Bob agreed.

Michelle's face turned pink at the thought that she might have been played. "Why in the world would Bella want to do that?"

Caroline turned in her chair, and asked Michelle, "Are you sure Bella was really kidnapped tonight?"

Blood in Michelle's carotid artery pulsed painfully against her neck as it flowed into her head. "I saw it! I—"

"Or," van der Pol added, "did you see exactly what she wanted you to see?"

Michelle bit her lip, unable to answer the counterintelligence officer's question.

"Michelle," Dagmar said calmly, "Thank you for giving us the details of what you saw and heard over the past few days. I very much appreciate the level of detail you've been able to recall. That's impressive and appreciated. I believe you when you say you believed what Bella told you. I'm sure this is confusing for you—it is for us, too. Right now, I simply don't know what to make of Bella and this event. What we've discovered here today is that Bella Cirrone either definitely did or did not manipulate you into bringing her to New York on your way to New Haven. Bella either definitely did or did not influence things to specifically visit or stay in the Times Square area. And Bella either definitely did or did not get kidnapped earlier this evening."

Phil Thompson chuckled. "Well, boss, that pretty much sums up the starting point of half of our investigations."

Michelle sat silently and felt her neck heat up as her level of embarrassment grew. "What's next? Will you get the police involved?"

Thompson and van der Pol looked at Bhoti.

The head of the Agency's counterintelligence office nodded and looked at her staff. "Yes. Phil, when we're done here, you and Caroline contact the FBI. Bob can make the introductions through the JTTF. Normally, the Bureau would handle a kidnapping as a criminal case, but because it's an undercover intelligence officer, Phil, ask them to handle it as a classified national security matter."

Phil Thompson nodded. "Will do. Caroline has the photos and biographical information we'll need. Michelle, you knew Bella the best and seem to be the only eye-witness available. Will you come with us?"

Michelle scrunched up her lips and nodded. She'd spent the majority of her professional life as the hunter who actively evaded law enforcement. Now, the back of her neck tightened painfully as she felt more like the prey about to walk into the lion's den.

Chapter 8

FBI Joint Terrorism Task Force, New York City

"I thought it would be bigger," Caroline van der Pol said to FBI Special Agent Ronald Poland.

"I'll bet he hears that a lot," Michelle added with a chuckle.

Caroline thought for a moment and her jaw dropped. She swiftly covered her open mouth with her hand. "*Oooh*! I didn't mean that, Ron. I meant—"

The FBI agent laughed. "It's bigger downstairs."

This time, the women giggled.

"What I *mean*," the FBI agent said, stumbling for words, "is that the watch center is downstairs. This is just the office cubicle bullpen. I—"

A female FBI agent walked around the corner and patted Ron Poland on the shoulder. She looked at Michelle and Caroline, and said, "That's been the rumor around here for a while, girls. Thanks for confirming it for us."

She smiled and walked off, leaving the CIA visitors smirking and Ron blushing and shaking his head. Chuckles rose from a few of the low-walled cubicles in the FBI office as Poland's squadmates enjoyed a *schadenfreude* moment.

Michelle tried to appease the FBI agent. "Ron, I'm so sorry. I didn't mean to start anything or make you look bad. I'm just a bit nervous. I've never reported a kidnapping before."

"No problem, Michelle. Kidnapping is new to us, too, on the national security squads. We don't usually handle cases like that."

"I never said I was new to kidnapping," Michelle clarified. "I've just never reported one before."

Caroline and Ron looked sideways at Michelle as they entered the small conference room. Neither could envision the five-foot-five brunette with trim, athletic legs jutting out from beneath her knee-length black skirt doing more in a kidnapping than making the ransom call. Both were getting to know Michelle. Neither knew her alter ego, Eden.

The CIA counterintelligence officer looked at the FBI agent and placed a color portrait on the conference room table. "This is Isabelle Cirrone," Caroline said. "She's an undercover CIA operations officer who was kidnapped from Times Square late yesterday afternoon."

Caroline dug into the bottom of the envelope of photos and data she carried and withdrew a blue thumb drive. "Everything's on here in digital form, so you don't have to take as many notes."

Poland thanked her for the digital archive and looked closely at Bella's photo.

Michelle related the story of what she saw of Bella's abduction from the hotel bar.

"This," Caroline said as she handed a sheet of paper to the FBI agent, "is biographical information on Bella. The vital statistics are recent—within the last week. We realize you'll have to involve NYPD in the investigation at some point, so the family and work information on that sheet is all fully backstopped undercover information. We'll share Bella's true background with the FBI, but we'd appreciate it if you'd keep that within federal channels. If NYPD starts poking around the background data on that sheet, we'll hear about it. They won't be able to penetrate the backstopping."

Ron Poland nodded and put the sheet down on the conference table. He explained the FBI's standard protocol for investigating kidnapping cases and read over the material the JTTF had provided to Bob McMillian. "Normally, we'd wait for a ransom call, tap a few phones, make the money drop and follow the kidnappers back to their hideout—just like in the movies, but a lot more high tech." He let the papers fall onto the table and looked at the women across the government's small round slab of Formica-covered particleboard. "But that's not the case this time, is it?"

Michelle shook her head. "No. Here's what's not in your files." She explained the relationship between Bella Cirrone and Wasif Ali, leaving out her own role in Bella's rescue in Iraq.

Poland leaned back, took a deep breath, and exhaled slowly as he digested the new information. "And I suppose *that* part of the file is classified?"

Caroline van der Pol nodded. "Consider it secret for now."

"No problem," Poland said, "every FBI employee is cleared to the Top Secret level, and everyone on the task force—including local agencies—is cleared for Sensitive Compartmented Information which allows access to intelligence source material."

The FBI agent straightened the papers, and said to Caroline, "I'll get a seven-matter case opened and request twenty-four-hour surveillance of Wasif Ali for the next week."

"Sorry," Michelle asked, "what's a 'seven-matter'?"

"Oh," Poland said, "that's Bu-speak for a kidnapping case. Opening that won't be a problem, but getting surveillances set up at this time of year could be an issue, what with New Year's coming up. There's no specific threat to the city, but there are always a dozen wacko groups planning to protest—some quite violently—against whatever they happen to hate this year."

"I'm sure you'll do everything you can," Caroline said. "We're talking about a woman's life, here."

"If it would help," Michelle offered, "I could scare up a small surveillance team and—"

Caroline shut her down immediately. "No, this is an FBI case, now, Michelle. The FBI has thousands of employees in New York City. It's *their* jurisdiction."

Ron Poland tucked the papers into a folder. "In fact, ten percent of the entire FBI is here in New York City. This is our largest office. We can handle it."

Michelle nodded slowly. "Glad to hear it." She wasn't going to agree to sit idly by, but saw that this was neither the time nor the audience with which she wanted to press the issue. "So, what's next?"

***

Michelle sat down in a guest cubicle in the CIA's National Resources Division office and dialed her team lead's number on the secure desk phone. After getting his voicemail message and hanging up, she dialed another number. Wilson Henry, the team's intelligence analyst, answered on the second ring.

"Holding down the fort back in Virginia?" Michelle asked.

"Oh, you know it." Wilson's distinct Boston accent was unmistakable over the crystal-clear connection. "Mike took his wife to West Virginia for a week. They're staying at the Greenbriar again."

"West Virginia's not my favorite place, but I know Mona likes it there. That's the big hotel that had Congress's never-used cold-war bunker underneath, right?"

"*That's* the one. They made that part into a museum. So, what are you up to in the Big Apple?"

"Unfortunately, not much. The FBI's got a good jump on their investigation. They've pulled all the background records they can, and they have a surveillance team set up on the apartment. I'd love to be out there with them, but they won't let me."

"I'm sure they have their reasons. And, besides, you of all people hanging out with a bunch of cops and federal agents does *not* seem like a match made in heaven."

"Yeah, I know, *right*? So, Wilson, I need to ask you do something for me. Call down to the Farm and ask the armory to send me two of my bags of equipment. I want disguise kit number two and technical equipment kit number one."

"Two and one, got it. Easy enough. So, is someone getting bored sitting in a cubicle all day?"

"You know me far too well, Wilson. How in the world can you sit in an office day in and day out without going batshit crazy? I can't stand not being out there on the street."

"Well, not all of us have your skillset, Michelle, nor your penchant for languages. While I'm ordering up your gear, are you going to want a weapons kit?"

Michelle hesitated. "I think the answers to whether 'I want one' and 'should I have one sent up' are entirely different. Let's go with 'no' for now, and if things change, I'll call you back. Just have the two bags I mentioned overnighted to the NR Division's Manhattan office." She read the address to Wilson and thanked him.

The following day, Michelle inventoried the disguise kit, lockpicks, and assorted electronics Wilson Henry had faithfully ordered up. She confirmed everything arrived in good shape. She set the disguise kit—a nondescript black duffel which looked like any other gym or overnight bag—next to her purse to take back to the Marriott after she made one small detour. From the other kit, she selected a small set of lockpicks in a thin leather case and secreted them into one of four hidden compartments inside the disguise kit's large purse. She left the rest of the technical gear in the NR division office and, even though it was still before lunchtime, left for the day.

At a supermarket two blocks from the office, she purchased a bottle of water and a brush. In the ladies' room, she changed into a new set of clothes, a blonde wig, and oversized sunglasses from her disguise kit.

In front of the store, Michelle flagged a taxi and rode north, past the 9/11 Memorial to City Hall Park. There, she switched cabs and rode to a corner four blocks from Wasif Ali's apartment.

She walked a route she'd planned at the NR office. To anyone observing her, she would seemingly be window shopping and making a couple of small purchases while in reality she studied her surroundings carefully to spot a surveillance team. She made her way along the memorized surveillance-detection route, traversing a stair-step pattern across a dozen city blocks, crossing streets at every other corner and stopping into three stores to look at women's clothing. Twice, she stopped to buy snacks and a drink at cafés into which she could enter from the street and exit into the interior of an office building. No one followed her.

Once on Wasif's street, she walked down the block slowly while drinking from the bottle of water she'd purchased and pretending to talk on her cell phone. All the while, she used the phone to record a video of the street-side scene outside his apartment for future reference.

The weathered façade of Wasif's aging apartment building sported cracks and an old-style stoop with a half-dozen steps leading up to the front door. Two men in jackets over long, white thobes—traditional Arab menswear—sat on the steps, talking. Michelle couldn't tell whether the men guarded the entrance or were just hanging out. Either way, they served as a significant disincentive for anyone who wanted to wander into the building to take a look—innocently or otherwise. She frowned when she concluded she wouldn't be able to sneak in and peek at the hallway outside Wasif's third-floor apartment.

Michelle stopped at a café three blocks away and ate a light lunch while replaying the video on the tiny screen of her cell phone. Thirty minutes later, she returned along the opposite side of the street, again videoing the scene, but from the opposite point of view. This time, she walked faster since she had to pass directly in front of the two men still sitting on the apartment building's front steps.

The men's silence disappointed her. She felt certain they wouldn't guess a random Western woman on the street would speak Arabic as well as she does, and she had hoped to hear what they were talking about. It was unlikely to be incriminating, but there was always a chance they'd be talking about people or vehicles that looked out of place. Often, people under surveillance make fun of their watchers openly. Michelle would have loved to hear that side of the conversation for once.

Few people walked down the block as Michelle strolled along the street on which Wasif lived. As she got to the far corner, she 'hung up' her phone and put it into her purse. She walked a dozen blocks in a zigzag pattern to detect anyone tailing her. When she decided she was still free of surveillance, she caught a taxi to Times Square.

In her hotel room, Michelle replayed the two videos a dozen times. At first, nothing seemed different between the two. She squinted into the small screen and paused it on one of six trucks parked along the side of the street opposite Wasif's building. She tapped carefully with her thumbs on the tiny screen, queued both videos to show the same particular area of the street, and flipped between the two repeatedly. She caught herself tilting the phone as if moving it up and down would change the angle of the video and show her something below its field of view. She snorted at her own expense and used the images she'd captured as best she could.

A brown-and-white Knickerbocker Plumbing truck caught her eye. In the before-lunch image, the truck sat lower on its suspension than in the corresponding image after lunch. She scoured the images for any sign that the owner had removed equipment from the truck. The same three ladders sat on top of the truck in both videos. Nothing she saw could account for how the truck could have shed several hundred pounds in the half-hour between her walks down that block.

She smiled at the one thing that could explain it.

Chapter 9

FBI JTTF Office, New York City

First thing the next morning, Michelle stood outside Special Agent Ron Poland's office cubicle and smiled at him. "*Sooooo*, Ron, how's the surveillance of Wasif's apartment going?"

"Fine. There's nothing significant to report. The team followed Wasif around town a few times and identified a couple of his customers, but there's been no sign of Bella."

"What about the guys on the stoop of his building?"

"Huh?"

"You know, the two guys acting as lookouts. I'm sure your team in the plumbing truck is watching them closely."

"I don't know what you're—"

Michelle cocked her head. "Are you *really* going to pull that crap on me? *Me*?"

Poland leaned back in his chair and looked at Michelle for a few seconds before responding. "Our surveillance teams use a variety of vehicles for surveillance. Some of them we own, others we just rent for the day."

"And some of the guys sitting in the vans all day get hungry and go out for lunch or take bathroom breaks, too. I noticed that."

"You were around the apartment? You really shouldn't—"

"Yeah, if you knew me better, you'd know I do a lot of things I 'really shouldn't' do. So, is your team using a shotgun mic to listen to the neighborhood gossip? Have they heard anything good?"

"No, we can't do that. It'd require a court order. We can't just—"

"Oh, warrant *shmarrant*," Michelle said, and waved her hand in dismissal. "There's a kidnapped woman at risk and we need to find her."

Caroline van der Pol walked around the corner. "Michelle, I'm sure he knows what's at stake. This is not the first kidnapping the FBI has worked, and—"

"Yeah, yeah," Michelle grumbled, "I know, but the best chance to recover a kidnapped victim is when there's a ransom demand which the family agrees to pay. There's been no such demand, right, Ron?"

Ron Poland looked at her sideways. "Know much about kidnappings, do we?"

Michelle shrugged. "I Googled it."

"Well, yes, that's true, but—"

"So, in *this* case, we have to be more proactive."

Ron crossed his arms. "Do you ever let other people finish their—"

Michelle smiled. "*Sentences*? Not when I need more action and less talking."

"We're already—"

"Then let me sit in the van for a day or two until I get bored. At least you'll have two days of peace around here without my interrupting you."

Caroline smiled at Ron, and said, "She has a point about that."

Poland dipped his head slightly. "Fine. I'll call the surveillance team lead and let him know to expect you at their staging area bright and early tomorrow morning." He looked at Michelle and furrowed his brow. "You didn't interrupt me."

"Nope," she said sweetly. "We're both getting what we want. See how easy life can be when I'm getting my way? Nicely done."

Ron Poland shook his head, and asked Caroline, "Does she always get her way?"

"I don't know her that well, yet, but I'm starting to think so."

"Well," the FBI agent smiled, and said, "at least if she gives the guys in the truck any problems tomorrow, they have guns. If they end up shooting her, I'm going to believe them when they say it was self-defense."

Michelle shrugged. "Okay, but just remember what happened to the last guy who shot me." She tapped her left thigh twice and walked back to her cubicle grinning.

***

The FBI's surveillance team lead selected a faux-electrician's box truck to keep "the eye" in front of the apartment on the next day's outing. Michelle stowed her backpack of lunch, equipment, and bottles of water under her seat and sat quietly. She resolved to not make a pest of herself in the hopes of getting an invitation to return the next day—or at least the next time she wanted to.

The agent who drove the van parked it halfway down Wasif's block and exited the vehicle in full view of anyone on the street. He wrangled a toolbox from one of the exterior compartments on the van to complement his look as a working electrician, and disappeared for the day, ostensibly on a job in the neighborhood.

In the back, Michelle watched silently as two FBI agents adjusted a half-dozen cameras. Special Agent William Hood pointed one camera at the three men on the apartment building's stoop and two others up and down the street. SA Paul McQueen attached another camera to a periscope concealed inside one of the supports on which the ladder tied to the roof rested.

A mobile surveillance team of eight FBI vehicles followed Wasif Ali on his travels around Manhattan. Michelle and the agents in the van listened to the radio transmissions reporting Wasif's stops and deliveries of electronics.

Rush hour traffic had already ebbed, and the trickle of pedestrians on the drab residential street stayed light for most of the morning.

Once an hour, Bill Hood conducted radio checks with the other surveillance vehicles parked across an eight-block radius surrounding the apartment. Every now and then, one of the FBI agents in the other vehicles would radio in a status code. Michelle quickly figured out the pattern: 10-7 meant they'd be temporarily unavailable, and 10-8 meant they were back from their meal or potty break. Her CIA team never used the typical police radio codes on their surveillances, so she enjoyed the challenge of deciphering the FBI's lingo.

Just after 4 p.m., the mobile surveillance team radioed news of Wasif's arrival when he parked his white van in a garage two blocks away. Bill Hood snapped a dozen photos of the tall, thin man greeting the two elderly lookouts sitting on the stoop as he walked up the steps and into his apartment building.

"The jaybird has entered his nest," Paul McQueen radioed to the mobile surveillance team.

Michelle cocked her head and looked at him sideways. "You guys really talk like that?"

"Not usually," McQueen replied, "but it's been boring as *fu*—ahem, *hell* here today. I was just having a little bit of fun."

"Okay," Michelle said with a wry smile, "I won't let that sour my opinion of Hoover's famous G-Men."

One of the FBI agents on the mobile surveillance team approached Wasif's white van in the parking garage and peeked through the windows to see if Bella were inside. He radioed there was no sound or movement and was returning to his car.

Michelle asked, "Are you guys allowed to break into the van and take a look?"

Paul McQueen shrugged. "Yes, in this instance, we could because it's a kidnapping case, but it's unlikely he'd keep anyone alone in the van overnight, so why risk it? And you heard on the radio that we had an eye on him all day. Unfortunately, he didn't stop anywhere long enough for a quickie with—"

"*Hey!*" Michelle said louder than she intended. She covered her mouth, remembering they were supposed to be pretending to be an empty truck. She whispered to Paul, "That's a friend of mine you're talking about. She's the victim, here."

"You're right. I apologize. It's been a long day for all of us. I want to get her back, too."

Michelle sat back and looked around the van. "Is this all you guys really have for surveillance? Radios and a couple of still and video cameras? Nothing high tech?"

Bill Hood nodded. "Nope. For criminal cases, this is standard fare and pretty much all we get. If Wasif were suspected in some kind of terrorist plot, then things would be different. The Technically Trained Agents on our tech squad—the TTAs in Bu-speak, because everything in the government has to be an acronym or it'll never get funded—have some cool gadgets they can use to follow subjects from a longer distance. In this case, we're looking for a kidnapped woman, and Wasif's not even trying to detect or evade our surveillance. He's not the KGB."

"It's the SVR, now," Michelle said offhandedly, and pulled her backpack out from under her seat.

"Yeah," Hood noted, "I know, but no one outside the intelligence business has ever heard of them by that name. They—what is *that*?"

Michelle pulled a tablet and two small sensors from her backpack. She stuck the pair of sensors to the tinted glass of the van's elongated side window and plugged their cords into the tablet.

SA Hood asked her again, "What have you got there?"

"Technology," Michelle said. "You should try it sometime. It's great. All the cool kids are using it these days." She focused the image on the tablet's screen at the right distance for the apartment building across the street and angled the sensors upward to scan the third floor.

"Seriously," Bill Hood asked, "what—"

"It's a thermal scanner," Michelle answered without taking her eyes off the tablet's screen. "Here, take a look. I've focused it on Wasif's apartment."

She turned the tablet halfway around so the two FBI agents could see the four white blobs representing heat in Wasif's apartment.

Michelle explained the image to the agents. "There are four large heat signatures—those white blobs. Two are stationary and two are moving. The two moving blobs are probably Wasif and Noor. I'm not sure what the other two are, yet."

Bill Hood pointed to the screen. "It's winter in New York and they live in an eighty-year-old building. Those would be radiators. For heat."

Michelle considered the possibility.

Paul McQueen agreed. "Yeah, we can check city building and utility records pretty quickly through the JTTF, but it's very likely this apartment has an old-style boiler in the basement which forces hot water up to the radiators in each bedroom."

Michelle scrunched up here nose. "Those are common in eastern Europe, but I didn't realize we still have apartment buildings with those kinds of things here."

"Yup. The lack of modern amenities keeps the rent down. I'll bet they're not paying more than about thirty-five hundred or so for that place."

"A *month!*" Michelle cupped her hand over her mouth. "Sorry...."

"Hey," Hood said through a chuckle, "welcome to New York. Just try living here on a government salary. That's why I live across the river, in Jersey."

"They're moving together," Paul McQueen said as he stabbed a finger into the tablet's screen. He looked out the window and counted the crowd gathering in front of the building. "Same time as yesterday."

Michelle checked her watch. "It's a little after four, so this is *Maghrib.*"

"Mah-*what?*"

"No, it's pronounced *mah*-grib. It's the Muslim afternoon prayer that comes right after sunset. They're heading to their mosque."

"Yeah," Bill Hood said, "the mobile teams followed them there and back yesterday. Check it out," he said, pointing to the two dozen people walking down the block. "Wasif's near the front of the herd, but look, third from the back. The woman in the black hajib."

Michelle peered through the tinted window. "I see her. The woman with the John Lennon glasses, right?"

"Yup, that's Noor."

Michelle looked at the tablet. Two stationary heat blobs adorned the screen. "Damn, just two heat signatures in the apartment, now. Wasif must be keeping Bella somewhere else. I was really hoping...."

She sat lost in thought for a few moments.

"Yeah," McQueen said, "that would have made it easy. Maybe *too* easy. Sorry it didn't work out like you hoped. Investigating these things take days or weeks. We can't finish every case in an hour like on TV."

"No," Michelle said, dejected, "I know."

The trio watched the front of the apartment building silently for the next forty minutes. The parade of faithful returned from the mosque and climbed the steps back to their apartments. This time, Noor walked in the middle of the pack and Wasif talked with another man as they lazily ambled at the rear of the group.

Michelle watched Noor enter the apartment and move around in a small area. The CIA officer checked her wristwatch, and said to the FBI agents, "Time for dinner."

"We'll knock off the surveillance before then," Bill Hood said.

Michelle shook her head and pointed to the slowly moving heat blob on the tablet. "No, I mean Noor is making dinner. Her movements look small because she's in the kitchen."

Hood looked at the screen and nodded. "Oh. Makes sense."

Wasif entered his apartment and walked from room to room. His heat blob overlapped Noor's and stopped. Michelle imagined he was asking—or demanding to know—when dinner would be ready. He walked into a bedroom. The blob dimmed slightly, and his heat blob shrunk in height and grew slightly in width.

"What's up with that?" McQueen asked.

Michelle looked at the image and adjusted the focus of the thermal sensors. The picture didn't improve. "I think he probably went into the bathroom, closed the door, and is sitting on the toilet."

"Oh, great," McQueen said, and turned away from the tablet. "I really did *not* need to know that."

Michelle rested the tablet on the workbench and propped it up against the FBI radio.

Wasif finished in the bathroom and the trio in the surveillance van watched him—or at least his heat blob—walk about his apartment. He walked back to the kitchen, through what Michelle imagined was most likely the dining room, and then over to the second bedroom.

Wasif entered the bedroom and his heat blob shifted to its shorter, wider version again, and stayed still for a few minutes.

The team watched Noor's blob meander around in the kitchen while the other three blobs sat unmoving on the screen. Michelle spent at least as much time looking at her watch as she did the tablet.

After five minutes, Wasif's heat blob moved, and so did the radiator. Michelle bent forward slightly and watched the white heat emissions of the radiator elongate until it was double its original size.

"What's going on?" Bill Hood asked under his breath.

Michelle leaned closer to the tablet and picked it up.

Wasif's heat blob merged into the radiator's, extending its length considerably.

"Oh, holy *shit!*" Michelle said, not caring how loudly she spoke. "I can't believe I missed that."

She dropped the tablet on the workbench, and it skittered into the radio handset. She reached for the door handle, and said, "We have to get up there. It's Bella. He's... He's on top of her again. We have to stop him! We have to save her. Come *on!* One of you, give me a gun."

Paul McQueen gripped Michelle's hand and held her firm. "Wait, we can't go out there. And how do you know she's even up there, anyway?"

Michelle ignored the FBI agent. "I should have brought my own gun. Give me one of yours. We have to get her out of there."

"Michelle," McQueen said quietly, "we're not going anywhere, and certainly not without a hell of a lot of back up before we charge into a building full of people unlikely to be even the least bit friendly. We're not equipped for that kind of tactical action. Besides, what makes you think Bella's even in there?"

Michelle reached for the tablet. She plopped down in her seat, rewound the video, and set the system to retain the entire record of the last quarter hour. The CIA officer queued up the video to the correct spot and jabbed her finger at the triangular "play" icon. Her pink-painted fingernail bounced off the tablet's smooth glass face. She slowed down, got her hands back under control, and tapped the icon again, this time more calmly.

"Here," she said, "is where Wasif enters the second bedroom and sits down again. See how his heat signature gets shorter like when he was on the toilet? This time, he's sitting in a chair reading poetry to Bella."

"How the hell can you know what he's reading to her?" Bill Hood asked incredulously. "Or that he's even reading at all? You can't hear through that thing, can you? It's not a parabolic microphone."

"I don't have to hear any of it to know what's going on. Bella told me what Wasif used to do to her. He'd sit and read religious poetry to her before sex, which was either his version of foreplay or maybe nothing more than self-justification for what he was about to do to her. I'm not sure. What I *am* sure of is this." Michelle fast-forwarded the video to the point at which Wasif stood up from the chair, and she pointed to the radiator's bright heat blob. "Look here. The radiator gets longer even before Wasif goes over to it. *That's* Bella. She's lying back waiting for the bastard. We didn't see her before because her heat signature was blocked by the radiator's. Or maybe she's chained to the damned thing and on these low-resolution images it all looks the same."

Michelle pushed pause as Wasif's heat blob covered Bella's and handed the tablet to McQueen. "I can't watch it anymore. We need to get up there and pull her out. Call in whoever you need to, but let's get this over with pronto."

McQueen and Hood looked at each other with pained expressions. Both knew they didn't have the authority on their own to decide to rush in, making an unplanned and ill-equipped hostage rescue. Best case, they'd get to the apartment door and have no way to force it open. Worst case, they'd create a tactical mess, get themselves and likely the hostage killed. Neither man could see an option likely to result in them getting Bella out successfully and no one getting hurt. Or killed. Especially them.

Bill Hood pulled his cell phone from his belt clip, called his squad supervisor, and explained Michelle's theory about the heat signatures on the thermal scanner. He ducked the question about why he and McQueen were using unauthorized intrusive investigative technology. Later, if he had to, he'd cast the blame for that onto Michelle and the CIA. An FBI agent blaming another agency—especially the CIA—pretty much guaranteed him a pass on any offense, especially when he had a fellow agent present as a witness.

Hood hung up the phone and looked at Paul McQueen. "The boss says to burn off the surveillance and regroup for a debrief. She's texting Jimmy to come back and drive the truck to the JTTF office."

He looked at Michelle, and added, "You can brief the team there and show them the video. They'll need to see it for themselves before either requesting a search warrant from a federal magistrate judge or authorizing an entry based on exigent circumstances."

Michelle stewed in her seat. She considered her options and didn't like either one. An unarmed, one-woman full-frontal assault on the apartment guaranteed failure and would certainly cause Wasif to move Bella. Right now, the FBI had the element of surprise. Her rushing in would sacrifice their one-and-only advantage for no apparent gain. On the other hand, the prospect of having to convince others she was right, and then waiting for another opportunity to save Bella, made her neck turn red.

She looked at Hood and McQueen and silently nodded.

The FBI agents packed up their cameras and waited for the agent posing as the electrician to return from one of the mobile surveillance units and drive them to the task force office.

For Michelle, it was the longest twelve minutes of her life.

Chapter 10

Michelle Reagan finished her briefing to the members of the task force by gesturing briskly at the conference room's big-screen TV. The wall-mounted video monitor displayed an enlarged snapshot from her thermal imager's video recording. "So, that's how I know it's her. I'm one-hundred-percent certain Bella Cirrone is in that apartment."

Caroline van der Pol asked the first question. "Why do you think you didn't see her earlier?"

"Her body heat," Michelle replied, "was overshadowed by the radiator's. I suspect she either spends her time sitting in front of the radiator or lying down next to it. If she lay very close to the radiator, her heat signature would merge entirely with the radiator's white blob and we'd never see them as two separate objects. Only when she lay back on the floor *away* from the radiator did she extend past that of the radiator's blob. That's when we saw her—when Wasif approached her to... well, you know that part."

One of the FBI's tech agents raised his hand, and asked, "Michelle, does your thermal scanner also show the intensity of the various heat blooms? By the way, they're 'blooms,' not 'blobs.'"

Michelle ignored his correction. "I don't know, but I'd be happy to give you the file from the tablet to analyze for yourself."

He thanked her and sat back.

FBI Supervisory Special Agent Nola Austin pointed to Bill Hood and Paul McQueen, the two agents from her squad with whom Michelle had spent the day. "Bill and Paul tell me you're recommending a tactical hostage rescue."

Michelle nodded. "I did it once. I can do it again. In this—"

Caroline van der Pol interrupted. "Nola, we recognize the FBI's jurisdiction in this case. The CIA will not take independent operational action on US soil."

Michelle glowered at Caroline and focused on SSA Austin again. "As I was saying, that's my recommendation, but in this case, I'll defer to you to determine the right path forward. As I understand it, you don't need a court order or search warrant to make rescues in kidnapping cases, but I'm not the expert. I just want to foot-stomp that a vulnerable and battered woman is at risk here. The longer we spend having meetings or debates, the more abuse she'll have to endure because of our delays. Anything Wasif does to Bella from this moment on is because of *us*—the dozen people in this room. I just want to get her back to safety as soon as we can—tonight, if possible." Having said her piece, she sat down and listened to the FBI discuss their options.

At the end of their deliberations, and much to Michelle's chagrin, Nola Austin announced they would reconvene the following morning at 10 a.m. for what she euphemistically termed a 'planning session.' Austin said she'd call in the FBI SWAT team's lead to join them and evaluate the situation from a tactical viewpoint. The JTTF analysts committed to getting the apartment building's complete architectural schematics from the city building commission and would review the surveillance team's reports and videos from the past few days. The tech agent enthusiastically said he'd scour the thermal scanner's data for any additional clues he might glean from it.

After the meeting concluded, Michelle approached van der Pol in the corner of the JTTF conference room and spoke quietly. "Thanks, Caroline. Way to make me look like a total shit in front of the entire group. You could have at least let me finish my sentence. I hope I can return the favor one day."

"Michelle, that was not my intention. I—"

"Save it for someone who cares," she said, and headed off to the Marriott's gym to work off her frustration and leg cramps from a long day of being cooped up in a surveillance vehicle.

***

The following morning, Michelle looked around at the mix of both new and familiar faces scattered throughout the JTTF's conference room. Bob McMillian, the CIA's liaison to the JTTF, sat to Michelle's left, and Caroline van der Pol to her right.

Within punching distance, Michelle thought, knowing she'd never actually do it. Well, probably not.

Supervisory Special Agent Matthew Decker, the New York Field Office's SWAT team leader, sat across from Michelle and next to SSA Nola Austin. He summarized his preliminary tactical plan for entry into

Wasif's apartment. "Whenever we decide to make the actual entry, the ingress and egress will be the same. We'll secure the rear stairwell and ascend to the third floor. The entry team will lead, and we'll leave two SWAT agents on each landing in the stairwell to prevent anyone from entering behind us on intermediate floors."

Nola Austin asked, "Do you have enough SWAT agents to do all that or will you need participation from my squad?"

"I'll bring two SWAT teams. We're used to working together. Your agents will stay outside the rear of the building until we've secured the apartment. Then, you can enter, take control of the hostage and anyone we've detained, and conduct whatever search you deem necessary. Unless we meet resistance upon our entry, we'll just detain anyone present, and then your agents can determine who, if anyone, to keep in custody and make the formal arrests."

Caroline's supervisor, Phil Thompson, spoke up from the far side of the table. "I understand your tactical plan, and that sounds fine. It's not my area of expertise, but I'd like to know the FBI's or JTTF's thoughts on what Wasif Ali is up to here in New York."

Nola Austin tapped her fingernail on the table. "What do you mean? This is a kidnapping, and it was your own agent who located the missing woman."

Phil Thompson let Austin's misnomer stand uncorrected—the FBI employs special *agents*; the CIA employs intelligence *officers*. "Yes, but... What is Wasif Ali doing in the United States in the first place? He's a retired Iraqi Air Force colonel and fighter pilot who fought against us in the First Gulf War. His son followed him into the Iraqi Air Force and apparently the US killed him during our invasion in 2003. Since Wasif rose to the rank of colonel, it's safe to assume he was a member of the Baathist Party until we destroyed it."

"Yes," one of the JTTF analysts said, "but he and his wife are legal permanent residents of the US—they have green cards, if you will. They're here legally, and they're not suspected of any terrorist connections. They're not on any watch lists—"

"Yeah," Thompson said, "got it. I'm not asking whether they *are* on a watch list, just whether they *should be*. Remember, we know that after the fall of Saddam Hussein the remaining Baathists formed the hardcore religious backbone of ISIS. What we *don't* know and should be asking ourselves is that when Isabelle Cirrone was kidnapped the first time, *why* was she given to Wasif Ali al-Bakkar in the first place? Why *him* in particular?"

The analyst sat back in his chair. "Foreign intel is the CIA's domain. You tell us."

"And then," Phil asked, "why after only six months did Wasif give Bella away, and again, it was to someone with a connection to ISIS, albeit a tenuous one?"

"Again," the analyst said, "you tell us."

"I wish I had the answers, but right now we should all be asking ourselves more questions than just which door to the apartment building to kick in."

Michelle Reagan spoke for the first time that morning. "We should go in through the front door like we own the place."

"*Excuse* me?" the SWAT team lead asked indignantly. "Sending two-dozen SWAT agents in the front door is the sure way to have someone start shooting at us. With the lookouts out front, they'll see us coming from two blocks away. We'll—"

"Not two dozen agents, Matt. Just one. And me."

"*You*? Not happening. With only one agent we couldn't control the environment, breach the door, and secure the apartment. We'd never get past the lookouts unchallenged. That's why we'll go in at four in the morning and go up the stairs quickly and quietly."

"I agree with the 'quietly' part, but we need to do it at 4 p.m., not 4 a.m."

"All right, I'll bite," the SWAT team lead said, and threw up his hands. "Why in broad daylight and not under the cover of darkness?"

"Because the building will be mostly empty. We've already seen that most of the residents attend mosque for Maghrib prayers in the afternoon. So, this afternoon we'll wait until the crowd walks away from the building and then calmly walk in the front door and up to the third floor."

The SWAT leader could barely stay in his chair. "What do you think the lookouts will do the second they see two dozen FBI SWAT agents approaching the entrance?"

Caroline van der Pol started to speak but stopped when Michelle held up her hand.

"Nothing," Michelle said, "because they won't know we're government. We—"

"You don't understand, there is no *we*."

"Why, because you speak Arabic so well, Matt?"

"What does that have to do with anything?"

"Even in disguises, we can't just walk past the one lookout they leave on the steps at prayer time without a formal greeting. How fluent are you, anyway?"

"I'm not, but the FBI has plenty of fluent Arabic speakers. We can find plenty here in New York."

Michelle smiled. "And how many of them are on your SWAT teams and you'd trust to go through a door with you?"

Matt Decker didn't answer.

"That's what I thought," Michelle said. "So, if we do it my way, you can keep the van full of uniformed SWAT operators two blocks away while you and I go upstairs. With the surveillance team using my thermal imager, we'll already know the apartment is empty, except for Bella. I'll get us past the lookout and, with the right disguises, we won't raise anyone's hackles. When we recover Bella, we walk down the rear stairwell to a waiting, unmarked FBI car or two. If things go bad, you radio the SWAT van and they're only thirty seconds away."

Decker sneered. "Why go through all these machinations instead of just rescuing the hostage using tried-and-true tactics?"

"Because my way preserves the FBI's freedom of action after we rescue her. I'm not an analyst or investigator, but if, as Phil suggests, Wasif's presence here is worth looking into further, then Bella's disappearance would be the only clue Wasif has that something may be amiss. You and I can make her disappearance simply look like she escaped on her own if we appropriately stage the scene. After we bring her back, Nola's agents can interview Bella, get her statement and whatever else you need to investigate and charge Wasif with kidnapping. After that, you can make an arrest at your leisure. You can stop him on the street one day instead of storming into the unknown of an apartment building he and his friends control. The follow-up is for Nola's squad to figure out later. Once we get Bella back, I'll be out of your hair for good."

Nola Austin said, "My primary concerns are a successful hostage rescue, if Bella is indeed in the apartment, and then the quick arrest of Wasif Ali for kidnapping. I—" She paused mid-thought.

After a few beats, Phil Thompson offered a compromise. "I have far more questions about Wasif than I have any evidence the guy's doing something wrong. Other than kidnapping, I mean. So, how about this. We try it Michelle's way this afternoon. If she can't get herself and Matt through the front door, they'll walk away and then SWAT gets to do it their way in the middle of the night. We'll bring the iron fist wrapped in the proverbial velvet glove."

Michelle looked at Matt Decker, and said, "I'll bet you'll look good with an Arab thobe over your SWAT body armor. Just don't wear a radio earpiece — those are dead giveaways."

Decker sat back and considered Michelle's plan. "Hmm. Sure, why not. It's been a few years since I did any undercover work, but on one condition."

"What's that?"

Decker gestured to the tall black FBI agent sitting next to him. "We bring Brian along."

Michelle shrugged. "Fine with me."

"And," Decker said, "you don't get a gun."

Michelle shrugged again. "Fine, if I need one, I'll take yours."

"You just try."

Michelle laughed. "*You* just try to stop me."

Chapter 11

New York City

At the JTTF office that afternoon, Michelle Reagan inspected Matthew Decker and Brian Jackson closely. The two FBI SWAT agents looked convincing in the thobes, skullcaps, and the oversized winter jackets Michelle picked out for them. The bulky jackets concealed the agents' body armor and .45 caliber handguns, of which each agent carried two.

"You guys look good. I'm glad you remembered to wear black dress shoes instead of tactical boots. When wearing disguises, it's the little details that matter most."

"And what about you? Are you wearing street clothes after making us get dressed up for Halloween?"

Michelle opened her backpack and carefully withdrew a large black garment. She donned the burqa, leaving the hood off until later. "Ta *da*. What do you think?"

"Do you always travel with that?" Brian Jackson asked as he felt the coarse fabric of her sleeve. A small stain near the cuff caught his eye. "You've worn this before, I see."

Michelle looked at the dried stain and made a mental note to have the burqa dry-cleaned again after this mission. *Well, not a mission, but a — whatever the hell it is.*

Jackson seemed fixated on the blemish. "Is that a food stain?"

Michelle pulled it away from him. "I don't know. Organic matter of some sort, I guess. Let's get going." She pointed at Matt Decker. "*Oh*, for the purposes of any conversation we have with people at the apartment, you're my brother." She looked at the few strands of gray hair in his otherwise light brown beard. "*Older* brother. They'll question why a woman is traveling with men who are not her relatives or husband. That's just the way it is in their culture. If you have to speak, only use our first names. If the conversation gets more complicated than that, I'll make our excuses, and we'll walk away. The danger word is 'popcorn.' If I say that, draw your weapons and shoot anyone you want to, except me. Any questions?"

A wicked grin formed on Matt Decker's face. "I'll reserve judgment on that last part."

Michelle mimicked his smile. "You're almost as cute as you are funny. *Almost*. Okay, guys," she said as she gathered a sheaf of papers, "let's go."

***

Decker parked his car four blocks from Wasif Ali's apartment, and Michelle led the way along the sidewalk at a measured pace. Each time she exhaled into the chilly December air, her breath crystalized in front of her burqa's veil. Matt Decker and Brian Jackson followed immediately behind. In the stress of the moment of approaching a possibly hostile tactical environment, both puffed white clouds like steam locomotives working overtime to get up a steep incline. Jackson adjusted his white knit skull cap nervously.

The CIA officer ascended the apartment building's exterior stairs and greeted the single lookout in Arabic. "*As-salaamu aaleyka.*"

"*As-salaamu aaleyki,*" he replied, and continued in Arabic. "Can I help you, sister? You're new here, no?"

"No, I've been here before," Michelle replied in Arabic. She held up the flyers she'd prepared in the JTTF office earlier that day. "I'm handing out flyers to invite the brothers and sisters of the neighborhood to hear a wonderful young guest speaker coming to the New York Public Library in a few weeks to share his experiences in Mecca when he made his pilgrimage last year. Would you like to attend?" She offered the man a flyer.

"If you're putting one on every door, I'll get mine upstairs." The elderly lookout pointed to the pair of FBI agents. "And they are?"

"My brother," Michelle replied, tapping Matt Decker on the arm, "and his friend who wants to make his pilgrimage next year." She held up the flyers, thanked the man politely, and continued forward before he could drag the conversation out.

When they were alone in the stairwell and halfway to the second floor, Michelle lifted her burqa's hood over her head, rested it against the back of her neck, and smiled at her FBI escorts. "Not bad play-acting, if I do say so myself."

Decker whispered back. "Not bad at all. So far, so good."

The trio climbed the stairs two at a time and paused on the third-floor landing. Michelle pulled her veil back down and stepped into the hallway. She rotated to look from side to side since the fabric mesh in front of her eyes significantly restricted her peripheral vision. The only people in the hallway were a young mother watching two toddlers play against the window at the far end.

To her teammates, Michelle whispered, "Follow me." She walked briskly down the hall away from the woman and children and stopped outside Wasif and Noor Ali's apartment. She pulled a W-shaped lockpick and L-shaped tension wrench from a specially sewn pocket in the sleeve of her burqa and picked the deadbolt open in seven seconds.

She attacked the lock in the door handle with gusto and flinched as the tension wrench snapped in two with a soft metallic *ting*.

"Shit," Michelle said under her breath.

"'Shit?'" Decker asked, the concern in his voice obvious. "What do you mean 'shit?' Don't say 'shit.' 'Shit' is never good. What the hell happened?"

"I broke my tension wrench."

"Well, use another one."

Michelle whispered back without turning around. "I didn't *bring* another one. They never break. It's always the picks that break, and I have plenty of those. Shit."

She felt inside her sleeve for other tools. A thin rake pick sat securely in its pocket.

Michelle turned around and held out her hand to Matt Decker. "Give me your car keys."

"My—"

"Just do it," she insisted, "and hurry."

The SWAT team lead unzipped his jacket pocket and fished inside for a set of keys. He held them over Michelle's hand, tilted his head, and paused.

Michelle tilted her head in response. When Decker didn't move, she opened her eyes wide—the only part of her Decker could see through the burqa—and shook her hand up and down.

Decker let the keys drop three inches into the CIA officer's hand and smiled.

Michelle turned back to the door and looked at the SWAT agent's key ring. The smallest key was a silver handcuff key. She selected the second-smallest one—for his gym locker's padlock—and inserted it into the door handle's lock about quarter inch. She used it as a makeshift tension wrench as she picked the lock, which popped open in less than ten seconds.

Michelle turned the doorknob and pushed the door open two inches. As previously agreed, she backed away and the two SWAT agents entered the apartment first. Once inside and out of sight of anyone in the hallway behind them, they drew their weapons from shoulder holsters concealed beneath their jackets. Instead of staying in the hallway as the agents thought she'd agreed to do, Michelle stepped through the doorway and closed the door behind her. She didn't want the woman at the far end of the hallway wondering what was going on.

Jackson and Decker pulled their radio earpieces from beneath their collars and stuck the telltale plastic pigtails into their left ears. "We're in," Jackson reported, barely audibly.

The surveillance team watching Michelle's thermal imager from the van outside reported that the coast remained clear. Neither SWAT agent was willing to bet his life on any tech gadget, and they proceeded to clear the apartment room by room, slowly and methodically.

When they got to the second bedroom, they found Michelle, sans veil, kneeling on the floor hugging a shaken Bella Cirrone.

Decker holstered his handgun and berated Michelle. "You were supposed to wait outside until we finished clearing the apartment."

Michelle continued to hold her friend in a firm embrace and didn't look up while replying. "You were too slow. Besides, there was some woman at the other end of the hall fawning over a couple of kids. If I stayed out there, it might have spooked her."

Bella sat up and pushed herself away from Michelle. "What are you doing here? You have to leave."

"Bella, we're here to rescue you. *Again,* I might add. I seem to be making a habit of this, but don't get used to it. Let's cut you loose and get you out of here."

Michelle tugged at the long chain secured to the radiator on one end and handcuffed above Bella's ankle on the other. The chain appeared just long enough for Bella to get to the bathroom in the hallway outside the bedroom. Michelle gestured to Decker. "Give me your handcuff key."

Bella pulled her leg away from Michelle. "No, you have to leave. *Now.* They'll be back from prayers soon. You have to go."

"Why? We're here to get you out of this hellhole and away from Wasif."

"No, Michelle, you can't. I have to stay."

Michelle extended Bella to arm's length and looked at the CIA officer closely. "What's wrong with you?" She ran her fingers through

Bella's hair. "Did they crack your skull open or something. Matt, uncuff her ankle, and let's get going."

"No!" Bella screamed and kicked her legs wildly.

Michelle scampered backward and tumbled to the floor. She sat up cross-legged and addressed Bella sternly. "So help me, girl, I swear this time I really *will* break your right kneecap and throw you out the window if that's what I have to do to get you out of this apartment. You—"

"No, Michelle. They're *planning* something. I think it's an attack."

Michelle quieted immediately.

Brian Jackson stepped forward, and asked Bella, "What do you mean, *attack*? Attack on what? Where? *When*?"

"I don't know. I don't know. I don't *know*." Bella hung her head in her hands, hiding her face. "I sometimes hear them talking in the kitchen. Usually, they run the water in the sink to cover up what they're saying, so I can't hear most of it. Not clearly."

"*They* who?" Jackson asked impatiently. "Is Noor involved?"

Bella shook her head. "No, she's just a woman. It's two or three younger men. I don't know who they are. I've only seen one of them, and then only once. But I can *hear* them. Sometimes better than other times."

Michelle turned up her lip at Bella's statement about women, but social inequality in Wasif Ali's world was the least important thing she'd talked about in the two minutes they'd been in the apartment. "Bella," Michelle said, "we'll take you with us now, and you can tell us all about it at the debriefing, okay? You'll—"

"*No*. No, leave me here and bug the apartment. Bug the kitchen especially. Bug this room if you can, and I'll get Wasif to talk to me when we have our private time together between Maghrib prayers and supper."

Private time? Michelle thought. *How could she call it that? How could she not call it what it was?*

Decker looked at Michelle and tapped her on the shoulder. "We have to go. If it were up to me, I'd drag Bella out of here kicking and screaming. But *you* wanted to come along, and she's your agent, so you get to make the decision."

Bella looked at Matt Decker, and said, "It's *officer*, not agent." She looked at Michelle, and said, "Well, maybe in this case since I'm staying behind, then *agent* is appropriate. What do you think?"

"Oh, Bella," Michelle said as her voice faded. "I...."

"Do the right thing, Michelle," Bella said. "We need to know what he's planning, right?"

"*Bel*-la," Michelle groaned. "Why are you doing this to me?"

Matt Decker gestured to his radio earpiece and said to Michelle, "Surveillance reports that prayers are over, and people are leaving the mosque. We have to go, and you know we didn't bring tech gear to install bugs. That's not what this was all about."

Michelle nodded and moved to kneel in front of Bella. "Bella, look me in the eye and tell me this is what you really, truly want."

"Yes," Bella said, staring into Michelle's brown eyes, "it's what I *have* to do. We collect information. That's what we train to do and work so hard at. It's what we sacrifice for. I can *do* it. You got me strong enough again at the Farm. Emotionally strong. Trust me when I say I know what I'm doing, and I can take it now that I know that the information I'll get Wasif to divulge is going to make a real difference. *Go*, please. I know you'll find a way to bug the apartment. I'll pretend to talk to myself quietly, but secretly I'll know you're listening to every word I say. Noor doesn't speak much English, anyway, so she won't understand anything. She's devoted to Wasif, but otherwise is pretty ignorant. I'll think of you every day, Michelle. You'll be my invisible motivation to endure Wasif and get him to brag about whatever he's planning. He's pretty self-centered. I can play to his ego."

Jackson stood up, and said resolutely, "We have to go, and while you probably didn't see it, there are electronics spread out all over the living room on a couple of tables. I'll snap some pictures on my phone on our way out."

"Electronics," Bella repeated, and her eyes lit up. "Yes, he sells electronics. It'll be easy to get him to talk about electronics. I'll start with that."

Michelle leaned forward and hugged Bella. "I can't believe I'm agreeing to this, but if you're sure—"

"Yes, I am. *Thank* you for believing in me. I *can* do this." Bella inhaled deeply and paused for a second. "A few weeks ago, you told me that Alex got Achmed in Iraq. This time, *you* can be the one to get Wasif. Or maybe you'll let me do it. Now *go* before they come back."

Michelle stood up. "The first time around I saved you from Achmed, and this time it'll be from Wasif. But I'm not going to let you do that to him or anyone else for that matter. Trust me. If nothing else, I'm going to save you from yourself."

Bella drew her lips back in a toothy grin. "I'm glad you trust me enough to continue working this case. I won't let you down."

Michelle waved her hand in front of Matt Decker. "Give me your handcuff key. Just the key."

Decker removed the small metal key from his keyring and handed it to Michelle.

She held it in front of Bella, and said, "Hide this somewhere, and use it if things get bad. Sneak out in the middle of the night, and go straight to any hospital, police station or fire department. Do you understand? You know the Agency's toll-free number to call in emergencies, right? Don't try to be a hero, Bella. Get yourself to safety, okay?"

Bella nodded and took the key.

Michelle rose and the two FBI agents headed for the door. Bella sat on her thin mattress and propped herself up by one hand. Before leaving the bedroom, Michelle turned and blew a kiss to the woman she never in a million years could have imagined leaving to the likes of Wasif. As she lifted the black hood of the burqa over her head, Michelle rehearsed in her mind the myriad painful things she would do to Wasif Ali al-Bakkar the next time she came into his apartment.

Chapter 12

CIA National Resources Division, New York City

Dagmar Bhoti screamed through the video-teleconference screen at Michelle. "You did *what*?"

Caroline van der Pol recoiled in her seat at the conference table as her mission center's chief spat out the last word, dripping with venom.

Michelle responded unphased. "I had to make the tough call on the spot and, as painful as it was for me, I made it."

"Are you out of your ever-loving mind, Michelle?"

"Maybe, but I also left a handcuff key with Bella, so she's free to leave that apartment any time she wants. Most likely at night, but—"

"*But*," Caroline van der Pol interjected, "now, we won't get to debrief her about the threat she claims Wasif Ali al-Bakkar poses. Some kind of non-specific attack, if there's any truth to what she told you. As of this moment, there's no indication that Wasif is anything but an electronics distributor."

"True," Michelle said, "we won't know more until the FBI gets the remote bug in place and we—well, they—can hear Bella."

Bhoti inhaled deeply and spoke more calmly. "And when will *that* be?"

Michelle answered, "At our debrief at the JTTF office earlier this evening, the tech agent assigned to the task force said they'll expedite the request and installation. He thinks it should be up and running the day after tomorrow."

"But," Caroline added, "they're only going to be able to aim the laser microphone at the window of Bella's bedroom because she's the one who specifically gave the FBI consent to listen to her. If the laser mic happens to pick up usable conversations from farther within the apartment, the FBI can use that freely. But to use additional listening devices on other rooms in the apartment, they'll have to apply for a FISA wiretap warrant from the Foreign Intelligence Surveillance Court in D.C. to bug the kitchen where Wasif and his cohorts meet and talk."

Dagmar Bhoti frowned. "How long will *that* take?"

Michelle and Caroline answered together. "Weeks."

"Great," Bhoti said, half under her breath. "Ladies, I'm going to fly up to New York tomorrow and bring Dr. Stone with me. We need to figure out what in the world is going on and decide what we're going to do about it. I'll meet you at the NR Division at 10 a.m."

"Yes, ma'am," Caroline replied, and clicked the VTC system off.

Caroline looked at Michelle, and said, "You know she's going to rake you over the coals tomorrow, right?"

Michelle swiveled her chair to face the counterintelligence officer, and said, "It may sound like bravado to you because she's your boss's boss's boss and you want to have her job someday in the distant future, but I really could *not* care less what Dagmar Bhoti thinks of me. She can't do anything to me. I know full well she doesn't approve of my methods. I've known that for years, but if you take her aside tomorrow, put her on the spot, and ask her directly, she'll admit she knows we're on the same side."

Caroline stood up, tucked her notebook and pen into her purse, and said, "Someday, Michelle, when this is all over, I want to put a bottle between us and pour six shots of tequila into you. I can't *wait* to see what comes out."

Michelle smiled. "I'm sure it'd get messy, so bring a mop. You know the old saying: one tequila, two tequila, three tequila, floor."

***

The following morning, Jordan Hastings, Chief of Station of the CIA's New York office, looked down the length of the NR Division's conference table as his guests kibitzed before the meeting started. He couldn't remember the last time he had so many visitors from Langley present at the same time, and not one of them had come to read him the riot act. Usually this many people coming up from D.C. meant someone very senior was about to threaten to rip off one of Hastings's arms and beat him to death with the wet end. This time, to his distinct pleasure, neither he nor his station were the focus of the group's concern.

Seated halfway down the table, Dagmar Bhoti and Ellyn Stone had parked themselves across from Michelle and Caroline.

Nino Balducci had reserved the seat between Hastings and Bhoti but busied himself working the room. To Jordan Hastings, Nino seemed to have worked with everyone present at one point or another during the short man's long and illustrious career. He wondered if there was anyone in the CIA Balducci *didn't* know?

Phil Thompson sat with Caroline to his left and CIA's JTTF liaison, Bob McMillian, to his right. Thompson smiled as Balducci finished relating the story of a case he worked in Medellin, Colombia, with one of Phil Thompson's former supervisors.

Dagmar Bhoti started the meeting by addressing Jordan Hastings. "Jordan, thank you for hosting us all on such short notice. Again, I might add."

"My pleasure, Dagmar," the Chief of Station replied. "I only wish it were under better circumstances. I thought we were going to have a welcome home party for Bella, but instead we're looking at a completely different situation. I'm certainly concerned about what Bob has been telling me about the possibility of another attack in New York. I'm not sure what to expect from Wasif Ali al-Bakkar. I don't know what you get when you cross a retired Iraqi Air Force fighter pilot with an electronics distributor, and I'm not sure I want to find out, but that seems to be the unenviable task in front of the JTTF."

Dagmar agreed. "We're going to have to leave the terrorism investigation to the FBI and the task force, but we do have an obligation to support them all, just the same."

"Yes, of course," Hastings said, "that's why Bob and his branch exist. Since 2001, we've greatly expanded our channels of communication with all the major law enforcement agencies in the local area. Both CIA and FBI can draw upon D.C.-based resources, as well. I do feel obligated to remind everyone that the FBI has operational jurisdiction. We can feed them whatever information is approved by headquarters, but not conduct joint field operations on US soil without approval from on high."

"Yes," Dagmar said, throwing a sideways glance at Michelle, "that does bear repeating. Jordan, I would like to introduce you to Dr. Ellyn Stone. She led Bella's therapy sessions over the past few weeks since Bella returned stateside."

"Thank you, Dagmar," Ellyn said. "Michelle, I'd like to ask you about Bella's state of mind when you spoke with her in Wasif's apartment. What did she act like? What types of words did she use?"

Michelle answered, "Bella was clearheaded. She didn't slur her words, and her eyes were not glassed over. She did not appear to be under the influence of any drug. She seemed perfectly lucid. Although I questioned the wisdom of her decision, she appeared genuinely concerned about the attack and saw herself as being in the perfect position to be able to get the inside scoop on it for us."

Dr. Stone jotted notes on the pad in front of her. "And what kind of language did she use when talking about Wasif?"

Michelle thought and shook her head. "I don't recall her exact words, and she really didn't say much about him. She mentioned that a few other men come to the apartment pretty frequently. Bella did say one thing about Noor that struck me as odd, however. She said Noor was 'just a woman,' so she couldn't be part of any attack planning. I don't agree, but I've worked enough in the Middle East that I can understand that Wasif thinks that way. It struck me as odd that Bella would say something like that. Nothing else she said stuck out in my mind."

Stone scribbled furiously and then looked up. She stared at Michelle for a few seconds, and said, "Now, tell me about the time in Iraq that Bella ran away from the medical clinic. You mentioned it when we talked at the Farm, but it's not in the Army's medical records from that day."

Michelle recounted the story of Bella's sprint from the clinic and how Michelle coaxed the petrified woman back to the doctor's office.

Dr. Stone didn't write anything on her pad this time. "When I first heard that story, it seemed to me that Bella was scared, hurt, and an invasive medical examination was simply too intimate at the time. That made sense to me at the time, considering what she'd been through for two straight years. But after hearing yesterday that she insisted on staying behind in Wasif's apartment, I have to say I'm now wondering if there might be something else going on."

"Such as?" Michelle asked.

"Stockholm Syndrome, in particular. That's where a hostage or group of hostages bond with their captors. Sometimes it manifests itself to such a strong degree that the captives, no matter how poorly they've been treated, will defend their captors both verbally and physically. Hostages become utterly reliant upon their captors for food, water, clothing, and even permission to use the bathroom. Living under such conditions day in and day out for long periods of time has led some hostages to become so dependent upon their captors that they stop seeing them as aggressors. Instead of wanting to escape, the hostages can start to see their captors more as benefactors they need to protect because their own well-being is so closely tied to that of their captors. In this case, Michelle, it concerns me that a few of Bella's comments seem to paint a picture quite different from the strong-but-injured woman you've described."

Michelle sat up straighter. "Bella has been through a horrible experience, and now she's volunteered to stay behind in an equally hazardous environment to elicit information for us on what may be an imminent attack. The FBI will have their window bug installed tomorrow, so we—"

"Yes, Michelle, I understand how this looks from the point of view of someone who has befriended her, but let me explain what I'm finding so worrisome about Bella."

Michelle gestured toward the doctor with an open palm. "Please."

"Thank you. I realize what I'm about to say may not be the popular opinion of Bella or how we'd *like* to think of her and, at this point, it's just a working theory and not my clinical diagnosis. Not yet. Let me explain. First, she ran away from the medical clinic. Bella didn't flee when the examination and testing started, did she? The medical staff— male medical staff members you said during the original debriefing— performed X-rays, drew blood, and took Bella's vital signs. Meanwhile, a male physician interviewed her about her care and condition. All that, you said, took about an hour."

Michelle nodded.

"Only when the doctor began to examine Bella's genitals did she react strongly. Some might even say violently. She pushed the doctor aside and ran from the room. At first, I thought it might just be sensitivity to what is a very personal and invasive exam by a total stranger. Now, however, I'm wondering if what triggered her violent reaction wasn't her own objection to the exam, but rather that she felt Achmed Hasan was the only man who should be touching her there and that *he* would be angry if he found out another man touched her in a place she had come to accept belonged only to him."

Michelle crossed her arms and leaned back in her leather chair.

"It's possible," Dr. Stone continued, "that Bella's reaction in the clinic was not caused by embarrassment, but rather was an act of defending what she felt was rightfully Achmed's."

Michelle couldn't believe what Dr. Stone suggested could possibly be true—not the Bella she'd come to know over the last few weeks. "I really can't see that being the case. Achmed *frightened* Bella. I can't see her defending him or feeling in any way that she or her body were his property. I don't buy it. Besides, at that point of the exam, Bella already knew that Achmed was... well, would never again be in her life." Michelle didn't want to get into a discussion of the sudden demise of Achmed Hasan and his entire family in front of the group.

Ellyn Stone slowly tapped her pen on the edge of the leather folio spread open on the table in front of her. "That may very well be, but what she may have *intellectually* known would not have sunk in, yet. Her *emotional* reactions were still likely to be centered on what Achmed—the man on whom she'd become dependent over the previous year and a half—would approve of.

"Second, is what you related to us about Bella's comment about Noor 'just' being a woman. I'm definitely concerned that during the two years Wasif and Achmed held Bella captive and inundated her with their culture and particularly warped philosophies so common in the Middle East that she not only became emotionally attached to and dependent upon both men, but also adopted several of their key attitudes. One of these is obviously the lower status of women in that culture. Another is the relative merits of our two cultures. Michelle, did you hear or see anything which might shed some light on whether Bella's attitudes on Western culture got changed by her extended, forced exposure to Wasif's and Achmed's rather tainted points of view?"

Michelle shook her head. "I never saw anything else from Bella."

The group sat silently for a moment until Phil Thompson asked the question several were thinking but didn't want to be the first to utter.

"There are so many unanswered questions in this case that we have to consider the possibility that this was not the kidnapping it appears to be, but for lack of a better term, a re-defection."

The room stayed silent, except for the tapping of Ellyn Stone's pen tip on her pad. Caroline scratched her chin and curled a strand of blonde hair around her finger. Michelle looked from face to face around the table.

Dagmar Bhoti's head dipped so slightly that Michelle couldn't quite tell if it were a nod or she simply exhaled. "Yes, Phil, that certainly is something we have to consider. It would also be a first. We've never had an Agency officer voluntarily join a terrorist organization."

Dr. Stone said, "I'm not going to argue Bella's actions here, but I think her true motivation is still unknown. I think it's likely—extremely likely, in fact—that through the traumas she experienced, her behaviors and thought processes have been manipulated to the point that she's not really the Isabelle Cirrone who got kidnapped two years ago. When we get Bella back this time, I'm going to recommend an in-patient evaluation, long-term treatment plan, and comprehensive deprogramming regimen for her. No offense intended, Michelle. I know how hard you worked with Bella for the short time you two were together, but this case is obviously far more complex than we realized a few weeks ago."

"You'll get no argument from me," Michelle said. "I just want to get her back safely, and then I'll be happy to leave her in the hands of medical professionals who are trained for this kind of thing. The FBI is continuing their physical surveillance of Wasif, and they should have the laser microphone set up on her bedroom window sometime tomorrow. That'll be welcome progress. Then, hopefully, we'll hear more from Bella about what's going through her mind."

Phil Thompson looked at Caroline, and said, "I want you to continue to be the CIMC's rep to the task force and work with Michelle, Bob McMillian, and the FBI."

"Will do," van der Pol replied. She looked at McMillian, and said, "Bob, since Bella's going to remain in the apartment and undercover for the foreseeable future, she should have the support of another case officer to handle whatever backstopping and communications planning you can do."

"I agree," the NR supervisor said. "I'll task someone in my branch to handle that."

"Actually," Nino Balducci offered, "if you'd don't mind, I'd like to do that myself. I know it's not what your teams in NR usually do, Bob, and Bella was one of my very promising officers in Baghdad. I'd like to help her get out of this situation. If this can be my way of contributing to that end, I would very much like to volunteer."

Bob nodded. "Fine with me. Jordan?"

The chief of station smiled. "We'd be happy to take you up on your offer, Nino. Few case officers in the Agency could do half the job you can."

Bob looked at Nino, and said, "Caroline, Michelle, and I are going over to the JTTF office after this. If you'd like to join us and get acquainted with the FBI's setup and plans for their audio coverage, you'd be welcome."

"Yes, thank you, Bob, I will. And while we're on the topic of the JTTF, what have they decided about the electronics in Wasif's apartment? Do they think they're components for a bomb?"

"No," Bob McMillian said, "they're stumped on that front. The inventory list the technical analysts and agents came up with looks nothing like a bomb detonator. They're running it by both the FBI's Bomb Data Center and DOD to see if anyone can make sense of it. It's an odd combination of electronics: a laptop computer with a bunch of handwritten notes about computer programming, four high-end Cobra-brand radar detectors, and a Raspberry Pi."

Dr. Stone cocked her head to the side, and asked, "A pie? Like for dessert?"

McMillian smiled. "No, sorry, the Raspberry Pi is a small programmable computer very popular with hobbyists. They cost about thirty bucks, and the FBI tells me that people use them to build home automation systems or, this time of year, to control Christmas lights."

"I'm not the expert," Stone said, "but a fancy Christmas light display does *not* sound like anything someone named Wasif Ali al-Bakkar would be building."

Phil said, "No, but it does sound like he's building something home-brew."

"Agreed," McMillian replied, "but the JTTF doesn't know what just yet. If it were a bomb, they'd expect to see a cell phone or garage door opener as a trigger, but none of those was present. When I get more information from the JTTF, I'll let you know."

After the meeting adjourned, Michelle found an empty cubicle and dialed CIA headquarters in McLean, Virginia, on a secure phone. Her boyfriend of more than a decade, Dr. Steven Krauss, answered the phone.

"Hey, honey. It's Michelle."

"Who?"

"That's not nice."

"Sorry," Krauss said, "I haven't seen you much in the last month, and I miss you."

"You could have led with that instead of making me feel bad."

"Okay, sorry. I miss you. How's New York?"

"Still dingy and gray, and it doesn't look like I'm getting out of here anytime soon. Nothing has gone right at all. This case gets stranger and stranger every day. I can't wait to be done with it."

"Well, if you're staying in the city for a while longer, then maybe I'll come up earlier than planned so we can spend some time together before we go to my aunt and uncle's place for New Year's. I was planning to pick my parents up in Jersey and drive us all to Queens, but if I'm already there with you, they can take the train up, and I'll meet them at Penn Station instead."

"I'll know more about my schedule in a day or two, and then I'll text you. I miss you and want to see you, too, but if you do come up early, I don't know that I'd even be able to get away that much."

"Okay, but think about all the Marriott points you're earning."

Michelle chuckled. "Yeah, I have more than enough now for us to spend another long weekend in Annapolis. That's always fun. But I have to check out of the Marriott in a day or two. It's getting too expensive. Christmas is next week, and the rates for a room in Times Square are skyrocketing. Tourists may be willing to pay a grand a night, but even Michael has his limits when it comes to paying my hotel bills for work that shouldn't even be something our team handles. I'm going to move to another hotel downtown, closer to the financial district."

"And that'll be *cheaper*? The banks are the ones with all the money."

"Yeah, I know, but when it's tourist season in Midtown, business travel slows to a halt downtown. For the next few weeks, everyone's going to be flocking to Broadway, the Rockettes at Radio City Music Hall, and ice skating in Rockefeller Center, so I'm heading *away* from Midtown and down here where paying *only* three hundred dollars per night is considered a bargain."

"Yeah, I forgot how expensive Manhattan can be. It's been a while since I've been there for New Year's. That's probably why my mom guilted me into bringing you up to see the family this year."

Michelle glanced at the floor at the entrance to her cubicle. A shadow that hadn't been there a moment ago darkened the industrial tan and brown carpet.

"Okay," she said to Krauss, "I'll let you know, but I have to go now."

"Love you," he said.

"You too," she replied, and hung up the phone.

Michelle turned to the cubicle partition, and asked, "Are you looking for me?"

Caroline van der Pol stepped into view. "Nino and I are ready to go, so whenever you are...."

"I'll be right there," Michelle said. "I have one more call to make."

Caroline nodded and walked off.

Michelle pressed three buttons in sequence on the secure phone's handset to erase the last number dialed from the phone's memory. Now, if Caroline van der Pol wanted to see who Michelle spoke with, she'd have to work harder at it. Michelle refused to make the counterintelligence officer's spying on her easy.

***

Bob McMillian gave his three fellow CIA officers the grand tour of the JTTF watch floor. The cavernous room had seats for over one hundred fifty people, but less than a third were filled that afternoon. Television screens covered ninety feet of the front wall. The high-resolution displays showed maps detailing power outages, the status of the three major and five regional airports in the Tri-State area, and a scrolling list of recent calls to 9-1-1.

McMillian led his guests up the back stairs to the JTTF's office bullpen where they found the FBI's Technically Trained Agent—or TTA in Bu-speak—working Bella's case.

The TTA told Michelle and Caroline the good news, that he received the electronics and coaxial cables for the laser microphone before lunch. Later that afternoon, he planned to meet up with two other agents on the roof of a building diagonally across from Wasif's apartment to install the equipment where it had good visibility of Bella's window and wouldn't be blocked by trees or passing trucks.

Michelle guessed that the two non-technical CIA officers wouldn't be welcome to accompany the FBI during the rooftop installation. Instead, she invited herself and Caroline to watch the FBI team install the equipment the next day in the remote listening post in the basement of a New York City Fire Department station a half-mile from Wasif's apartment.

The TTA looked briefly at the two attractive women and readily agreed they'd be welcome to join him at the fire house. Even though he was married, the opportunity to have the two in close proximity for the afternoon was not something any tech nerd would turn down.

***

The cleanliness of the fire station's main floor impressed Michelle. The three bright red-and-white engines awaiting their next call-out gleamed brightly under fluorescent lights. To her chagrin, the basement looked like it hadn't been used for anything but storage of items that both time and the FDNY had forgotten about long before the turn of the millennium.

No wonder the station captain readily agreed to let the Feds use it. He probably hoped they'd have to clean it up for fear of dust and grime shorting out their electronics.

The FBI TTA, Special Agent Clayton Curtis, greeted Michelle and Caroline as they entered the basement storeroom. Michelle fanned her hand in front of her face as she looked around. Clayton introduced the women to another TTA and an electronics technician helping with the install.

"We have the antenna installed on the roof," the electronics technician, or ET, reported to Clayton in a strong southern drawl, "and are feeding the cable down the side of the building so we can get it over to the receiver. There's a conduit for a phone line we can use to string our cable into here."

The ET pointed to a table on which were stacked a half-dozen black boxes resembling a 1970s-era hi-fi component stereo system. "That's the receive and recording gear over there. We'll have headsets for y'all to listen in on once we get everything connected and set up. Speaking of that" — he looked at Clayton Curtis — "I have to show you something."

The ET led the FBI agent to the table of electronics components, and they spoke quietly out of earshot of the CIA officers.

Caroline opened a folding chair and brushed a thin layer of dust off before sitting down. She looked at Michelle, wrinkled her nose, and said, "I didn't think of bringing a towel."

Michelle grimaced and pinched her nose with two fingers. She remained wary of the counterintelligence investigator and disliked the woman's accusatory tone when she spoke of Bella. However, Michelle recognized that they each had their respective jobs to do. A little bit of bonding over the rank room in which they'd be spending the next few days or weeks couldn't hurt.

SA Clayton Curtis frowned and watched the ET leave the room and jog up the stairs.

Michelle approached him, and asked, "Well, *he* did not look happy. What was that all about?"

Clayton put his hands on his hips and shook his head. "Just another Bureau snafu."

A crease appeared on Michelle's forehead. "I'm afraid to ask...."

"Oh," Clayton said, and exhaled deeply, "it's.... Here, I'll show you." He walked over to the table of electronics and held up the end of a black coaxial cable the ET had fed down the conduit from the roof. "The laser microphone we installed across from the subject's apartment yesterday broadcasts its signal to the antenna we installed on the roof of this fire station. The other end of this cable is plugged into that antenna. This is the end of the cable that needs to go into the receiver, but — "

"But what? But it's too short? But it's the wrong color? But it doesn't match your shoes?"

Clayton held up the end of the cable and showed the two CIA officers where yellow insulating fuzz surrounded a solid copper core that stuck out of the unfinished end of the wire. In his other hand, the FBI agent held a small, round, silver plug.

"Okay," Michelle said, "I officially don't like where this is going. I've taken enough electronics classes to be able to guess that *that* plug is supposed to be secured to the end of *that* cable."

"Exactly, but—"

"I already said I don't like where this is going."

"Me neither," he said, and groaned. "We don't have the right crimping tool I need to attach the connector to the cable. Without that, I can't plug the antenna into the receiver. No cable, no audio from the laser mic aimed at the apartment window."

"So," Caroline asked, "don't you have tools like that back at your office?"

"Or," Michelle added, "can't you just bite down on it or something? That's what works in every movie ever made."

"No. Dental bills aside, that's not going to do the trick. The ET said that all our crimping tools were signed out for other cases. I'll be able to get one from our shop in a couple of days."

"Days?" Caroline asked.

"*Days!*" Michelle screamed.

Clayton Curtis recoiled a half-step.

Michelle didn't even try to conceal her displeasure at the news. "We don't have *days*! There's a woman doing everything she can to tell us about an attack being planned, and we're not able to listen to her feed us critical intel until we get that thing plugged into that other thing. How much do those tools cost? Can't you just go buy another one?"

"They're only fourteen or fifteen dollars, but—"

"*Fifteen* bucks?" Michelle said. "We're standing around talking about *fifteen* lousy dollars? Surely with the billions of dollars in the FBI's budget you can find fifteen measly dollars?"

"Unfortunately, no," Clayton said as he braced himself for another outburst from his CIA visitors. "You see, we can buy the coaxial cable from covert case funds because that's an expendable item we'll use just for this case. But for a crimping tool, well, that's considered a capital equipment purchase because it's a durable piece of equipment we'd be able to use on multiple cases. Because we're operating under another Continuing Resolution until Congress passes the final budget for this year, we can't legally purchase any capital equipment. So, I'll have to wait to get one —"

"Are you fucking *kidding* me?" Michelle screamed. "What kind of fly-by-night agency do you work for, anyway?"

Clayton took another step back and tried to remember why he decided to leave his sidearm locked in his van outside.

Michelle's cheeks puffed out, and her face turned red. "I've never heard such bullshit in my life! There's a woman suffering things you can't even *imagine* five blocks from here, and you're going to let fifteen dollars stand in the way of finding out about whatever terrorist attack Wasif and his friends are planning? Are you *serious*?"

"I'm sorry. We don't have to like the law, but we still have to follow it. I —"

Michelle took a half-step forward and spoke slowly. Her eyes narrowed into slits, and her nostrils flared. "Where do they sell crimping tools? I'll go buy one myself, and after you're done using it on the cable, I'm going to ram it —"

Caroline stepped forward and put her hand on Michelle's shoulder. "I think I'll join you, Michelle. Clayton, can you maybe look up the address of the closest hardware store or electronics store or wherever we might find one? Then text me the specific model we should buy, all right?"

Clayton nodded silently and thumbed at his phone for twenty seconds. He handed Caroline his phone, and said, "That's the address. Type in your phone number, and I'll text you the part number."

Michelle shook her head, stomped up the stairs, and exited through the front door five paces ahead of Caroline. Michelle hailed a taxi, and the women traveled eight blocks in silence.

At a red light, Caroline turned to Michelle, and said, "You didn't have to tear into him like that."

Michelle said nothing in response.

When they arrived at the hardware store, Michelle paid the driver and told him there'd be an extra twenty for him if he waited ten minutes while they shopped before taking them back to the fire station.

Michelle purchased the crimping tool Special Agent Curtis specified, and the women returned to the waiting cab.

Halfway back to the station, Caroline said to Michelle, "You're both right, you know. It's a crazy situation, and it shouldn't be this way, but you're both doing what you each need to do to reach the proper resolution."

Michelle looked at Caroline and knew she was — in her own way — giving Michelle rare praise. "You know for damned sure that *we'd* never let some crap like that get in our way."

"I know."

Michelle hefted the crimping tool like a pipe wrench she wanted to swing at someone's skull, but upon returning to the dank storage room, she handed it to Clayton Curtis without comment. She unfolded a chair next to Caroline's, sat down, and simultaneously crossed her arms and legs.

The FBI team completed its setup and phoned the JTTF to report they'd started recording the feed from Bella's bedroom. Michelle and Caroline listened intently for an hour to little more than background noises and some hissing that Clayton said was probably the radiator which sat immediately below the window pane at which the laser microphone was aimed.

FBI Special Agent Ronald Poland arrived mid-afternoon with two Arabic-speaking agents in tow. As the FBI's designated case agent for Bella's kidnapping investigation, Poland wanted to hear the audio intercept for himself in real-time. The other two FBI agents served as the monitoring team for the afternoon shift. At midnight, another pair of agents were scheduled to relieve them and, in turn, they would be replaced at eight in the morning.

Poland listened for a while, and asked the women, "Has she said anything?"

Caroline shook her head. "No, not a word."

The FBI radio on the table holding the monitoring equipment crackled out a report from the surveillance team. "The crowd is gathering for their walk to the mosque."

Almost as soon as that transmission ended, Bella's voice came through the monitoring equipment's speaker. She spoke softly, and the assembled FBI and CIA team strained to hear her through a *whooshing* sound that distorted her voice. "They've gone to Maghrib prayers. I hope you can hear me."

Michelle didn't notice that she nodded in silent response.

Thirty minutes later, the FBI's mobile surveillance team reported that several large groups left the mosque. The monitoring room remained quiet until what sounded faintly like a door closing came through the speaker like a pop.

Michelle leaned closer to the speaker, and asked, "Are those voices in the background? I can't tell."

One of the FBI agents from the JTTF lifted a pair of headphones over his head and rewound the audio recording thirty seconds. He replayed the audio on different settings and tilted his head as if that would change the timber of the digital recording.

He removed the headphones and shrugged. "I *think* so, but I can't be sure. We'll ask Quantico to post-process the audio to improve the signal-to-noise ratio, but it'll take them a day or so to work on it. Combining what we can hear of the background conversations with the additional physical surveillance Nola Austin put in place will give us a better chance of identifying the two or three men who visit Wasif."

The team continued to listen to the clicks and pops of the audio intercept until Bella's voice came through clearly. "Hello, Wasif."

Without returning her greeting, Wasif Ali read aloud in Arabic.

As if on cue, Michelle and the two JTTF linguists leaned forward while the rest—non-Arabic speakers—leaned back in their chairs.

Wasif's voice streamed through the speaker for several minutes. His intonations rose and fell rhythmically through a dozen verses of poetry. He read with confidence and, perhaps, Michelle thought, even pride. At one point when his pace quickened, he seemed on the verge of breaking into song.

After five minutes of listening in silence, Caroline asked Michelle, "What's he saying?"

Michelle replied softly. "It's hard to understand. I recognize many of the words, but not the context."

One of the JTTF analysts clarified Wasif's poetic recitation. "It's religious poetry, so the grammar is unusual in the same way that poetry in English doesn't follow the rules or syntax of daily conversation. The vocabulary certainly isn't what they taught us at the Defense Language Institute, I'll tell you that. It sounds like some of the words are archaic while others are probably religious in context."

Michelle added, "Yeah, I'm not sure that understanding the words would really help us at all. Bella told me that he uses the poetry as both his form of foreplay and a way to justify the whole situation. I doubt there's any value in a literal translation of any of that."

Wasif ended his reading on a high note, and the sound of a book slapping closed burst from the speaker.

Michelle stood up. "I don't want to hear what comes next."

The JTTF agent picked up a headset and turned the speaker off. Three others joined him in listening through their own headsets. Caroline waved away the offer of a headset and sat quietly next to

Michelle. The women watched as the men stared intently at the receiver as they listened to what the laser microphone returned from the window of Bella's bedroom.

Michelle wanted to count off thirty seconds, hoping that would be as long as it would take for the man she despised to finish. Instead, she read two news articles on her cell phone and breathed a sigh of relief when one of the JTTF analysts removed his headset and said that Bella told Wasif that she hoped his business was going well.

The agent activated the speaker in time for Michelle to hear his reply.

"What did he say in return?" Caroline asked.

Michelle translated. "He said it's none of her business. She replied that she owes him gratitude for his food and the roof over her head."

When Wasif spoke again, his voice strained as he stood up from the thin mattress on the floor of the bare bedroom.

Michelle said, "He told her that she has a role to play in *Allah's* plans, and so does he. But his role is fit for a man."

"What does that mean?" Caroline asked.

Michelle shrugged. "Could mean he's planning an attack, or it could mean that he just needs to get his rocks off more frequently than Noor is willing to put up with. I don't know."

The younger of the two JTTF agents smiled, drawing an elbow from the more seasoned agent.

The senior agent said, "We'll send the audio to Quantico tonight and ask them to translate the poetry, assuming that's what it was. I also want them to clear up the background noise as best they can so, if we're lucky, we can hear what Wasif and Noor were saying in the kitchen."

Michelle stood up, and said, "It's probably not worth their time. It's unlikely to be important."

"True," the agent said, "it's probably not, but it will do two things for us. First, it gives the Engineering Research Center in Quantico time to work on the background audio when it's not important. Then, once they have the right filters developed to allow them to more clearly hear what's going on in the kitchen, they can send them to us. When we get that file, we'll program it into our receiver. That way, later, when the two or three other bad guys show up, we'll have a good chance of being able to listen to them in real-time as they talk in the kitchen or dining room. Second, the specific poetry he's reading may have some contextual meaning if we know what the subjects of the poems are, even if the specific wording itself is not relevant."

"Makes sense," Michelle said, and turned to Caroline.

Caroline stood, and said, "I don't think we'll hear anything else of interest tonight, guys, but if you do, can you give us a call?"

The JTTF agents agreed readily.

"Michelle," Caroline asked, "we've been so busy I haven't had a chance to look around Times Square, yet. I'd like to see the electronics store firsthand and walk around the area a bit to get a feel for the layout of the place where this all started. Will you go with me, since your hotel's up there?"

"Sure," she said, and pulled her heavy purse that came with the disguise kit from the back of the chair. She missed her small purse— she'd have to get the broken strap repaired once she got back to Virginia.

FBI Special Agent Ronald Poland jingled his car keys in front of Michelle. "I'd be happy to give you ladies a ride up to Midtown, if you'd like. It's more or less on my way home, and I need to earn my overtime pay somehow. I might as well play taxi driver on Uncle Sam's nickel."

The ladies followed him to his car for the forty-five-minute drive through rush hour traffic. Along the way, Poland regaled them with tales of his counterintelligence work on the JTTF. He and Caroline compared notes on their respective agencies' methods of investigating cases.

The two women alighted from the FBI agent's car in Times Square and thanked him for the ride. They walked down the long city block across the street from the Marriott, and Michelle played tour guide.

She pointed to the Marriott's eighth-floor bar, and said, "See that rounded area protruding over the digital billboards? That's the bar where I was sitting when she was grabbed."

Caroline squinted as she looked through the bright lights and flashing billboards. "The windows are so dark I can't see anything inside except a slight glow from the ceiling lights."

"After she was taken, I stood out here for a few minutes planning my next move. I don't remember how long I stared at those windows trying to figure out if I could convince myself that Bella either could or definitely could not see me up there. I knew right where our two glasses of wine were, but I couldn't see them through the darkened windows. I've been beating myself up ever since trying to figure out if she could see me or not. If she could, then maybe, just maybe, this really was staged. I've come out here most nights to look up at different times, at different angles, and try to come to a different conclusion. But I can't. I don't think Bella could have seen me."

Caroline walked up and down the sidewalk to peer up at the bar's windows from different angles. Michelle followed her to the end of the block and stopped outside the gift shop.

Caroline shook her head. "I don't see how she could possibly have seen you up there. I think sometimes I can see shadows inside, but not always. There's no way she could have identified you, other than—like you said—the bar was mostly empty that afternoon, so it's a shot in the dark that anyone moving up there would have been you. Or a waitress, I suppose. But, from down here, *mmmmm*, Bella couldn't have known how many people were in the bar at that moment. So, yeah, I'm with you on this one."

"Okay, finally something we agree on. Well, that and a fondness for tequila."

Caroline smiled. "My offer still stands."

"Speaking of standing," Michelle said quietly, "let's not stand in front of this particular store any longer, and the two cops over there are making me nervous. Let's walk down the block a bit."

Caroline looked over her shoulder and saw two uniformed NYPD officers across the street. "Cops make you nervous? You must spend wa-*ay* too much time overseas. What makes me nervous is that store a block away."

Michelle looked at the garish neon sign in front of the M&M World store and smiled. "Looking at it is free, but you gain two pounds simply walking past both that one and the two New York-style pizza restaurants further down the block. It's delicious but comes at a cost. Let's go this way, instead."

The women walked east on West 47th Street, and Michelle pointed out where she'd jumped up on the hood of the Chrysler on the night of the kidnapping.

"You didn't mention that in the debriefing. You said you ran down the street but lost the van."

"Okay, maybe I *didn't* mention jumping up on some guy's car in my high heels and probably scratching the hell out of his hood. I also spared you from all the curse words he used to shoo me off. Maybe I didn't mention the FedEx and UPS trucks double-parked on the block, either."

"True, but those were in the videos and stills we saw. The cameras don't cover the side streets nearly as well as the main arteries of Times

Square, but I remember seeing at least one boxy, white truck in the slideshow Bob got from the task force the day after. Probably the FedEx van. I'll have to check my notes."

As the women walked and talked, Michelle pointed to the stage door of a theater a dozen yards in front of them. "That night, I walked as far as that door, then turned around. I went back to Times Square and accosted just about anyone I could find, asking them if they saw what happened. One woman in a church group singing Christmas carols looked at me like I was crazy. Maybe I was—a bit."

"I'm sure we all would have been crazed after something like that."

Caroline walked past the cinderblock alcove concealing the theater's stage door and over to the base of a stairwell secured behind a metal cage.

Two vagrants warmed themselves over the outflow pipe of a steam vent a few yards past the metal stairs.

Michelle quickened her pace along the empty sidewalk and caught up with the counterintelligence officer at the base of the stairs. She nudged Caroline's elbow, and said, "Let's head back to the hotel, and I'll show you the bar."

The two men in jeans and hoodie sweatshirts who had been standing over the steam vent surged at the women. The taller—a white man with a scraggly gray beard and stained dark-blue hoodie—jumped in front of Caroline.

An older, bald, black man crossed behind his friend and blocked Michelle's path. He held a semi-automatic pistol in his hand and waved it between the two women, not sure who he should threaten first. In a voice made gravelly by decades of smoking, he growled, "If you got money for buying drinks, jes hand it over. Give us your purses. Both of 'em. Now."

At the sight of the handgun, Caroline let out a shrill yelp and raised her shaking hands.

"Come on," the white mugger added. "We ain't got all night."

Caroline wore her purse under her jacket with the strap strung across her body. She fumbled with her coat's zipper, which repeatedly slipped out of her quivering fingers.

Michelle lifted her hands to waist height but made no move to take her pocketbook off her shoulder. She held her palms outward to show she was unarmed, but she kept her hands low.

Michelle looked from the man standing in front of her holding his gun in front of him, to the one in front of Caroline who kept his hands inside his sweatshirt pockets. That man's right hand, smudged with dirt, stuck out of his sweatshirt farther than his left hand did. Whatever gun he carried, she noticed, was considerably smaller than his friend's Berretta.

The black man in the black hoodie scowled at Caroline's inability to unzip her jacket. He chewed his bottom lip and waved his gun in her face.

At the sight of the weapon just inches from her nose, Caroline screamed shrilly. Instinctively, she abandoned her latest attempt to unzip her jacket and thrust her arms above her head.

At the intersection eighty yards behind the women, two NYPD officers on a Times Square foot patrol heard Caroline's wail. From that distance, they couldn't see what was going on, but a yell and a woman with her hands over her head counted as probable cause to investigate. The senior patrol officer grabbed the sleeve of his junior partner. The two trudged through one of New York's seemingly endless construction zones and along the sidewalk on the opposite side of the street from the blonde woman with her hands fluttering above her head.

The man waving the Berretta in a circle in front of Caroline's face cursed at her and repeated his demand for the women's purses.

Michelle cleared her throat loudly and the thug swung the pistol in her direction. In one fluid motion, she swept her arms forward as if to clap. The fingers of her left hand curled over the top of the semi-automatic pistol, and she wrapped her thumb underneath. She used the man's momentum to her advantage, pushing the weapon's barrel safely past her in case it discharged. At the same time, she swung her right hand as hard as she could at the inside of the gunman's right wrist, hitting it with as much force as she could generate.

Her two-handed sweep dislodged the weapon from his grip, and it came away in Michelle's left hand.

Caroline watched in horror and screamed in Michelle's ear.

The man across from Michelle grunted and flicked his wrist in pain from Michelle's blow.

Michelle transitioned the Berretta from her left hand to her right and lowered the barrel. She pulled the trigger once, firing a 9mm bullet into the man's left knee.

His legs buckled, and he fell to the ground, howling in pain.

Caroline screamed in surprise.

Two NYPD officers yelled from a dozen yards away for everyone to put their hands up.

The white man in the blue hoodie pulled his right hand from his sweatshirt exposing a subcompact Glock pistol.

Michelle fired a second round which shattered his left knee.

He shrieked in pain and dropped to the sidewalk, writhing.

Caroline yelped in surprise and then went silent. Her hands few over her eyes and she cringed.

The NYPD officers screamed conflicting orders at everyone. One wanted everyone to freeze, while the other ordered them to put their hands over their heads.

The two men thrashing on the ground ignored everyone and howled in agony.

With her right thumb, Michelle pressed the release button on the side of the pistol, dropping the magazine into her left hand. She ignored the orders of New York's finest and casually tossed the mag over her left shoulder.

Caroline dropped her hands to her mouth, but they barely squelched her next scream.

The two men on the ground shrieked and convulsed as they both grabbed their left knees and rolled from side to side.

Michelle took a half-step forward and pulled the slide of the Berretta back. The weapon ejected a single 9mm cartridge, and she caught it in mid-air. She flicked the lone bullet over her left shoulder, and it landed on the sidewalk with a *dink*. She pushed her left hand over the weapon's slide and nudged it forward an inch. With two fingers, she pinched the release buttons on the side of the weapon's frame, and the spring-loaded slide glided off easily. One at a time, Michelle tossed the gun's skeletal remains over her left shoulder.

Caroline screamed through her fingers again. She had never experienced gunfire outside of the CIA's firing ranges and could not understand how Michelle remained so calm at a time like this.

The senior NYPD officer skidded to a halt ten feet from the women and again screamed for both to put their hands up.

Caroline raised her hands as high as they would go. The whites of her eyes shone brightly in the dim side street.

She looked to Michelle like a teacher's pet desperately wanting to answer whatever question had just been posed to the class. Reluctantly, Michelle raised her hands as well.

The junior patrolman ordered the women against the wall and grabbed for his handcuffs.

On the ground, the two muggers rolled and whimpered.

Michelle's left foot made a scraping sound as she slid it in an arc from in front of the muggers, across the sidewalk, and toward the officers. She lifted her foot and kicked the Glock toward them, and said, "You may want to worry more about the man with the gun, first, and the unarmed women with their hands in the air, second."

The NYPD officer growled. "I'll worry about you at the station. Now, up against the wall, both of yous."

He jingled his handcuffs in the air as the two CIA officers moved to the wall.

Michelle looked over her shoulder at the officer with the handcuffs, winked, and said, "You need to step up your game. My boyfriend makes the whole handcuff-thing *so* much more appealing at home."

Chapter 13

NYPD Midtown South Precinct, New York City

The female NYPD officer escorting Michelle Reagan and Caroline van der Pol into the police station's dank holding facility closed the cell door behind them. The metal door slid into place and locked with a resounding clank, causing Caroline to jump.

An obese woman perched on the narrow bench on the cell's right side looked at the newcomers and smiled. She chuckled at Caroline's nervous reaction. "Oh, *honey*, is this your first time?"

Without thinking, Caroline nodded.

"Well, Blondie, it's true, you know? You never forget your first. Too bad we can't give you a proper welcoming here, but my friends and I are going to just *love* getting to know you better once we all get to Rikers Island."

Michelle scanned the twelve other women occupying the fifteen-by-thirty-foot cell. Eight sat to her left—four squeezed onto a bench and four on the floor. Four others sat to her right—three on the bench, including inmate-zilla who seemed to want to make Caroline her pet project. A rail-thin woman sat on the floor at the large woman's feet having her hair stroked by the self-proclaimed queen of the cage.

The hefty queen asked Caroline, "And who's your little friend?"

Michelle looked around the cell again, fixed her gaze on the large woman, and said, "There's something you should know."

"Oh, and what's that?"

Michelle smiled, and said, "You're in my seat."

***

FBI Special Agent Ronald Poland stepped into the holding room behind the NYPD detention officer as she caught the G-man up on the goings-on in the precinct that evening.

The NYPD officer looked back at Poland, and said, "Some of the women were giving your two girls a bit of attitude, earlier. You know, a

'warm welcome,' but that's normal for newcomers here. They didn't—
what the *hell*?"

As the heavy metal door thudded closed behind them, the NYPD
officer stopped short and SA Poland bumped into her. The officer stood
with her mouth open as she stared in disbelief at the sedate scene in the
holding cell in front of her.

Michelle and Caroline sat alone on the right-hand bench. The thin
woman who'd been at queen-mama's feet sat cross-legged all the way to
the cell's right where the cinderblock wall met the metal cage's bars.

The other eleven women sat on and around the left-hand bench.
Queen-mama, as Michelle thought of her, sat in the middle of the bench
with a squiggly, burgundy line of dried blood leading from her nose to
her upper lip. A smear of blood stained her right earlobe where a
dangling stainless-silver earing once hung. The woman next to her
rubbed a sore shoulder and held her arm as if in a sling. One of the
women on the floor alternatingly rubbed her left knee and right eye.

Michelle greeted the NYPD officer and FBI agent with a finger
wave.

The officer repeated her stutter. "What the...."

"Oh," Michelle said, "the ladies and I had a bit of a getting-to-
know-you conversation earlier, but we're all good friends, now." She
looked at the former queen of the holding cell, and asked, "*Aren't* we?"

The women on the other bench sat expressionless, their eyes
darting between Michelle and the NYPD officer unlocking the cell's
door.

She slid it open, looked from one end of the cell to the other, and
said, "Caroline van der Pol and Jane Doe, you're free to go."

Caroline jumped to her feet and practically bolted to freedom.
Michelle, on the other hand, stood casually and headed out of the
holding cell calmly.

On her way out, Michelle turned to the large woman sitting on the
other bench and said, "Too bad we didn't get to meet your other friends
at Rikers. I'm sure it would have been quite a party." She waved, and
said, "Toodles."

The large woman extended her middle finger to the undercover
CIA officer, and Michelle smiled.

Once safely in the front seat of Ron Poland's car, Caroline asked the
FBI agent, "Are they going to press charges against us?"

Poland chuckled. "*You*? No, you didn't do anything wrong. The
detective who caught the case talked to the arresting officers and got the

details he needs from their statements. Last I heard, the two guys Michelle shot were both still in surgery. By the way, Michelle, they couldn't find any identification in your purse, and you wouldn't give them a name, which is why they logged you in as Jane Doe. Don't you carry a wallet?"

Michelle tapped the purse the NYPD detention officer had returned to her upon their exiting the precinct. "The strap on my personal purse broke last week when I ran after Bella, and the only other one I brought was a small, formal clutch. So, I've been carrying this Agency-issued one instead. It's not exactly off the rack. I use the hidden compartments in it to hold multiple identity documents, lockpicks, small disguise items, and the like."

Poland smiled. "Must be part-and-parcel for your overseas work."

"Yeah, I don't do much domestically, but using the hidden compartments is second nature to me since getting caught with IDs and credit cards in multiple names just causes problems."

"True, and so does shooting people on the streets of New York."

Michelle shrugged. "Meh."

Poland said, "Not to worry. I squared your involvement in the incident with the case detective through the JTTF. The two uniformed officers saw enough so that neither of you should have to testify if this goes to court."

Caroline's voice quivered as she asked, "Do they need us to press formal charges, or something?"

Poland shook his head. "No, since the attempted robbery happened in the presence of the officers, they can press the charges directly and not involve you. One of the muggers had an active felony warrant in the system, and the other has two misdemeanor convictions on his record. I think the case will end up rattling around the local courts for six months or so and then those two schmucks will just plead guilty. Neither of them is going to walk free for the next decade."

Softly, Caroline said, "Neither of them is going to walk at all for a while." She shivered.

Michelle reached forward from the rear seat and gently rubbed the rattled woman's shoulder.

Poland added, "And on that note, the detective told me the emergency room doctors marveled that your bullets hit both of the subjects in the same part of the knee—right into the patella and through the knee joint. He commented at how uncannily similar the wounds were."

Michelle shrugged again. "Beginner's luck."

"If you say so." Poland glanced at his watch. "Well, it's two in the morning. Do you want me to drop you off at your hotels?"

Michelle looked at Caroline. "What do you say? You want to get that bottle of tequila in front of me, now, and see what comes out?"

Caroline shook her head. "I just want to take a shower and go to sleep. I can't—"

Michelle smiled and patted Caroline on the shoulder. "I'm *kidding*. I'm wide awake, so I think I'm going to work out in the hotel gym and then turn in, myself."

Poland drove to the New York Marriott Marquis in Times Square and pulled up in front of its famously large and brilliantly lit overhang.

Michelle stepped out, thanked him for the ride, and said to Caroline, "No more than two."

"Two what?" she asked.

"Glasses of wine. You'll think you want more, but trust me on this. No more than two."

Caroline looked at Michelle expressionlessly, then nodded.

"Okay, I'll see you about three tomorrow afternoon at the fire station. I think we've both earned a sleep-in day. What do you think?"

Caroline nodded energetically.

***

In the basement of the fire station the next afternoon, Michelle strained to hear the voices through the headset. She pressed the earcups tightly against her head, but it didn't help much. "Nope," she said.

The JTTF agent shook his head. "I can't tell, either. I'm getting about every fifth word. We'll have to see what the audio engineers at Quantico and the linguists at the National Virtual Translation Center say. The sound is too muddled by the hissing of the radiator in Bella's room."

Michelle looked up as Caroline van der Pol entered the FBI's monitoring room in the basement of the fire station. Large, dark Oliver Peoples sunglasses hovered above pale pink lips, obscuring the blonde woman's face.

Michelle frowned, and said, "You didn't follow my advice, did you?"

Caroline shook her head twice and stopped abruptly. She slid a white knit cap back and off her hair, sat down next to Michelle, and cradled her forehead in her hands.

Michelle handed her a bottle of water and twisted the cap off for the counterintelligence officer. "I have Tylenol, if you want some."

Caroline spoke without moving her head. "I took two at the hotel. It's just a headache. Or three."

"Well, you chose a good day to sleep off a hangover. Bella hasn't said a word. Wasif has at least one guest over, and they're talking in the background, but we can't hear what they're saying."

"Are they running the water in the kitchen to mask their conversation?"

"No, but it's a cold day, so the steam radiator in Bella's room is providing lots of white noise for them. Even if they didn't plan it, it's working like an audio smokescreen."

Caroline tried three times to roll up her sleeve to look at her watch. The cuff kept falling back over her wrist before she could see the time.

"It's almost five o'clock," Michelle said. "Why don't you go back to the hotel and rest? I'll stay here. You're not missing anything, anyway. Just take today off as a mental health day or something. You had a rough night."

"I need something to eat, first."

"If you'd like, the guys upstairs made Italian meatball subs for lunch. They've invited everyone here up about a million times over the past day or two. I think they just want to know what the big secret going on in their basement is." She elbowed Caroline gently. "It's a perfect situation for a counter-intell officer like yourself to mess with them, don't you think?"

Caroline smiled. "I think we can safely stick with the 'no comment' line here, but a sub sounds good. I'm officially off my diet, now."

"You don't need a diet. You just need something to soak up the last of the wine still swirling around in your system. You didn't finish the *whole* bottle, did you?"

Caroline shook her head slowly. This time, the world didn't spin. "No, but after three large glasses, I... well, I poured the rest down the sink this morning. I think that may have been more in anger than preventing it from happening again."

"Destroying the evidence? Maybe there's hope for you, yet." Michelle reached her arm around Caroline's shoulder and helped her up two flights of stairs.

A half dozen firefighters sat around a table playing cards in the station's second-floor dining room. Michelle introduced Caroline to the junior staff tending to the chili they were preparing for dinner. The firefighters were happy to reheat a meatball sub for their guest.

Michelle sat across from Caroline at an empty table in the corner of the room and watched as the hungover woman slowly nibbled a sandwich dripping with homemade marinara sauce. The FDNY's red, white, and blue logo and the engine company's number outlined in gold stood out prominently in the center of the black rectangular table. Michelle traced the logo with her fingertip.

"This is really good," Caroline said as she licked her fingers. "No diet *and* no manners, today."

"I won't tell if you won't," Michelle said, and handed her two napkins from the dispenser on the table. "Maybe that's why Big Bertha didn't like me last night—no manners. I think when I booted her off the bench, I forgot to say *please*."

"When you and I first met, you made the offhanded comment that you were better at taking people apart than putting them—and specifically Bella—back together again. I wrote that off as nothing more than you posturing to get released from this case and the kind of bluster typical of so many of you guys in the Special Activities Center. Until last night, that is. But now, in all seriousness, when you and I go to jail," Caroline said as she balled up a red-stained napkin and placed it alongside her plate, "I *definitely* want to be your cellmate. You can have all my cigarettes."

Michelle smiled. "*Aww*, gee. You say the sweetest things. So, why are you still single?"

Caroline smirked. "I'm married, I just don't wear my good jewelry in the field. Sometimes when interviewing subjects, it helps to appear single. It gives them less information about me. What about you?"

"Oh, sorry. I didn't know. I just meant to pile my own joke on top of yours. I have a special someone waiting for me at home, too."

Michelle barely got the last word out of her mouth as the station's klaxon blared its pulsating alarm. Caroline buried her ears in her hands trying, unsuccessfully, to block the eardrum-piercing noise.

The loudspeaker blared instructions to the station personnel. "Engine Two, respond. Engine Two, respond to Code 10-24. Automobile on fire."

Two firefighters abandoned their card game and ran down the stairs. Four others, not assigned to Engine Two, set aside their scorecard and drew up new teams, unphased by the blaring alarm.

Caroline squeezed her eyes shut as if to keep the sound from penetrating her skull through her baby blues, but to no avail.

A minute later, the fire engine left the house and the alarm died down with an extended whine. Michelle walked Caroline outside to catch a cab back to her hotel, and then returned to the FBI monitoring room downstairs.

The two JTTF agents listened intently through their headsets. Michelle joined them for a few minutes.

One of the agents excused himself to use the bathroom and, when he returned, Michelle asked him about the conversation going on in Wasif's apartment. "It sounds technical, but I don't really understand it."

"Another guy showed up a half hour ago, and now we can hear the conversation more clearly. I think it's because they're speaking louder and not whispering like you can do when it's just two people. Noor offered the newcomer some tea, and then the men got down to talking about computer programming. Wasif doesn't seem to understand the software side of things. He's the hardware guy, which I guess makes sense. I mean, you don't necessarily have to understand the hardware just to sell it, but it seems like he has a pretty good grasp of the equipment they're using."

"So," Michelle asked anxiously, "what are they using it *for*?"

"No idea," the agent admitted with a shrug, "but they're making progress on whatever it is. The two guys figured something out, and we heard them very clearly say it's working. More specifically, one said pretty loudly, 'that worked.' So, obviously they've made some kind of breakthrough. But so far, they haven't discussed its purpose. It might not even be illegal, after all. We just don't know, yet."

Michelle bit her top lip, and asked, "What can you make out of the equipment they have?"

"Not much, really. The Raspberry Pi is just a processor and some memory. By itself, it doesn't do anything. These guys are programming it through the laptop computer, so my guess is they're not going to deploy the laptop with the final product."

"So," Michelle said as she sat back and crossed her legs, "they're making something out of four radar detectors and a portable computer — the pie-thing. What's it all for?"

The FBI agent shrugged again. "Best I can guess, the radar detectors are a trigger for something. We've alerted the physical surveillance teams to be on the lookout for additional hardware or a big shipment of something."

"Something?"

"Yeah, explosives or fertilizer. If you mix that with diesel fuel—"

"ANFO, I know. Ammonium nitrate and fuel oil is a powerful combination. That's what Timothy McVey used to bomb the Oklahoma City federal building a bunch of years ago."

"You can't outlaw fertilizer or diesel fuel, so it's still easier to get those than large quantities of plastic explosives or TNT, at least here in the US. But we still watch out for large quantities being purchased by people not in the agriculture business."

Michelle crossed her arms. "But how would you trigger a truck bomb like that with a couple of radar detectors?"

"We're definitely not the experts on *that*. Offhand, I can't figure it out, either. Maybe if you park the truck on the side of the road and a cop drives by with a radar speed gun?"

Michelle tapped the toe of her leather boot on the concrete floor. "But, man, that sounds *sooo* inexact, you know?"

The agent shrugged. "I'm not the expert."

The other agent removed his headphones and rubbed his ears. "They're making progress, but at what, I have no idea. They're just talking about programming... stuff. They're using a language called Python to read inputs from one computer port and display it on the screen. I have no idea what they're planning to use it for, though. The engineering section at Quantico may be able to figure out more, but not me. I don't know the computer vocabulary in Arabic, although half the tech jargon they use is in English, which only helps a little bit. It might as well be Greek. Do you want to listen?"

For lack of anything else to do, Michelle agreed, knowing she'd not be the one to break this case wide open from listening to the audio intercepts of computer programmers speaking techno gobbledygook.

***

The following day, Michelle entered the FBI's monitoring room and found Caroline van der Pol talking with Nino Balducci.

"Ah, Michelle," Nino said, "just the woman I've been looking for."

Michelle removed her jacket and hung it and her purse over the back of a chair. "I'm usually here from noon to midnight."

Nino smiled. "Except when you're clearing the streets of New York of its would-be muggers, I hear."

Caroline blanched.

Michelle wasn't sure why that would embarrass her.

The two JTTF agents removed their headsets and silently watched. The rumors had been running rampant throughout the JTTF. The men both chomped at the bit to hear the rest of the story from the horse's mouth.

"Well," Michelle said, "I think too much has been made of that incident already." She looked at the agents, and asked simply, "*What?*"

One looked at the other who got up the nerve to speak. "Ron Poland specifically told us to not ask about that. But he didn't say we couldn't mention that the story—or, at least *a* story—is going around, and we'd love to hear the rest of it."

Michelle sighed, and sat down. "Okay, it's nothing, really, but here's what happened." She related the events that befell her and Caroline near Times Square to her eager audience.

"Quite impressive," Nino said.

Caroline agreed. "She knew just what to do. I never saw it coming."

Nino smiled. "That's life in the Clandestine Service. The opposition never sees it coming. That's the whole idea. So, anyway, I'm glad I ran into you here. I need your help."

"Help?" Michelle parroted. "With what?"

"Several days ago, I agreed to be Bella's handler, and the first order of business for a case officer when dealing with an agent or undercover officer in place is to establish a communications schedule. Even with my decades of field experience, I couldn't come up with any combination of the tradecraft we regularly use that would work in this particular case. Bella doesn't get out of the apartment, and we can't go in. We can't call her on the phone or mail her a care package. After all, we're not even supposed to know where she is. I thought long and hard about having her use the handcuff key you left with her to get herself out of the apartment at night to meet with me—or us, as I'm confident your field tradecraft is certainly up to par. But none of that matters because I have no way of getting a message with instructions to her in the first place. Or at least I didn't until two days ago."

"What did you come up with?"

"*Me?* Nothing. All the credit goes to the technical wizards in the Directorate of Science and Technology. I called a division chief over there who used to be a Technical Services Officer with me in Bangkok a million years ago. He put me in touch with a young TSO to work with and *she* came up with the other half of the puzzle."

Michelle cocked her head slightly. "What was the first half?"

"Your laser microphone," Nino said, and pointed at the receiver on the table. "Communication is a two-way street. You and the FBI set up this way of getting communications out of the apartment, but we have no way to get messages *in*."

Caroline asked, "And the answer turned out to be...?"

"Another laser," Nino said, and leaned back in his chair. "Have you ever seen a fireworks show at which they display messages in the smoke left by the explosions?"

"Yes," Caroline said, "I think I saw that at Disney World a couple of years ago. It was more than words, though. They showed images of a lot of Disney characters until the smoke dissipated. My kids loved it."

"Yes, that could be the same thing. Right." Nino said. "It's not magic, but I'm sure their engineers made it look like it is. We can use the same principal here."

"Okay," Michelle said, "how's it all going to work?"

Nino waved his hands in front of him. "Same way the CIA always does things, smoke and mirrors. Except this time, there'll be no smoke — we won't need it. What the TSO will do tomorrow is install another laser on the same rooftop as the FBI's laser mic. The new one will use the wall of Bella's bedroom opposite the window as the smoke. Or, in this case, maybe the term movie screen is more apropos. Once it's installed, we'll be able to sit here, type messages for our laser to shine into Bella's room. Then, we'll listen through the FBI's laser mic to her acknowledging the message or telling us the answers to whatever questions you want to ask. It'll be like having two telephone lines installed where, on one, you only talk and, on the other, you only listen. It seems crude and makeshift but given the limited time we have available to us and Bella's limited ability to move independently, it should suffice."

Caroline looked at Nino with concern etched on her face. "They're going to install it tomorrow? That's Christmas Eve."

Michelle said, "I don't think Wasif is likely to take the holiday off or give Bella a one-day pass to go to midnight Mass."

"No," Caroline said, "I was just thinking that I was going to take a couple of days off for the holidays." She looked at Nino, and continued, "But DS&T is going to work?"

"Yes."

Michelle waved a hand at Caroline. "Take the time off. You deserve it and probably still need the rest somewhere away from the city. I'll be here and can help Nino out on the roof."

Nino said, "I'll be on the rooftop with the young lady from DS&T during the installation. We'll need you here, actually, to radio to us when Bella sees the test messages we send. Literally, when she sees the light."

Michelle nodded. "Sure thing. But why use radios and not just call each other's cell phones?"

Nino looked at the FBI's communications equipment on the table against the wall of the room and chuckled. "You're right, of course. I'm so used to working overseas under the watchful eyes of foreign security services that I've forgotten how easy it can be to work more openly at home. We not only don't have to worry about a security service working *against* us, here, but in fact, they're part of our plot, aren't they? Well, even at my age, we're never too old to learn something new. Very good."

Caroline looked at Michelle, and said, "If you're staying, I can stay, too. I don't mind changing my plans if it helps the case."

"Don't be silly," Michelle said, "you definitely need the time off. I'm planning to take a couple of days off around New Year's, although I'll still be here in New York. So, how about this? I'll work *this* holiday, and maybe you'll work *that* one, if we're still at it? Besides, after what happened two days ago and the shock you had, you need a break. The best way to get over a bad experience is to get under your husband for a good one."

Caroline's eyes involuntarily narrowed as she processed Michelle's comment. In an instant, her eyes went wide, and her hand flew over her mouth.

The two FBI agents put their headsets back on, tried hard not to smile, and turned toward the radio receiver to pretend something interesting was happening.

Chapter 14

Lower Manhattan, New York City

Nino Balducci braced himself against the biting wind whipping across the rooftop and through his light-brown scarf. The gray skies above the city looked ominous, but the forecast called for wind, not snow. There'd be no white Christmas this year.

Katherine "Katie" Tolliver, a technical services officer from CIA's Directorate of Science and Technology, had arrived on the first commuter shuttle from Reagan National Airport outside Washington, D.C., that morning. Nino had picked her up at JFK, and now the lanky redhead in blue jeans and Muk Luk boots knelt next to the two-inch-wide pole to which she had secured the laser transmitter. She grunted as she tightened the last of the four bolts holding it securely to the metal pole.

"Okay, Nino," Katie said as she rubbed her hands for warmth. "I'll fire it up. Go ahead and give the listening post a heads-up, so they can make sure that only your person is in the room on the receiving end before you send the test message."

For security reasons, Nino had not told Katie Bella's name, only that an undercover CIA officer is the intended recipient of the messages they'd be sending. Within the agency, compartmentation of information is a double-edged sword, simultaneously wielded for protection of sensitive sources and methods of collecting intelligence, as well as to concentrate as much political power in the hands of the few who have the authority to control its flow across the United States government.

Nino fumbled with his cell phone, but the touchscreen wouldn't respond to his fingertip through his glove. He removed his black leather glove and tapped a stubby finger on Michelle's phone number.

"Are you guys ready?" she asked immediately.

"Yes," Nino answered. "Katie is entering the first calibration message now."

"Okay," Michelle said, "give me a minute for the FBI agents here to contact the surveillance van and see if she's alone."

"I'll hold," Nino said. He listened to the conversation in the background and heard the affirmative response. He nodded to Katie even before Michelle relayed the green light to him.

"Okay," Michelle said, "the thermal scanner shows she's alone. Go for it."

"We're transmitting the wide beam now. Let us know what our friend says. Just text me the answer, okay? We don't need to keep the voice line open unless a problem arises."

Michelle looked incredulously at her cell phone to see that Nino had unceremoniously terminated the call mid-conversation. She shook her head, thinking that Nino was so used to operating overseas he didn't appreciate the full value of the luxury they enjoyed in New York without an opposing intelligence or security service mercilessly hunting them down.

Michelle tapped one of the agents on the shoulder and asked him to put the audio on the speaker. He readily agreed, and the three of them leaned back in their chairs to listen for anything that might confirm Bella got the message.

The background hissing from the speaker proved the audio intercept's laser system worked even in the high winds of a cold, late December day. The radiator to which Bella remained shackled worked overtime to heat the small apartment.

Michelle looked around the monitoring room and surveyed the small chamber. Without Caroline, who'd flown home that morning, the room somehow seemed even more diminutive than before.

"Blue," the faint voice from the speaker said. "It's blue."

Michelle clapped and let out a *whoop* as she pawed at her phone. She sent the single word to Nino: *blue.*

His reply arrived quickly: *Good.*

Bella cleared her throat, and asked, "If that's really you, name your school."

Michelle smiled broadly. She texted instructions to Nino: *Send the single word 'Columbia.'*

Why?

Michelle typed feverishly with her thumbs: *Challenge/response confirmation.*

Okay.

Bella's voice came through the speaker clearly. "Green."

Michelle texted Nino: *I think we're mixing messages and crossing in the mail. She saw green this time.*

Yes, Nino replied. *Katie had that message queued up first. Already sent the other.*

No sooner had Michelle read Nino's reply than Bella's ebullient voice streamed through the speaker. "I *knew* you'd find a way to make this work. I'm so happy. I—"

Bella stopped mid-sentence. Michelle leaned forward and gently laid her hand on the shoulder of the agent nearest to her as she strained to listen to the captive woman on the other end of two laser beams.

Bella's voice came through the speaker in a whisper and far less confidently. "I think it's supposed to say *red*," she said softly, "but it's very faded. I can't really make it out, but going by the pattern of what you're sending, I think that's what it's supposed to be."

Michelle decided she was not going to type that much on her phone's tiny keyboard. She called Nino to explain it directly, and he relayed the message to Katie.

"Michelle," Nino said, "Katie thinks it's the glass in the window, or maybe an infrared film layered onto the glass to cut down on how hot the apartment gets in the summertime. Those apartments are so old they probably don't have air conditioning unless the tenant installs a window unit. Katie will configure the transmitter to use the blue and green portions of the visible light spectrum more and avoid red. Between you and me, I'm glad we have tech officers who know this stuff. I couldn't handle it."

Michelle chuckled. "You and me both. I live and die by their gear in the field. All I know is how to use it. I'm glad they know what makes it tick and why."

The voice over the speaker came through clearly. "That's better. It's good. I can read it clearly."

Michelle relayed the message and smiled at their successful afternoon. "Nino, ask Katie to tell Bella we'll send more tonight. Then bring the laptop to me here at the fire station."

She hung up the phone, stretched out her legs, and debated what she wanted to tell Bella first. She took out a notebook and began asking the two FBI agents a string of questions. After she had a few good ideas jotted down, she hurried out for some fresh air and a quick bite to eat.

Two blocks away, Michelle sat at a small table in the corner of a Peruvian chicken restaurant. She texted her boyfriend: *Miss me?*

He replied: *Of course. Hung out last night with Jon Brady. Fun, but not the same.*

She smiled. *What did you do?*

Had dinner. Brought in chicks to lay.

Michelle's eyes narrowed and her eyebrows met in the center. She stared at the phone, unable to decide what to reply.

Sorry. Meant Chick-Fil-A. Damned autocorrect.

Michelle laughed so hard she nearly knocked her plate off her table.

After lunch, Michelle returned to the monitoring room and slung her purse over the back of a chair. Nino Balducci watched over Katie Tolliver's shoulder as the technical services officer completed her installation of the messaging laptop in the FBI's monitoring room.

"Ah, Michelle," Nino said warmly, "let me introduce you to Katie Tolliver. She's the technical wizard who adapted and installed the laser transmitter to go with the FBI's laser receiver. Quite the 'his and hers' lash-up, I must say. Katie has done an absolutely *mar*-velous job. Without her genius, we wouldn't be able to talk to our undercover officer at all. This is a fantastic turn of events and will make all the difference in our ability to bring this case to a successful conclusion."

Michelle smiled, but inwardly she cringed. She felt that Nino's sparkling compliments toward the DS&T officer went too far. He laid it on too thick for her tastes, but perhaps that's why he's been such a successful case officer over the past thirty-plus years. Buttering people up to get what he wants is his stock in trade.

Michelle played along. "That's wonderful! I'm looking forward to seeing it in action." She pointed to the laptop. "Katie, can you show me how to use it?"

Tolliver gave Michelle a crash course in sending messages, which turned out to be easier than sending email since there's only a single possible recipient. The DS&T officer left her contact phone number with Michelle and Nino in case they needed to reach her for technical support.

Nino and Michelle wished her a Merry Christmas and thanked her on her way out.

To Michelle, Nino said, "Glad you came back in time to hear how to work the system directly from her. They make it pretty easy to use, thank heaven, but computers are not my thing. Not by a long shot."

"Mine neither," Michelle agreed. "I was out for lunch and did a bit of shopping. Those are more my speed, not the tech stuff."

Nino smiled. "Last-minute Christmas gifts, I hope?"

"No," she replied with a frown. "This two-day trip to New York turned into a long week, then two weeks, and now there's no end in sight. I've run out of clothes twice now, so I bought practically an entire new wardrobe *and* another suitcase to put it all in." She slapped her thigh and said, "But from now on, it's jeans every day for me. I'm done dressing to impress."

Nino nodded. "Who can blame you? Sitting in a basement for twelve hours a day listening to the hiss of a radiator is nothing to get gussied up for." He flared his nostrils, and said, "And the musty smell of this old storage room...."

Michelle chuckled and pointed to the electrical outlet in which a Glade PlugIn sat. "I know. I purchased that air freshener after the first day. Caroline and I stopped by a grocery store the first evening and both ended up buying the same kind of air freshener without the other knowing it until we pulled them out of our purses first thing the next morning. It was pretty funny."

"I hear that you two had quite an adventure in Times Square the other night."

"Well, she's not a field officer, and I'm not much for sitting at a desk all day, so...." Michelle shrugged. "I think she was really worried about what Dagmar Bhoti or Security Division might do to her or her security clearance."

"And you have no such worries?"

Michelle laughed. "*Me*? No. They're the least of my concerns. Right now, my only concern is Bella."

"Mine, too. What can I do to help?"

"Well, the laser transmitter is going to be a huge help as we load Bella up with suggestions on eliciting information from Wasif. Let's create a list of the information we want to get from Bella, and you can make some suggestions based on your big bag of case officer tricks. Your experience is sure to help Bella phrase things the best way, okay?"

Nino smiled broadly. "It would be my pleasure. I do have a few ideas, but first, tell me more about Wasif Ali al-Bakkar. What are his hot buttons? What makes him tick? What is he afraid of? What motivates him?"

"*Hmm.* I'm not really sure. I've jotted down a few things Bella told me back at the Farm. That seems like it was a million years ago, but actually has been just a couple of weeks. Let's see... She said he's a retired Iraqi Air Force colonel, was a fighter pilot, and is very religious."

"Military and religious. Okay, those two tend to go together since it takes a strong set of beliefs in some foundational ideology to be willing to risk one's life for more than your own self-defense or that of your immediate family. What else?"

"Well, he served in their military under the Saddam Hussein regime, so politically he was a Baathist and religiously a Sunni. His connection to the Baathists seems to also be how he got aligned with ISIS and in, *umm*, possession of Bella in the first place."

"Yes, let's use some of that. While you were out and Katie was setting up the tech gear, I spoke with the very nice FBI agents monitoring Bella about things she's said to Wasif."

Michelle scrunched up her lower lip. "It's not much, unfortunately."

"No, but I listened more for *how* she spoke to him and *how* he responded rather than what information he related to her, which admittedly was very little."

Michelle leaned forward slightly. She longed to learn more about elicitation techniques from an experienced CIA case officer. "What did you find out?"

"Bella probed him carefully and revisited topics she learned about during her first captivity, but Wasif didn't bite. Then, she took a new tack. A few days ago, she played to his ego. She complimented him and, well, not to sound crude about a terrible thing, but she... shall we say, made him believe she enjoyed the sex."

Michelle nodded. "Yeah, I heard that and couldn't wait to rip the earphones off my head. I got the gist of what she was doing and why, but I didn't like it."

"Understandably. And after a couple of days of that, what happened?"

"Nothing that I could tell. Did you hear something subtle?"

"No, Michelle, that's my point. Her techniques didn't work. When we do this in the field, it's never just one case officer making things up on the spur of the moment as he or she goes about their job. We game plan these in group sessions. Sometimes we call upon the expertise of a psychologist or specialty consultant. Only then, once we have a good picture of a potential source's weaknesses, motivations and desires, will we have a case officer with a decade or two of experience help the newer members of the team craft their approaches and messages. Bella doesn't have that support system in place."

"Well, with you here, she does now."

"Exactly, my dear. You and I are going to give her all the support we can, help her craft her messages, and improve her tradecraft."

"Okay, Nino, you're the expert. What do you suggest?"

"Since playing to his ego didn't work for Bella, this time let's try something bolder. We call it a 'provocative statement.'"

"Sounds aggressive. What do you have in mind?"

Nino explained what he wanted Bella to tell Wasif and wrote down the message Michelle should send word for word.

Michelle looked at the completed sentence on the notepad and whistled. "Wow, if the FBI didn't know in advance we were feeding this to Bella ourselves, they may be just as likely to arrest her as Wasif."

Nino leaned back in his chair as the two agents monitoring the laser mic's receiver looked on. He pointed to the notepad, and said, "Wasif doesn't seem inclined to talk to Bella, so we need to give him a push. Whether it's a push forward or off the cliff, I have no idea, but this should get him talking, one way or another."

Michelle turned the notepad over on the table and set her pen on top of the cardboard backing. "I'll send it to her tonight for her to use tomorrow after *Maghrib* prayers and they have their 'private time,' as she calls it. If we get anything from him tomorrow, it'd be a nice Christmas present for all of us."

Chapter 15

FBI Monitoring Room, New York City

A partly overcast sky greeted Michelle Reagan on Christmas morning. She worked out in the hotel gym and returned to her room to find a voicemail waiting on her cell phone. Her boyfriend, CIA executive Dr. Steven Krauss, had called to wish her a Merry Christmas.

She called him at their condo in Arlington, Virginia, and Krauss answered on the second ring. "Hey, babe," Michelle said. "I got your message. Thank you so much. How's Virginia treating you?"

"Whenever you're on travel I work too much, so... pretty typical, I'd say. But I'm looking forward to seeing you in a week. Less than a week, in fact, if I come up early like we talked about."

"I haven't had a really consistent schedule for a while. At the moment, I'm working noon to midnight every day, but not much has been happening. It's been slow but should pick up speed tonight. I can't go into details, but I'm hopeful that over the next few days we'll hear something useful one way or the other. One thing this whole case has made me realize is that there's no *way* I'd ever make a good DS&T officer. I can't just sit around with headphones on all day. I'd last, like, a week at most."

"Well, I doubt they'd last even that long in your shoes in the field. But, hey, enough shop talk. How about we firm up my travel plans?"

"Yes! Much better, hon. What did you have in mind?"

"What if I came up on Amtrak on the twenty eighth? I'll tell my parents to take the train up from south Jersey on the thirtieth. I can meet them at the station up there, then we all take a cab to my aunt and uncle's house in Queens. That way, you and I will have at least part of two days together before the rest of the family arrives. I miss you, and it'd be great to spend some time alone with you in the city before the big anniversary party on New Year's Day. Even if you are still working, we'll still have some time in the mornings together."

"I miss you, too, Steven, and some 'us' time sounds great. I can easily cut my hours down to just the late afternoon and evenings, which is when things are most likely to happen. Besides, the team has my cell phone number, so they can reach me whenever they need."

"You gave them *this* cell phone number? Really?"

"No, no. I keep a burner in one of my equipment kits to use for field work. I don't care if they have *that* one. I'll turn it in and get a new one when this case is over."

"Ahh, now *that* sounds like the paranoid Michelle I know and love. Okay, sounds like a plan. I'll text you when I get on the train. Love you!"

Michelle air-kissed the phone, hung up, and jumped in the shower.

She arrived at the fire station shortly after noon to find only one FBI agent on duty in the monitoring room. He told her that the holiday schedule called for a single monitor in the morning, but a second agent would arrive to join them on the four-to-midnight shift.

"Okay," she said, "I'm going upstairs to get lunch. Call me if anything happens."

Michelle walked upstairs and joined a table of firemen for lunch and a game of gin rummy. They did their best to pump her for information on whatever secret caper was unfolding in the basement which their captain had made clear was off limits to all station personnel. Michelle easily deflected the discussion since, in truth and much to her dismay, little to nothing had been happening downstairs.

Between card games, she checked in on the agent in the basement monitoring room and strolled around the block a few times for some fresh air. She appreciated her decision to dress casually, even if it was for 'office work,' as she thought of it. Caroline always dresses to the nines, and Michelle felt obligated to dress more professionally when she's around. The more relaxed atmosphere of the past few days suited her tastes far better.

Shortly before six o'clock, Michelle returned to the monitoring room and greeted the newly arrived monitoring agent. The three of them sat in the storage room and listened to Bella's radiator hiss through the speaker.

An hour later, Michelle sat up straight when the FBI surveillance team radioed that the crowd returning from the mosque turned onto Wasif's street.

Nino Balducci came through the monitoring room's door and eased it shut behind him. "Merry Christmas," the CIA case officer said. "Let's see what Santa's brought us."

Michelle waved a silent greeting and brought him up to speed. "The days are getting longer now that we're past the winter solstice, so sunset and *Maghrib* occur a few minutes later each day. Noor does all the meal prep before they leave for the mosque, so it doesn't take more than about a half hour for it to cook once they return."

"And Wasif still visits our girl right before dinner?"

Michelle nodded silently. 'Visits' was a polite way of saying it. Or not saying it, as the case may be.

The team of two FBI agents and two CIA officers listened to Wasif's rendition of poems from his favorite book. The FBI's Virtual Translation Center identified the book, and the JTTF had purchased two copies in Arabic and English to help the monitoring team and analysts determine if the poems themselves had relevance to anything that might be overheard via the laser microphone. The two agents followed along as Wasif read—one reading the Arabic and one the English—and jotted notes in a log they provided to the JTTF daily. So far, the poetry turned out to be religious and not especially meaningful to the eavesdroppers.

As Wasif ended his recital, a JTTF agent plugged in headphones and prepared to turn the speaker off, as Michelle had always preferred. This time, she waved him off, and said, "No, tonight I need to listen to it all."

Several times over the next five minutes, Michelle grimaced when Bella uttered a few guttural *mmm*s feigning pleasure.

Nino Balducci looked at Michelle, and said, "She's just buttering him up, and I'm glad to see she's not overacting the part. Half of the job of a case officer is acting, half is proper planning, and half is holding your breath and hoping it all works out well in the end."

"That's a lot of halves, Nino."

"In this business, we work a lot of overtime."

Michelle nodded, not happy, but fully understanding the role Bella volunteered for and was playing out this evening.

After Wasif finished, the monitoring team tensed. None realized they were all leaning forward anticipating what might come from the speaker next.

Bella spoke first. "Noor said she's making lamb again tonight. I like her *Quzi*. You do too. It gives you strength."

"She cooks well, like her mother did."

"I never learned. American mothers don't teach their daughters things like that anymore."

"Americans are weak. Your military has strong weapons, but the country produces feeble men."

Michelle held her breath for fear of breathing too loudly and drowning out the sound of Bella's voice, practically whispering through the speaker.

"That's why," Bella said, "you will win. Because you're strong and *Allah* wills it."

"We have already won. These fools have no idea what's coming."

Nino Balducci slapped his thigh and a toothy grin exploded across his face.

"You're strong with me," Bella agreed.

Michelle grimaced. "I wish she could just ask him straight out what it is that's coming."

Nino shook his head. "It doesn't work like that."

"I know...."

Wasif continued, "Americans have all gotten fat and lazy."

The sound of flesh slapping flesh rumbled through the speaker as Bella patted her stomach repeatedly, and said, "I'm not fat."

"All you do is lie around here all day."

"I can help in the kitchen, if you'd like. I can help cook for you and your friends when they come over."

"They won't be coming over anymore. We're done after tonight."

"They sound like smart men. I don't understand any of that stuff."

"Maybe you'll go serve Fasil next week," Wasif said.

Shuffling sounds came through the speaker like static as Wasif stood up.

"You want to get rid of me *again*?" Bella asked. "You did that once. Have I done something wrong this time?"

"No, but I won't be here to...." Wasif's voice receded into the distance. "Noor will bring you dinner later."

Michelle sat back and closed her notebook. She looked at Nino, and said, "Wow, you guys are *good*. I'm impressed. After a week of nothing, the script you sent Bella made all the difference. This is real progress."

The two JTTF agents looked on as Nino thought about what the team just heard from Wasif Ali al-Bakkar.

"Okay," Nino said, "let's recap. Number one, his technical project finishes tonight."

One of the JTTF analysts picked up his cell phone. "I'll let the surveillance team know. They've identified the three computer programmers, but still haven't figured out what they're doing. They need to know this is the last time they're likely to see them around Wasif's apartment."

Nino continued. "Number two, Wasif has something planned over the next week. What it is, we don't know."

"Could be the attack," the other JTTF analyst said.

"Could be," Michelle agreed. "Either way, it sounds to me like Wasif will be out of the picture afterward. He said he might give Bella to one of the programmers, Fasil. The last time he did that, he sold her to Achmed just prior to leaving Iraq for New York. That point has to be significant. He's going somewhere, but where? And why? The last time he gave Bella away he moved to America. Maybe this time he's moving back to Iraq."

"We don't know," Nino said, "but right now, the two most likely scenarios seem to be that either his part in the preparation for an attack is done and he's going to leave town, or he's going to participate in an attack and... what? Be martyred? His part in preparing the electronic device is apparently coming to a close tonight. What they're going to do with it, however, is still anyone's guess."

Michelle drummed her fingertips on her notebook and looked at the FBI agents. "Well, either way, you guys have *got* to keep him in your sights twenty-four-seven."

"Already do," the agent confirmed. "We'll relay what we heard tonight to the JTTF and give them a transcript once we translate it. The mobile surveillance teams stay on him all day and night. Wasif doesn't even try to slip away from them."

Michelle shook her head slightly. "I'm not sure if that makes me more confident or less. From what we've heard so far, I can't figure out what he's up to. Can the FBI do something else, like try to get an undercover agent into one of the electronics shops he sells to?"

The FBI agent shrugged. "I know the JTTF has been looking at options like that, but it's a tightly knit community. I doubt they'd be successful doing that. Through DEA, the JTTF got a wiretap up on one of the shops he supplies because they're also trafficking heroin through that store, but, so far, they haven't heard anything of interest. The National Virtual Translation Center monitors that line from Virginia and the JTTF gets daily transcripts."

Michelle sighed. "I don't like just sitting here twiddling my thumbs."

Background sounds of dinner conversation wafted through the speaker.

Michelle typed a sentence into the laser transmitter's laptop computer and sent a message to Bella: *Good job. Any idea what he's up to?*

"No," came her whisper through the speaker, "but it sounds like we'll know in the next week. I don't want to be given away again. I...."

Michelle typed furiously. Don't worry, I won't let that happen to you. I promise!

Bella's whisper came through the speaker clearly. "Thank you."

Nino's head tilted slightly. "Doesn't she still have the handcuff key that you gave her?"

"Good question. I'll ask."

Michelle typed her question and Bella answered in the affirmative.

"Good," Michelle said, and leaned back.

"To me," Nino said, "it's somewhat concerning. She shouldn't be dependent upon you to rescue her again — for the third time. She has the means to effect her own escape."

"Yeah, I'm with you. She should be able to walk out on her own anytime she wants."

"Right," Nino said. A frown crossed his face. "I'm hesitant to call Dr. Stone, but not being the expert in these matters, I'm concerned that Bella is not showing that she's able to take care of herself anymore. I don't agree with what I heard Dr. Stone say about Stockholm Syndrome, but I don't like that our young friend in there may simply be too scared to fend for herself anymore.

"If we only have a week, then it's time to get more aggressive. I hate to ask direct questions, but we've got a bit of a time problem here." Nino turned his notebook for Michelle to read what he'd been writing. "Have her say something like this to him tomorrow night."

Michelle looked at the notebook and typed the message: *Nino says hello and that you were superb tonight. Since we're up against the clock, he suggests you ask Wasif the following or something similar: Will Noor go with you to paradise right away, or will she join you there later?*

Chapter 16

FBI Monitoring Room, New York City

Michelle slept in after a long night at the fire station waiting for answers that never came. She ate a light mid-day breakfast and then worked out in the hotel's gym. After doing a load of laundry and checking in by cell phone with FBI Special Agent Ron Poland, she walked to the fire station refreshed.

She arrived just before 4 p.m., and the surprise of seeing Caroline van der Pol showed on her face. "I didn't expect to see you here tonight."

Caroline smiled. "Happy Boxing Day."

"Yeah, right. You too," Michelle said with a chuckle. "If we were British, it might even matter. How was your Christmas?"

"Good. My girls always love opening presents, and I especially enjoyed watching their excitement yesterday at the crack of early. I flew up right after lunch today."

Michelle tugged at her jeans with her thumb and index finger. "As you can see, we're in casual mode this week."

Caroline pulled the jacket of her pantsuit closed. "I don't like flying in skirts. But anyway, what have I missed?"

Michelle back-briefed her on the conversation of the previous evening.

Caroline crossed her arms, and said, "Well, that sounds both too vague to be useful and too terrifying to ignore."

"Exactly. We're still trying to piece it all together."

Caroline opened her notebook and jotted a few lines. "Before you got here, the FBI agents said the physical surveillance is going well, but they haven't seen Wasif do anything of interest. If there's an attack planned, shouldn't he be out, you know, plotting and gathering supplies, or doing reconnaissance, or something obvious?"

"Yeah, you'd think," Michelle said, and shrugged.

Nino Balducci entered the monitoring room and looked around. "Good afternoon, Ms. van der Pol. I didn't realize you'd be joining us this evening. Welcome back."

Caroline waved. "There seems to be a lot of that going around. I didn't know I needed an invitation."

"No, no, I'm glad you're here. Michelle and I were talking about Bella last night, and specifically her state of mind. I think your connection with Dr. Stone may prove quite helpful."

"How so?" Caroline asked.

Nino recapped his concerns about Bella's state of mind.

The radio crackled with a report from the FBI's surveillance team watching Ali's apartment noting a group of residents gathering on the sidewalk for their walk to the mosque for prayers.

"We have at least a half hour until they get back. Want an early dinner?" Michelle asked Nino and Caroline.

Both joined her upstairs where they found the fire station's junior firefighters preparing Gumbo and spiced shrimp for dinner. Somehow — Michelle wasn't quite sure how it was possible — the food in the station got better with time. To combat the food and her sedentary assignment, she availed herself of the hotel's gym each morning for extended workouts.

The trio returned to the monitoring room to find Wasif and Bella already engaged in their 'private time.' Afterward, the apartment remained eerily quiet for several minutes, with only the low hiss of the radiator to confirm the laser mic continued to listen in.

Bella's voice came through the speaker distinctly. "Before you go, have you decided whether you'll give me to Fasil or Malik?"

Michelle translated in real-time for Nino and Caroline.

Caroline's eyes went wide.

Michelle shook her head. She whispered, "We won't let that happen. *I* won't let that happen."

Wasif responded simply, "Not yet."

"If they're not going with you, why can't you stay, too? Noor will miss you terribly."

"*Allah* has told me what my destiny is."

"After he brought us back together again, it's disappointing that we have to be separated again so soon. Being together is his will. I know that now. I see that's the truth, and I don't doubt it in my heart anymore. It must be comforting that you know the path your life will take and that it will make a difference."

Caroline put her hand over her mouth and stared piercingly at Nino.

"It's all an act, I assure you."

Wasif continued. "Yes, we both do his will."

"Will Noor go with you to Paradise?"

Wasif paused. "No. You women are meant to serve men in this life. Allah provides for us in the next." The sound of ruffling clothing came through the speaker as Wasif dressed.

Everyone in the monitoring room jotted notes in their notebooks.

Bella's whisper was barely audible above the radiator's hiss. "He's gone."

One of the FBI agents monitoring the audio intercept called the JTTF to report the latest: an attack was imminent and Wasif Ali was planning to die in the process. But when and where, they didn't know.

Chapter 17

JTTF Office, New York City

The following morning, Michelle Reagan and Caroline van der Pol found seats against the conference room's back wall. FBI agents, CIA officers, and NYPD detectives assigned to the task force packed the room.

SA Ronald Poland spoke from the podium. "Based on last night's intercepts from an FBI wiretap, we now assess the likelihood of a terrorist attack on New York City over the next week to be a virtual certainty. Unfortunately, we don't know the nature of the attack, the target, or the specific timing. This investigation has only been underway for two weeks, so we haven't had as much time as we would have liked to get in front of it. Bob McMillian from the CIA will brief on the information they've developed."

McMillian stood and presented the information the team learned from Bella.

One of the NYPD detectives who recently joined the expanded investigation asked, "If your undercover operative can't get close enough to the subjects, can she introduce one of our undercover detectives? Maybe a man would have a better chance of getting in good with a male-dominated group like this and could offer to assist the subjects with their plot?"

"No," McMillian said with a scowl, "unfortunately that's not possible in this case. It's not because we don't want to, but because there's no possible way to introduce an undercover into the mix through our officer. I wish there were—"

"*Oh*, come on," the detective said, throwing his hands in the air, "you guys are just trying to protect your sources again, but the city's under a *real* threat here."

"No, detective, believe me, we've already looked at this from every angle, and the FBI agrees. In this case, we're fully willing to burn our officer's cover if it would stop an attack. The situation is just not at all conducive to our UC introducing anyone into this group. It's not a matter of risk to the operation or the officer—there's just no possible way the subjects would trust anyone introduced through this particular officer. I'm sorry."

SA Poland retook the podium, and said, "I agree with Bob on this one. We've looked at it from all angles, and there's simply no way it could work. We are, however, making incremental progress on another front. The FBI's lab in Quantico is still analyzing the photographs of electronic components one of our SWAT agents took while inside the apartment a week ago, but they don't have a final determination on what the subjects are building. Since the device is programmable through software, we're going to focus on two possible types of attacks. First, a cyber attack. Where's our rep from the Department of Homeland Security?"

A full-figured woman with short red hair raised her hand.

"As always, DHS's Cybersecurity and Infrastructure Security Agency, CISA, is leading the interagency preparations for prevention of and recovery from any wide-scale cyber attack. They routinely work with critical infrastructure owners such as electrical grid operators and metropolitan transit agencies to prevent attacks and will continue to do so. Post-attack—if we're not able to stop it in time—DHS will work with industry and the city on the cleanup, the FBI would be the lead law enforcement agency for a criminal investigation and we'll all work closely with NYPD. The second most likely type of attack is a roadside bomb. The electronics we found in Wasif Ali's apartment included four high-end commercial radar detectors like you'd buy for your sports car. It's little more than speculation at this point, but he could be using those to somehow remotely trigger a bomb in a vehicle, maybe on a bridge or in a tunnel."

Caroline shifted in her seat. The thought of being on a bridge collapsing from a truck bomb or trapped in a tunnel flooding when a bomb caves the ceiling in sent goosebumps racing down her spine. She crossed her arms and pulled her Cardigan sweater closed at the neck.

Michelle leaned in closely and whispered, "Don't worry. We'll stop him before he gets that far."

Caroline nodded weakly.

Poland concluded his briefing, saying, "The two most likely days for an attack are December 31st and January 1st. We're not going to let it go that long. We have surveillance teams covering all four male subjects twenty-four-seven. If we don't have a line on the specific target by then, we're going to move in and arrest all four no later than 10 p.m. on the thirtieth. We'll interview them to identify the target and means of the attack well before anything actually happens. Refer to your briefing packets for additional information including surveillance photographs and vehicle descriptions."

After the briefing, Michelle stood up and lifted her jacket off the back of her chair. She leaned down, put her lips close to Caroline's ear, and said, "If they need help with the interrogations after they arrest these bastards, I have a few friends in some very out-of-the-way places who'd be happy to help."

Chapter 18

Michelle's Hotel Room, New York City

"You got thrown in *jail*?" Dr. Steven Krauss practically yelled.

Michelle Reagan pulled the bed's top sheet up and tucked it under her armpits. She punched the two feather pillows behind her head into submission until they formed the shape she liked. "No, not really. It was just an NYPD holding cell, not really *jail*. We never got to Rikers Island."

Steve looked at his girlfriend of more than a decade, and asked, "Have you ever been in jail before? A *real* jail?"

"No, not exactly," she said slowly. "I mean, just in training, you know?"

"That's not a course *I* ever went through."

Michelle smiled at the Senior Intelligence Service executive from CIA's Directorate of Analysis. "No, of course not. And besides, it was before I met you."

"So, how did you handle it in real life?"

"Well, it wasn't anything like training. The CIA's class was much more physical. The instructors really roughed us up, and the interrogations were pretty intense, by design. They want to see if you're going to break cover or crack under pressure. Here, in New York though, it was just like the movies, you know? I just went up to the biggest person in the cell, let her know that there was a new sheriff in town, and I wasn't going to take any of her crap."

"I'm afraid to ask how exactly you did *that*, but okay, go ahead and tell me."

"Just like they say in the movies: you go directly up to the biggest person in the place and beat the shit out of them. After she said what she and her friends were going to do to Caroline once we all got to Rikers, I walked right up to her and, without telegraphing it in advance, I kicked the big woman right in her face. Her head snapped back and slammed into the cinder block wall behind her. I wouldn't be surprised if she got a concussion from that. After she was out of the picture, two of her gal pals thought they could take me."

Steve put his hands behind his head and interlaced his fingers. The top sheet slipped down, exposing his bare chest. "Okay, this I *do* want to hear. They obviously don't know you like I do."

"Well, you have an advantage. You saw me in action the day we met."

"And that other time—"

"But we don't ever talk about *that*," Michelle said, and gave the love of her life a stern look.

"Okay, so what happened with these other two women?"

"Well, one came at me, and I wrapped her up quickly in a wrist lock. The other must have thought that since I was in high heels and she had on flats, she could maneuver around me and punch me from the side."

"Oh, the best-laid schemes of mice and women often go awry."

Michelle smiled. "I like that. It's not one of your Shakespeare quotes, is it?"

"No," Krauss said, shaking his head, "I paraphrased a Robert Burns poem from the seventeen hundreds."

Michelle said, "Okay, well, leave it to a history major like you to know that. Anyway, I spun the one girl around by her arm and her friend ended up punching her right in the jaw."

"Ouch!"

"Yeah, then I got creative, cranked on her shoulder, and pushed her forward into the punchy girl. There's a distinctive sound that's made when one skull cracks into another. It can be rather satisfying."

"As long as it's not *your* skull."

"True. After that, neither of those women had much fight left in them, so I pushed them over to the other side of the room and gave the queen bee the choice of walking to the other bench herself or having me, umm, help her."

"*Help*. Yeah, right."

"Well," Michelle said with a smile and a shrug, "at that point, I was back to being 'nice Michelle.' And, after that rather rousing introduction to the women in the cell, Caroline and I had a whole bench to ourselves for the next couple of hours."

"If I ever end up in jail, I want you on my side."

"Too late. Caroline already called cellmates. She's a smart woman and emotionally strong, but not one to—shall we say—mix it up physically. In return, I get all her cigarettes."

"You don't smoke."

"And *you've* never gotten more than just that one speeding ticket, so I don't see you suddenly turning to a life of crime or ending up with a government-provided retirement in Sing Sing or Leavenworth."

"I'm not really well suited for a stretch in the big house."

"Oh, I'd give you until the second night before someone made you his bitch."

"The *second* night? Gee, thanks for your vote of confidence."

Michelle gently dug her knuckle into Steve's side. "I'm just saying...."

"*Anyway*... How's your case going?"

Michelle's wagged her head from shoulder to shoulder. "Ehh, I *think* it's going well, but I don't know. It *should* be wrapped up in two days, or three at most, but there are still a lot of ifs. The FBI is going to take down the cell before the terrorists can do anything. They've got surveillance on 'em twenty-four-seven. I'm playing a central role in communicating with Bella. She and I spend a lot of time chatting by remote control. At least I'm able to pass her some ideas we come up with and keep her spirits up."

"That's good. And since it'll wrap up soon, I'm looking forward to having you all to myself for a day or two before my parents arrive, and we all go to my aunt's for New Year's. You know how the Queens part of my family is. It'll be a madhouse."

Michelle smiled and rolled toward her boyfriend. She ran her fingers through the hair on his chest, sidled up to him, and gave him a long kiss as the bedsheet slipped halfway down her bare torso.

Chapter 19

Michelle's Hotel Room, New York City

Michelle awoke early on December 30th, anxious to start her day. After her workout, she kissed Steve Krauss goodbye as he left for Queens. Michelle walked to the fire station under an ominous-looking gray sky.

She arrived in time for lunch and stood on the sidewalk outside the station as an ambulance and a stream of firetrucks emerged from the cavernous garage with their sirens blaring. The procession wailed its way down the street, responding to an oil fire at an autobody repair shop six blocks away.

As Michelle entered the second-floor dining room, Nino Balducci stood at the large stainless-steel-topped island in the kitchen. He stirred a cauldron of something steaming while Caroline placed two bowls on the island and then laid soup spoons and napkins atop placemats on the table.

Michelle snickered. "They've finally pressed you two into service, I see. Time to earn your keep, is it?"

Nino beamed from ear to ear. "Exactly right! I don't cook well, but I can stir like a champion."

Caroline looked up, and asked, "Hungry? I'll get you a bowl."

Michelle draped her jacket over a chair, and said, "Yes, thank you."

As Caroline pulled a blue bowl from the cabinet, she said, "They all had to respond to a multi-station callout and would have had to turn the stove off. The beef stew would have just sat here and probably gone bad. We're not doing much of anything downstairs, anyway. The FBI has the monitoring covered, and Bella only sees Wasif once or twice a day. Since all the firemen are gone, I figured Nino and I could chat while we eat and discuss what to tell Bella about tonight. No one's here anymore to overhear us. Glad you can join us."

Michelle searched several drawers and wrestled a ladle out of one. She placed it near Nino and slid the three blue bowls closer to him.

The trio ate, and all helped themselves to seconds.

When she finished, Michelle leaned back in her chair and rubbed her stomach. "Wow, that was good. I don't even want to ask what was in it."

Nino patted the corner of his mouth with a napkin. "The rookies on cooking duty today said the station's recipe has a secret ingredient. Instead of using the amount of salt and black pepper specified in the official FDNY cookbook, they replace half of it with Old Bay seasoning. It gives the broth the same saltiness, but an additional kick beyond what the black pepper would provide by itself."

"*That's* what it is," Michelle said. "I'm used to having Old Bay on steamed crabs at the Inner Harbor in Baltimore, you know? But now that you mention it, I can certainly taste it. Okay, good to know. They do a wonderful job with the food here. Last week, I gave one of the lieutenants a hundred bucks from my expense account to cover our share of the food."

Nino broke out in a hearty laugh. "I gave him forty yesterday in appreciation. He didn't mention your donation. I guess we should have compared notes in advance, eh?"

"I didn't give them anything," Caroline said as she folded her napkin neatly. "Now I feel bad." She placed the serviette next to her empty bowl and spoke softly. "Okay, well, before they get back from the fire, let's figure out what we should tell Bella. The FBI is going to make the arrests tonight at the latest. What do you guys think?"

Michelle drummed her thumbs on the edge of the table. "Two things come to mind. First, this is the last chance she'll have to draw information out of Wasif, so maybe we can be more aggressive? It's not like we're going to spook him or anything. Second, we need to tell her not to fall asleep. If the FBI barges into their apartment at 10 p.m., she should be awake and ready to keep her head down after the SWAT team kicks in the front door. When they enter the apartment, I expect they'll use flash-bangs as distractions, and it'll seem like all hell's breaking loose."

Nino shook his head slowly. "I've only seen them used in training and, even then, only from a distance. They're not like the M-80 fireworks I played with as a teenager."

"No, not at all," Michelle agreed. "They're deafening up close, even if you know they're coming."

"So," Caroline asked, "if we start with this being the last time she can solicit information from Wasif, what should she say to him?"

Nino and Michelle discussed a few options. Michelle pulled her notebook from her purse and laid it open on the table. Nino provided specific phrases, and Michelle wrote the script longhand. When they were done, she read her notes back to Nino, and he nodded in agreement.

"Now," Caroline said, "about the other matter. I have instructions that Bella is not to be told about the FBI's raid or any arrests beforehand."

Michelle's eyebrows contracted as she looked at the blonde counterintelligence officer. "Are you saying you still don't trust her? After all she's been through, you think she'd leak that to... him?"

"All I'm saying is that on orders from Langley, Bella is not to know about the FBI's planned arrests in advance. I understand you want her to be ready, but she is *not* to know what's going to happen before the SWAT team arrives. Besides, Bella is in a separate room, and her bedroom door doesn't face the apartment's front door. She won't be affected by the entry, so I don't think it'll matter whether she's asleep at the time, or not. Don't you think it'd be safer for her if she's not running around the apartment at the time a heavily armed SWAT team barges in?"

Michelle looked at Caroline and realized it wasn't worth fighting a battle that did not appear to have a clear benefit. Ron Poland would brief the SWAT team on exactly where they should expect to find the hostage in the apartment. Bella would not be in any danger from the entry team. Michelle nodded her assent silently. No doubt remained in her mind that Dagmar Bhoti gave that particular order to Caroline.

Before long, the fire station's personnel trickled back in from their callout. With an exaggerated waving of his arms, Nino ebulliently showed them that their lunch remained on a low simmer, awaiting their triumphant return.

Caroline and Michelle cleaned up their table, and the three CIA officers trudged down two flights of stairs to the monitoring room. The FBI agents on duty put down the books they read "between innings," as they termed it, and advised the arrivals that they missed absolutely nothing during their extended lunch break.

The early afternoon passed slowly, punctuated by a few instances of Noor speaking in the background. The CIA team alternated playing cards with fire station personnel in the dining room and transmitting instructions to Bella.

Shortly after 3 p.m., the station's alarm sounded again and the announcement of a car hitting a pedestrian sent the station's ambulance crew racing for the scene. The instructions blaring from the loudspeaker almost drowned out a harried radio transmission from the FBI's mobile surveillance team.

"*What* did they say?" Michelle asked as she craned her neck toward the radio on the table.

One of the FBI agents scooted his chair closer to the radio and turned the volume up. "It sounded like they said, 'he's gone.' But—"

The voice of an FBI agent assigned to a mobile surveillance team came through the radio's speaker clearly. "Wasif's van remains double parked in front of the store. He went in with a handcart full of boxes, like he always does, but never came out. Unit three, what's going on in the alley behind the store?"

An FBI agent on foot surveillance repeated his transmission. "The subject is gone. The alley's empty. Just a couple of trash dumpsters and a guy smoking a cigarette farther down the block. Want me to check with him?"

The answer came back after a short delay. "Affirmative. See if he saw anything."

Michelle muttered under her breath.

Caroline looked at her, and said, "Sorry, I didn't catch that. What?"

Michelle crossed her arms and leaned back in her chair. "It was nothing lady-like, I assure you."

"Where'd he go?" Caroline asked.

Nino scratched his throat, and said, "If he's really gone, it sounds like he used a textbook evasion maneuver."

Michelle nodded, and said, "Yup. When you have enough time to set expectations appropriately, it works like a charm."

Nino explained Countersurveillance 101 to Caroline. "In the field, the subject of an extended surveillance will set up patterns of behavior he wants the surveillance team to see. For example, let's say you go to a particular dry cleaner and gym every Saturday. The surveillance team sees you take an armload of clothing and a gym bag with you out of your house every Saturday morning and drive to the same dry cleaner and gym. If you do it every week for months on end, you end up lulling the surveillance team into a false sense of security. One day at the gym, however, you take your bag in as usual, but instead of working out, you simply walk in the front door and right out the back. Most of the time in the Clandestine Service, we don't evade surveillance teams. We need to execute our operational acts *while* they're watching us. That's what makes it *clandestine*, instead of what Wasif did, which is *covert*."

Michelle added, "Wasif seems to have pulled a switcheroo on the FBI today. Everything looked like he was making a routine delivery of electronics to one of his customers, but in reality, he walked in the front door with his handcart stacked high and then went right out the back door with whatever was really in those boxes. If *that's* what happened, he knows his van will be towed and searched by NYPD. It's a write-off for him. He knows he won't get it back, and he'll never see it again. He planned it that way."

Nino agreed. "Exactly. And whatever was in the boxes he wheeled into the store was probably the electronics he built in his apartment. That's my speculation, anyway."

Caroline looked at the radio over which increasingly frantic calls between FBI agents on multiple surveillance teams streamed nonstop. The rapid pace of their communications and frequent use of four-letter words made it clear that the team which had so successfully followed Wasif for two weeks had lost him today to a beginner's countersurveillance maneuver. To no one in particular, she asked, "What do we do now?"

The FBI supervisor in charge of the surveillance provided the answer over the radio. "Bravo team, continue vehicle and foot surveillance and conduct a grid search out to six blocks. Alpha team is inbound to assist you and take the lead. Bravo team leader, report to the JTTF office for a debrief."

Michelle said, "We should go, too."

Caroline looked back and forth between her and Nino.

Nino spoke first. "I'll stay here. I'm Bella's handler. My job is to stay by her side. Text or call me with any instructions or questions for her, and I'll transmit them with the laser system."

Michelle and Caroline rose simultaneously. "Okay," Michelle said as she hurried to put on her winter coat, "let us know if you hear anything."

Michelle and Caroline hailed a taxi outside the station and rode to the JTTF office in silence. Neither wanted to verbalize the thought that they—or, more specifically, the FBI—had lost their best chance of finding out what kind of attack Wasif Ali planned to conduct against the city of New York.

Both women felt bad for the Bravo team lead who would surely be on the receiving end of a shit storm once he arrived at the JTTF that afternoon.

Chapter 20

The JTTF conference room filled with a steady stream of FBI agents, NYPD detectives and detailees from a dozen federal agencies and city departments. A task force analyst dialed the Polycom connecting the conference room to the JTTF watch center on the floor below, then put the phone on mute. Analysts on the watch floor downstairs would relay any important surveillance-team radio traffic up to the secure conference room, in which radios and cell phones were not permitted for security reasons.

Special Agent Ronald Poland smacked his open palm on the podium three times to get the murmuring crowd's attention and spoke from the front of the room. "Ladies and gentlemen, tomorrow is New Year's Eve, and the subject we believe is planning an attack on this city slipped through your fingers this afternoon. You had a surveillance team of seventeen experienced FBI agents and NYPD detectives following Wasif Ali al-Bakkar all day in anticipation of an arrest tonight! And now you're telling me that he simply walked in one door and out another?" Poland looked at the surveillance team lead, and asked, "You *lost* the terrorist plotting to do who-knows-what? Please tell me that's not the case."

From his seat, the Bravo team lead briefed the assembly on what he and his team saw throughout the day and detailed how Wasif slipped through their net.

Poland shook his head. "Not our finest hour. Okay, here's what's going to happen now. As we speak, FBI agents are applying for arrest warrants for Wasif Ali and his three computer programmer buddies. We should have the warrants from the federal magistrate's court within the hour. NYPD is posting Ali's photo at all train stations, bus terminals, toll booths, and the airports. JTTF analysts are working with NYPD to scour traffic cameras for any sign that Wasif Ali got into a car, van, bus, or, hell, even on a moped. They're also adding his photos to their facial recognition databases in case he takes the subway. Where do we stand with that?" He pointed to a woman sitting at the conference table.

She said, "No hits on the face cams, yet. We've pulled as many analysts as we can spare from all other tasks and put them on traffic cam analysis. They've identified over six hundred vehicles that drove past at least one part of the block behind the store from which Wasif Ali disappeared in the thirty minutes between the time his van arrived and when the FBI confirmed he was in the wind."

A wave of groans flowed over the crowd of law enforcement professionals in the room.

"It'll take hours for our analysts to trace that many vehicles," she continued, "and, well... I'll update you if I get any positive results."

"In the meantime," Poland said, "the FBI is gathering three teams of agents and NYPD officers, both plainclothed and uniformed, to make arrests of Ali's three accomplices. We'll conduct interviews continuously throughout the night, starting from the moment we pick them up and going non-stop until we find out what the hell they're up to."

A lone voice from the back of the conference room spoke, probably louder than the NYPD detective intended. "*Interviews*, eh? I'll bring the rubber hose."

Poland ignored the comment but instinctively looked at Michelle. After he finished his briefing, he walked toward where she and Caroline were sitting against the conference room's side wall. Seven JTTF personnel lined up to ask Ron Poland questions. It took him a dozen minutes to make his way the forty feet from the podium to where the two ladies patiently waited for him.

"Ugh," he said as he rubbed his eyes and dropped into the chair next to Michelle. "What else can go wrong today?"

Michelle shrugged. "The coffee machine could break."

Poland gasped. "Don't even *joke*."

Caroline held up the cup in front of her. "There's a Starbucks on the corner downstairs."

"Caroline," Poland offered, "this is New York City. There's a Starbucks on *every* corner."

Michelle looked around the room at the few lingering agents and analysts and lowered her voice. "Ron, what about our girl? We prepared her with some rather pointed questions to ask during her time with Wasif tonight, but now —"

"Yeah, Michelle, honestly, I don't know. I'd say let's leave her in place for now in the hopes that maybe something weird happens and

Wasif will show up back at home. If he does show up later and she's still there and not acting like anything's awry, then maybe we will end up getting that one last shot at questioning him. We still have Echo team on surveillance around the apartment, and they'll stay all night, if need be. We're calling in agents from the outer boroughs to cover the overnight shifts and can request support from Albany and Newark, if it comes to that. For now, though, we have enough personnel here in the New York Field Office."

"Okay," Michelle said, "we can leave her there for the night. It might even be interesting to hear Noor's reaction when Wasif doesn't come home. Tomorrow, I can tell Bella to use Matt Decker's handcuff key to let herself out, and I'll be there to pick her up."

"Keep us posted," Poland said.

"Will do," Michelle said, "Nino is staying on communications duty with the monitoring agents in the listening post. If you want me to tell Bella something specific, just let me know, and I'll text Nino the details."

"Thanks," Ron Poland said as he stood up.

"Ron," Caroline said, "you said you were applying for arrest warrants. I don't know why, but I expected you would have gotten those days ago."

"We didn't want to," Poland said, "because the timing gets tricky. Legally, once we have a warrant for someone's arrest, we have to serve it as soon as we can. In this case, we had Wasif under surveillance and wanted to continue following him to identify additional accomplices and learn more about the nature of the attack they're planning. Obviously, we couldn't do that if we'd already arrested him. It's always a balancing act, and I realize now that it might come back to bite us on the ass this time."

"Yeah, that sucks," Michelle said. "You know, Ron, when you were talking about interviewing Wasif's three computer programmers after you arrest them tonight, I noticed you glanced at me. I could have sworn I heard you telepathically use the word *waterboard*. Maybe it was just my imagination."

"Well, at this point I'm less concerned with the admissibility of evidence or prosecuting the subjects than I am in stopping the attack they're planning. But no, there'll be no waterboarding."

"Ohh-*kaa*-ay," Michelle said with a toothy smile, "but you know how to reach me if you change your mind. I just so happen to have friends in some rather dark and remote places around the globe."

"Good to know," the FBI agent said. He tapped the edge of the conference table with his index finger twice, pointed at Michelle, and walked away.

Caroline looked at Michelle with a pained look on her face, and quietly said, "Michelle, you *do* know we can't do that anymore, right?"

Michelle stood, looked down at Caroline, and laid her hand gently on the blonde woman's shoulder. "Are you *sure*? I don't recall having gotten *that* memo." Michelle winked at the CI officer and squeezed her shoulder.

Chapter 21

JTTF Watch Center Floor, New York City

Michelle Reagan and Caroline van der Pol slowly paced along the back row of the Joint Terrorism Task Force's watch center. They alternated between peering down at the computer monitors in front of the two dozen analysts, and up at the ninety-foot-wide video wall in the front of the room. The big screens displayed everything from lists of emergencies phoned into NYC's 911 call center, Intelligence Information Reports filtering in from around the globe, color-coded status maps of New York's critical infrastructure and the anchors on the evening's cable news shows.

At the left end of the room, law enforcement officers sat elbow to elbow sharing status updates on open terrorism cases, tips received from informants and maps of key neighborhoods in which various agencies' surveillance teams were operating. At the other end of the cavernous room, representatives from CIA and NSA sat next to their DOD counterparts. The IC agencies fed foreign intelligence reports to the task force and the DOD rep prepared graphics detailing the scope of the Air National Guard combat air patrols that would fly protective missions above the city the following night.

Michelle checked her watch. The luminescent hands showed 6:11 p.m.

One screen on the large video board displayed driver's license photos of Wasif Ali's three computer programmers. A single word in red letters crossed the center image diagonally: Captured. The screen listed the home addresses of the other two below their photos.

Caroline leaned down and spoke to the JTTF analyst who had updated the status board most recently. "How much longer until they get the guy they arrested back here and begin interrogating him?"

The analyst shook his head. "They won't bring him here. They're taking him to the FBI's main office at 26 Federal Plaza. We'll get the video from the interview when they get him into the room. We'll get the one-way video. I can put it up on the big screen, if you'd like."

"Okay, thanks."

Michelle offered to buy Caroline a Starbucks coffee, and the CI officer told her what she wanted.

When Michelle returned, half of the analysts in the room stood along the left wall or in the aisles as they watched the silent video of two FBI agents sitting across a narrow, white table from a bearded man fidgeting with his handcuffs.

Caroline asked the FBI analyst, "Why don't they broadcast the audio?"

"Too many managers would become backseat interviewers and try to run it by remote control. It would be a nightmare for the agents in the room. Nothing would get done. But don't worry, those two guys are experts."

A voice from the center of the room spoke up. "Got another one! They arrested Fasil."

The analyst in front of Caroline updated the big screen, overlaying the word "Captured" over the photograph of Fasil Mahmood.

The evening progressed slowly, and Caroline volunteered to make the next Starbucks run. As she stepped onto the sidewalk in front of the JTTF's office, a gust of frigid wind blew down the street and swirled around her ankles. She shuddered and pulled up the collar of her jacket as she walked toward the coffee shop.

On the corner, she looked across the street at an elderly Santa Claus ringing his bell. A woman dropped a few bills into his red Salvation Army bucket, and the bearded man in the red velvet suit waved politely to his benefactor. On the other side of Santa, a hot dog vendor stomped his feet while standing next to his iconic silver cart with the brand name "Sabrett" emblazoned across the yellow-and-blue umbrella.

Caroline turned slowly and took in the scene of bustling pedestrians and honking cars battling a fleet of yellow taxis for position and right of way. She stopped, gathered her tan pashmina tightly under her chin to ward off the cold, and stared at the vendor in front of her.

She imagined how the scene on the busy street corner would change in an instant if *that* hot dog cart or *that* delivery truck suddenly exploded with whatever bomb Wasif Ali planned to unleash on the city. Images flooded her mind as she imagined people fleeing in panic and the bloody carnage of the dead and dying lying on the sidewalk amidst shards of glass and twisted steel while dozens of wounded New Yorkers pled for help.

A thump in the middle of her back jolted her forward and brought her back to the present.

The voice of a harried pedestrian rushing past her hissed, "Watch where you're walking, lady!"

Caroline turned and made a beeline for the Starbucks on the corner. The warmth of the busy shop and aroma of expensive coffee displaced her visions of what the aftermath of a terrorist attack on the frigid streets of New York might look like.

When she arrived back in the JTTF Watch Center, a second silent video of an FBI interview room played on the front wall adjacent to the first.

Michelle reached for the cup Caroline offered, and said, "Thank you. Ron said that the first guy they arrested lawyered up. The second guy seems like he might eventually crack."

Caroline thought back to the street corner downstairs. "I hope *eventually* doesn't come too late. So, if the first guy asked for a lawyer, why are they still interrogating him?"

Michelle took a sip of her coffee, and said, "The FBI calls it *interviewing*, not *interrogating*. I guess the difference is how many stress positions you can put someone in. I can't imagine the handcuffs are comfortable, but they're not breaking out the rubber hoses. Anyway, because there's an imminent threat to the city, the agents are going to continue to question him. If they get anything out of him now, they can use it for intelligence purposes and to stop the attack, but probably not for a prosecution later."

"Okay, well," Caroline said, "as long as they stop the bomb."

"I agree," Michelle said, "but at this point, we're still just *assuming* it's a bomb. What information do we really have that—"

"No, you're right," Caroline said, and crossed her arms. "You're right. I... I was just downstairs and looking around. I tried to visualize what would happen if a bomb exploded on the street corner in front of the coffee shop. I can't even imagine...."

"I can," Michelle said, and placed her cup of coffee on the desk. She lifted the right side of her blouse a few inches and showed Caroline a scar in the shape of a jagged number four. "I've been on the wrong side of a large explosion. I don't want to see it happen again. I want to get Bella out of Wasif's apartment and get us all the hell out of here."

Caroline looked at Michelle's side in amazement. "Where?"

"Overseas. Doesn't matter where. We were operating somewhere we don't operate, doing something we don't do, and an idiot did something stupid. Bad shit happened that night. Real bad." She tucked her shirt back into her waistband and took a sip of her coffee. "I don't want that happening here."

"Me neither," Caroline agreed.

"Or me," the FBI analyst at the desk in front of them added.

Michelle patted him on the shoulder and pointed to the twin video feeds displayed on the large screens in the front of the room. "If those agents are good enough at extracting the information we need, we can prevent anything bad from going down."

"That's the plan," the young agent said, "and then it'll truly be a Happy New Year for everyone."

The trio watched one of the FBI agents interviewing Fasil Mahmood stand and leave the small, white box of the interview room. The second agent unscrewed the plastic top from a water bottle and placed the drink in front of Fasil. The young man emptied the bottle in a long, single draw.

A few minutes later, the agent reentered the small interview room and Ron Poland burst into the Watch Center and called for everyone's attention.

"Okay, everyone, listen up! I just got word from the team interviewing Fasil Mahmood. The subject claims he doesn't know the entire plan, but said the attack involves commercial aircraft, is planned for tomorrow, and New York City is definitely the target. The interview team will continue to press him hard for additional details, and maybe if he continues to cooperate the prosecutors will take the death penalty off the table for him. In the meantime, DHS will add all four subjects — the three programmers and Wasif Ali — to the No-Fly list, but that'll take some time because it has to be approved down in Washington."

Poland pointed to teams of analysts in the room and barked orders. He assigned several to check airline reservations for Wasif Ali and all his known associates. TSA reps on the task force stabbed the speed-dial buttons on their desk phones to call their agency's intelligence center in Arlington, Virginia. Poland tasked other JTTF analysts to write summaries of the case and send them to the mayor's office and FBI Headquarters. Additional task force employees filtered into the watch center and manned unoccupied desks to take up the growing workload.

When Ron Poland finished tasking the teams, he approached Michelle and Caroline in the rear of the room. He took an empty seat at a desk and fiddled with his gold wedding band. "At least now we know more about what's behind this plot. Bella was right. Without her, we wouldn't have known about *any* of this. We owe her — and you — a lot. Now, we're going balls to the wall to find Wasif. We still have a full day to do that before the shit hits the fan, but the clock's ticking."

"This is terrific progress," Michelle said to him, and smiled. "Congrats on getting that guy to crack."

"Yeah, well, he's not a hardcore jihadist. He's just a graduate student at NYU studying computer science and doesn't want to see his whole family get deported. Someone at the mosque introduced him to Wasif Ali and the rest is history. He's just a cog in a machine that was not of his making."

"Well, good job, just the same, Ron. I'm not used to working large cases like this with two hundred or so people involved. I feel like the same kind of small cog in a large machine."

"Yeah, some days are like that around here. People can get lost in the shuffle sometimes. That's life in the big city."

Michelle asked, "Speaking of that, what about Bella? It's after ten o'clock, and Wasif hasn't returned to his apartment."

"Well, she doesn't seem to be in any imminent danger, and we won't have personnel to spare anytime soon. She's probably best-off staying in place and reporting back anything she hears from Noor. She's still our only eyes in that apartment, and you're the key connection we have to her. She trusts you. That's worth its weight in gold."

Michelle grumbled at the thought of Bella staying in place with Wasif Ali in the wind but couldn't come up with a better idea. She told Caroline that she was headed for the fire station to tell Bella what she should do next.

Caroline added, "I think I'll join you."

Chapter 22

Michelle and Caroline entered the monitoring room and the agent on duty told her the news: nothing interesting had happened.

Michelle asked him to check with the surveillance team outside Wasif Ali's apartment to confirm Bella was alone in her room. The radio call came back quickly and reported that Noor appeared to be in her own bedroom and Bella was indeed alone.

Michelle tapped on the keyboard: *B, it's M. Any news?*

The soft background hiss of the radiator confirmed the laser mic continued to work perfectly. Bella remained silent. Michelle considered the possibility that Bella might be facing the other way or had her eyes closed. She waited a minute and sent the message again.

"No, nothing," came the soft reply.

Did Wasif come home?

"No," Bella whispered, "not after he left this morning. I'm worried."

Caroline bit her bottom lip, and asked Michelle, "Worried *about* him or worried *for* him?"

Michelle glanced at Caroline and typed: *Did it seem like Noor expected him home for dinner?*

"No. She ate at a friend's house, I think. After that, she brought me a slice of pizza."

Caroline looked at Michelle, and said, "So, Noor knows what Wasif's up to, or at least that it's going down now. For the first time in forever, she didn't make dinner for her husband, and she put no effort at all into caring for Bella."

"Yeah," Michelle said, "you're right about that. Noor may not know exactly what Wasif is up to, but she definitely knew in advance not to expect him home for dinner tonight. I wonder if that means she doesn't expect to see him again. I mean *ever*."

Caroline twisted her lip.

Michelle typed to Bella: *Have you heard Noor crying at all?*

"No," Bella said. "Why?"

I'm just wondering whether she thinks she'll be seeing Wasif again. I have no idea what his timetable is. Do you?

"No."

Michelle frowned at Caroline, and typed: *Do you still have the handcuff key?*

"Yes. Are you saying I should leave?"

Michelle looked at Caroline. Neither had a good answer. If Bella left and Wasif returned, they might be tipping their hand and also lose a chance for one more opportunity to question him. If, on the other hand, Bella remained behind, the risk of her being handed over—or sold—to another man increased by the hour.

Michelle typed her response. *No, wait until tomorrow. If you learn anything, someone will be listening all night, so let us know immediately. I'll stay here awhile to keep you company, and then you can get some sleep. Tomorrow, we'll make plans to get you out.*

Chapter 23

Allentown, Pennsylvania

Wasif Ali al-Bakkar joined his seven compatriots around the long oval dining room table for lunch and lifted a small glass of black tea to his lips. The sweet liquid had a hint of bitterness which disappointed him. Over the decades of their marriage, Noor learned to brew tea to his liking: strong and sweet. At his host's house, the man's young wife had not yet learned all the techniques she would need as a proper wife of an Iraqi man. Perhaps her next husband would demand more of her after her current husband, Gabir Wahab, followed Wasif to Paradise.

"Brothers, it is good to see you all again," Wasif said in Arabic. He gently placed his glass on the table, being careful to not spill it on the cardboard box in front of him. "We are on the precipice of a monumental achievement. You have trained for years to reach this point, and I have waited decades to avenge the death of my son at the hands of the American Air Force. We will finally do what no other group of the faithful has done since Usama bin Laden's hand-picked martyrs brought this wicked country to its knees a generation ago. Together, we will make these heathens regret the destruction they continue to inflict on our country. The eight of us will remind them that *we* will always win because we are doing *Allah*'s will."

One of the men raised his tea glass, and said, "*Allahu Akbar!*"

Two other men at the table repeated his call to victory.

"Yes, brother, indeed," Wasif said, and smiled. "Between your pilot training, new air-charter jobs, and my experience in the Air Force of our homeland, we now have the tools we need to succeed." Wasif took the lid off the box in front of him. "And, we now have this."

Piece by piece, he lifted electronic components from the box and laid them on the table. He pointed to the equipment and explained how the four radar detectors fed the laptop with data, so its screen could display the custom-programmed calculations and displays for him.

"Have you tested it? Will it work?" one man asked.

SCOTT SHINBERG

"We've tested it as best we can on the ground, so if *Allah* wills it, we will be successful. I have my faith in him and will thank him in person in two days' time."

Wasif boxed up his equipment and set it on a chair in the corner of the room. He withdrew a series of aeronautical charts from a tan backpack hanging from the back of Gabir's seat and distributed them to the pilots sitting around the table. "Now, brothers, we make our final plans. Our host has graciously provided us with these charts of the airspace between here at the Lehigh Valley International Airport and New York City. You have already been assigned your specific aircraft. Gabir will be my co-pilot. Each aircraft is large enough and carries a sufficient load of fuel, so each will burn brilliantly and send hundreds of heathens to their deaths. Then, they will burn for all eternity in *Jaheem*. I marked your specific flightpath on each of your charts and noted the takeoff times, as well. Do not let these charts leave your sides before we take off."

Around the table, the men nodded vigorously.

Wasif pointed to the man next to him, and said, "Gabir and I must depart first since we have the longest distance to fly. Our plans require us to come in from the north. The rest of you will take off fifteen to thirty minutes later to conserve some fuel but also to ensure that security or police on the ground cannot stop you. Once we are all airborne, nothing can prevent our success. We will use the Americans' own aircraft against them." He looked at Gabir, and asked, "You are sure we can steal the aircraft we need? It's too late to turn back now. We must be successful."

"Yes, brother," Gabir answered enthusiastically. "We will be. I have the combination to the safe in which the keys are kept, and there should be only two people in the office at that time of day. We can take care of them easily."

"Excellent," Wasif said, and his thin lips drew back into a broad smile. "Then we celebrate tonight, for we will spend tomorrow in prayer and on December 31st, we fly into history! *Allahu Akbar!*"

In unison, the men around the table joined Wasif in cheering to the success of their plan to triumphantly enter Paradise after gloriously crashing their aircraft into the buildings of New York City on live TV as the illuminated ball drops in Times Square at midnight on New Year's Eve. "*Allahu Akbar!*"

Chapter 24

CIA National Resources Division, New York City

Michelle Reagan entered the CIA conference room a few minutes before their 11 p.m. start time. Caroline van der Pol chatted with her branch chief, Phil Thompson, at the front of the room as Phil dialed a number on the video teleconferencing system.

Dagmar Bhoti's face appeared on the large screen in the front of the room. She greeted Nino Balducci and the others as each took their seats around the table.

Phil began the meeting by recapping the events of the past few days.

Dagmar Bhoti said, "I'm sorry I can't be there in person, but official travel to New York City and the surrounding areas is being limited for a few days."

"So," Michelle asked, "what does that mean, Dagmar? It's too dangerous for *you* to come up, but the rest of us are expendable?"

Silence engulfed the room, and no one spoke for a few heartbeats.

"Michelle," Dagmar said, "I wouldn't put it quite that way, but I understand your angst. All non-essential travel to the Tri-State area has been curtailed. All NR Division personnel supporting the JTTF will remain in place while all others and their families are being instructed to quietly depart the city before noon on the thirty-first—tomorrow. A previously scheduled visit by the vice president to Radio City Music Hall to see the Rockettes perform will be cancelled tomorrow afternoon due to a last-minute scheduling conflict, or at least that's the story that will be released by his office. The NR Division will continue to support the FBI, but the Counterintelligence Mission Center's primary interest in this case is with Isabelle Cirrone. Where do we stand with her?"

Caroline cleared her throat, and said, "Ma'am, she's still in place in Wasif Ali's apartment. Michelle and I spoke with her earlier this evening, and she's in good spirits. Ali has not returned to his apartment and the FBI and NYPD are still actively searching for him. At this point, Bella appears to be out of immediate danger, and tomorrow, we'll be finalizing our plans to get her back."

"Good," the CI Chief said. "Phil has made arrangements for her medical care post-return. Speaking of that, if Wasif is not back home, why aren't you pulling Bella out sooner?"

Caroline said, "The FBI case agent asked that she remain in place for one more day just in the off chance that Noor says something relevant or Wasif does, for some reason, return home. That would give us one last chance to question him through Bella. Once we have enough first-hand intel to confirm his presence, the FBI will swoop in and arrest him before he can escape again."

"I see," Dagmar said. "Ms. Cirrone volunteered for this, otherwise I would never want to keep her in that apartment a minute longer than she's already been there."

"Dagmar," Nino Balducci said, "Bella is an experienced operations officer. She knows the risks and, as you pointed out, volunteered to remain in place to enable us to gather as much information as is humanly possible. I hate the thought of what she's been through to help us all. I know we all do. That young lady has certainly gone above and beyond what anyone could or should ever have to do."

"I agree, Nino. She volunteered to do something no one else I've ever met would have. I just want to make sure she's doing it for the right reasons. When she's back in Virginia, she'll get whatever psychiatric and medical care she needs."

Michelle leaned back and thought about Dagmar Bhoti's backhanded compliment of Bella. Clearly, the CIMC chief still questioned Isabelle Cirrone's loyalty.

***

Michelle walked down the street and away from the NR Division's office in Manhattan's Financial District. She thumbed her cell phone's contact list and pressed the button to dial her boyfriend.

"Hey, Michelle, I'm glad you called, even if it is almost midnight. I didn't want to bother you but wanted to ask when you're going to join us. My folks have already gone to bed but are looking forward to seeing you again."

"Yeah, about that, Steven, I think you should go home."

"*Home*? What do you mean?"

"In fact, I think you should suggest everyone leaves the city with you. Maybe go down to your parents' place in New Jersey. You can suggest everyone celebrate New Year's Eve tomorrow at one of the casinos in Atlantic City or something. Don't they have fireworks on the boardwalk, or something?"

"What? *Why*? Is it because of my mom? Michelle, I know she can be a bit overbearing, but—"

"No, honey, it's not that. Other than my continually disappointing her because I won't be giving her grandchildren, your mother and I get along just fine. I can't go into details, but I think you should all get out of town for New Year's no later than lunchtime tomorrow. You and I can pay for your aunt, uncle, and cousins to stay in a hotel down by your parents. It doesn't matter where, just as long as it's not in New York."

"Why? Michelle, this isn't like you."

"Steven, honey, listen to what I'm saying, will you? I'm in New York City *working*, and you're here on *vacation*. I shouldn't have to say this, but you really don't want to be anywhere near me when I'm *working*. Do you understand?"

"I don't know how I'd convince everyone to leave. What am I supposed to say? Michelle, is everything all right?"

"If it were all right, Steven, would I be urging you to hightail it out of town, or just hopping in a cab to come join you?"

"I guess you're right, but... I can't just—"

"Steven, I have to go. For such a smart man, sometimes you can be so dense. You need to go, too. I *mean* it!"

Chapter 25

The next morning, Michelle typed her question for Bella and hit send. *Did he come home last night?*

"No," Bella replied immediately.

Caroline entered the room and rolled her suitcase up against the wall. As quietly as she could, she placed her cup of worth-what-you-paid-for-it free hotel coffee on the table next to Michelle's laptop and draped her jacket across the back of a folding metal chair.

Michelle looked at the late arrival, and asked, "Did you get the rental car?"

Caroline pulled a set of keys from her jacket pocket and jingled them. "The firehouse captain is letting me keep it in the employees' lot behind the station for now."

Michelle nodded and typed her instructions to Bella. *When Noor leaves the apartment, use the handcuff key and free yourself. First, tell us you're leaving. Then, we'll pick you up at the rear of the apartment. We have a rental car.*

"No," Bella said. "I think I should stay to see if Wasif comes back. That may be our only chance to get more information."

Michelle grunted and repeated her instructions. *You've already done more than anyone could ask of you. It's time to come home.*

"I'm okay, Michelle. Really. Right now, I'm just bored. I pass the time by thinking of how I'm going to decorate my new apartment when I get back to Virginia. Of course, I have to find one, first."

I'd be happy to help you go house hunting, but first you have to get yourself out of Wasif's apartment. Along the left side of the building's main hallway, you'll see a stairway leading down to the basement. It's marked by the typical illuminated emergency exit sign over the doorway. You can't miss it. The door at the bottom of the stairs exits directly into the alley behind the building. I'll meet you there.

"Not yet," Bella replied. "Later. Or tomorrow."

Caroline fidgeted with her leather portfolio and slipped her pen back into its elastic holder. She looked at Michelle, tilted her head slightly, and asked, "Do you still think she's acting rationally?"

Michelle looked at the counterintelligence officer, and said, "I think she's been under more stress than you can possibly imagine."

"Put yourself in her shoes, Michelle. If you had the handcuff key and could simply walk out of that apartment any night of the week, how out of whack would your loyalties have to be to keep you from leaving? She's literally chained to a radiator on a cable just long enough for her to reach the bathroom."

Michelle crossed her arms over her chest. "I don't do this kind of undercover work for a reason—I'm not well suited for it. And neither are you. You wouldn't last a day in her job, and we already know you wouldn't last a minute in mine, so don't be so quick to judge people, especially when they're in impossible situations."

"You call it judging, but in the counterintelligence field, we call it assessing someone's motivations. At this point, I'm not sure what Bella's real motivation for staying is. Is it as she claims, to gather information for us? Or is she instead demonstrating strong personal loyalty to Wasif and not wanting to leave his side when he might need her particular services the most? I don't know, yet, but I *do* know that the only way for us to find out is to get Bella out of that apartment and into a treatment facility where she can be helped by Dr. Stone and her team."

"Believe me, I want Bella to get the help she needs, too. I just don't want to save one person at the expense of hundreds or thousands of others. I'm looking at the big picture, here, and so is Bella."

"That's mighty altruistic of you, Michelle. I wonder if you'd be so willing to stay there if it were you and not someone else who had to tolerate what Bella's going through."

Michelle raised her voice more than she would have liked. "You heard her yourself. Her biggest problem right now is fighting boredom, not terrorists."

"I hope you're right. Who knows what'll happen if Wasif does return to his apartment?"

"Well, I for one hope he does. If he goes home, the FBI will hear about it immediately. They'll storm the place, arrest him and rescue Bella. Problem solved. And if he doesn't go back, Bella continues to mentally decorate a virtual apartment and picks out, I don't know, imaginary purple window treatments to match her equally non-existent bedspread."

Caroline looked at her watch, and said, "Well, it's less than twelve hours until the ball drops. Let's hope that by this time tomorrow everyone's safe, and Bella is free."

"Yeah," Michelle said. "Let's hope."

Chapter 26

Lehigh Valley International Airport, Allentown, Pennsylvania

After feasting on an early dinner and celebrating their last day before entering Paradise, Wasif Ali led seven men across the General Aviation parking lot toward the Keystone Air Charters office. He pulled the glass door open, and Gabir Wahab rushed in first, followed closely by Gabir's cousin.

The seating area of the small, private terminal frequented by well-healed passengers sat empty in the late afternoon. The last charter flight—a family of six heading to Colorado for holiday skiing in Aspen—lifted off almost an hour earlier. The only other flight of the night, an arrival from Orlando, was behind schedule and not expected to land until shortly before 9 p.m.

Gabir and his cousin drew identical 9mm pistols from their waistbands and ran to the narrow counter behind which a Keystone employee tapped at her computer. She squealed in shock as Gabir swatted her hands away from the keyboard. His cousin grabbed her roughly by the hair, and two of the other pilots yanked her into the center of the small terminal and away from the computer and telephone on the countertop.

Wasif and three of his men surged into the adjacent office where the shift manager sat at his desk streaming the movie *Airplane!* on his computer over Netflix.

Wasif instructed his team to push the two Keystone employees into the women's bathroom in the main terminal. As the men shoved their prisoners forward, Wasif stepped back and glanced at the posters lining the walls. Scenes of the Swiss Alps, Mount Rushmore and a dozen other destinations popular with Keystone's wealthy clientele hung between photographs of the charter company's fleet of gleaming Gulfstream aircraft. That night, Wasif planned an entirely different destination for Keystone's opulent jets.

Four gunshots echoed from the bathroom. Gabir closed the door behind him and nodded to Wasif.

Wasif raised his arms above his head, and said, "Brothers, it has begun! We are Allah's soldiers and will be victorious tonight!"

Shouts of agreement and praise for the almighty resounded throughout the terminal.

Wasif waved to his followers to gather around him, and said, "Now, we have work to do. Gabir, get the keys. Amed, make sure everyone has his aeronautical charts." Wasif continued tasking his team, and they set about the terminal locking doors and dimming the lights.

"Brother," Gabir said from the office doorway with a wide grin, "they haven't locked the safe yet." He held up the keys for all to see. "Now we have everything we need to take the jets."

"Excellent, Gabir. All right everyone, it's time! You have trained for years to fly and put in many hundreds of hours in these jets for what is to come. Gabir, use the computer in the office to file the flight plan with the FAA for our jet. Everyone else will fly by visual flight rules, so watch your altitudes and stay low enough to keep out of controlled airspace. That can be difficult in jets, but I have faith in all of you. Tonight, brothers, we fly to Paradise in luxury!"

Chapter 27

Airborne over Long Island, New York

The US Air Force's E-3C Airborne Warning and Control System aircraft, the venerable AWACS, flew in hundred-mile-long ovals at an altitude of thirty thousand feet above the north shore of Long Island. The AWACS, built on a now-ancient 1960s-era Boeing 707 airframe, had lifted off from its home at Tinker Air Force Base in Oklahoma four hours earlier and assumed the role of *Mother*, relieving the previous E-3C which had diligently watched air traffic over the Mid-Atlantic seaboard since early afternoon for signs of any wayward aircraft entering restricted airspace in or around the nation's most populous city.

Thirteen Air Battle Managers aboard *Mother* monitored the crowded airspace of the Tri-State area from north of Boston's Logan airport, south to Delaware, and west past Philadelphia in the same way their predecessors had done on every New Year's Eve since the September 11th attacks in 2001. The powerful thirty-foot-wide black-and-white striped radar dome atop the AWACS rotated every fourteen seconds as it stared unblinkingly at the horizon. At that moment, over eight hundred commercial and private aircraft operated within its half-million square mile field of view.

Mother also clearly saw and tracked four Air National Guard F-16C Fighting Falcons. One pair of fighters patrolled the night skies north of the Big Apple while the other duo patrolled to the south. Armed with heat-seeking missiles and 20mm cannons, the ANG jets defended the two busiest approaches to New York City to identify aircraft not responding appropriately to civilian air traffic control or, if necessary, intercept troublesome aircraft and escort them to a designated airport for investigation by the FAA, FBI, or both. Only upon the direct order of one of two designated US Air Force brigadier generals — collectively referred to as *Castle Control* — would any of the military pilots engage an aircraft over US soil with deadly force.

That evening, Brigadier General Timothy Denton drank his third cup of black coffee aboard *Mother* and served as *Castle Wind*. His land-based counterpart, *Castle Rock*, planned to watch New Year's Eve festivities unfold around the world from a secure conference room in her building on Peterson Air Force Base, Colorado. The designator *Rock* persisted for years, even after the Air Force closed its hardened command center deep inside Cheyanne Mountain and the North American Aerospace Defense Command, NORAD, moved to more comfortable, albeit less protected, offices on "Pete Field."

Aboard *Mother*, Captain Anthony Winters studied the multi-colored computer display at his workstation. He keyed the microphone in his headset to transmit instructions to the northernmost pair of F-16s, indicated on his monitor by a pair of blue triangles. "Mountain flight, Mother. Be advised, commercial traffic to your eight o'clock inbound to LaGuardia. Turn right to heading two-one-zero. Climb to flight level two-five-five and maintain."

Vermont Air National Guard Lieutenant Colonel Jordan Kelly acknowledged the transmission. "Mother, Mountain flight copies turn and climb." With his left hand, "Machine Gun" Kelly—Gunner for short—pushed his single-engine F-16's throttle forward an inch and deftly tilted his right wrist to put his agile aircraft—callsign Mountain 3—into a gentle bank. Off his left wing and two-hundred feet away, Captain Stephen "Railroad" Zeller flying Mountain 4 duplicated his flight lead's movements, and the pair of fighters maneuvered to their new altitude and heading to avoid the potential for a mid-air collision with the commercial jet.

Gunner keyed his tactical radio so only Railroad would hear him. "It's hard to see at night, but just ahead at your one o'clock is West Point."

Railroad squinted through the plexiglass canopy of his supersonic fighter and raised a one-finger salute to the Army institution that he and other Air Force Academy graduates, including Gunner, referred to as Hudson High. He keyed his mic, and replied, "Do you think anyone would mind if I dropped my external fuel tank on their parade ground? It's empty, so...."

Gunner laughed. "Why bother? We beat them again this year and won the Commander-in-Chief's trophy away from Navy."

"Yeah," Railroad replied, "that's true. Okay, I guess I can be a good sport and gracious winner. But one of these days...."

Gunner smiled and glanced down at the radar screen in the center of his console. To him, flying above friendly territory waiting for the remote possibility of another enemy attack seemed like the exception to every rule. But that was the mission of both his unit and that of the Atlantic City ANG fighters, callsign Casino, eighty miles to their south.

As Casino flight patrolled over the Atlantic Ocean, Major Alexandra "Buck" Hamilton guided her two-ship flight of F-16s northeast and away from shore. Asbury Park, New Jersey, receded behind her and her wingman, Captain Peter "Limo" Bentley. She looked at the bright stars shining above as the encrypted transmission from the AWACS came through her headset.

"Casino flight, Mother. Two unidentified fast-moving contacts forty miles to your south at low altitude are non-responsive to civilian air traffic control. Both are squawking one-two-zero-zero for VFR in legal airspace. No threat. Repeat, no threat identified, but you are directed to intercept and identify."

"Mother, Casino flight, copy intercept and identify."

Limo mimicked Buck's righthand turn to a southerly course, and the pair of F-16s descended to fifteen thousand feet. Both pilots turned the same gray dials on their cockpit controls to extend their AN/APG-68 fire-control radar's horizon to sixty miles.

"Did you have plans for tonight, Buck?" Limo asked.

"Nah," the senior pilot replied. "I'm sure my husband has already tucked the kids in, and he usually turns in early, himself. I haven't seen the ball drop in at least five years. I'm an early riser, so I can't stay up that late. You?"

"No, I'm still so new to the unit that I need the flying time before New Year's to get enough service points for the year to count toward retirement."

"Yeah, you'll be on the short end of the schedule until you get more seniority. Okay, radar shows we're ten miles out and ten thousand feet above the two inbound aircraft. They're flying in a two-mile extended trail formation. Are you up for a Split-S tonight?"

Limo keyed his mic. "Let's see... night flying, in a two-ship formation, making an inverted dive at three-quarters the speed of sound, just to level out behind the bogeys? Sounds like fun. Lead on, Buck."

"Roll on my mark. Three. Two. One. Mark."

On cue, the pair of Fighting Falcons rolled upside down and the pilots reduced their throttles in unison. They eased the fly-by-wire sticks back with their right wrists and the aircraft completed the planned half-circle maneuver at 4 Gs. Both fighters pulled through their dives behind the rear-most unidentified aircraft and resumed straight-and-level flight.

"Mother, Casino flight," Buck radioed. "Two aircraft appear to be medium-sized commercial business jets flying straight-and-level in two-mile extended-trail formation. Their wings are clean. Can't tell from this distance if they're Learjets or Gulfstreams."

Buck knew the powerful radar atop the AWACS clearly showed its Air Battle Managers the flight characteristics of the two unidentified aircraft. Her stating that the wings of the aircraft were *clean*—that the airplanes carried no external fuel tanks or visible weapons—served to answer the real question Mother had tasked Casino to investigate.

"Casino, Mother. Copy. Stand by."

Buck led Limo to a position five miles behind the rear-most jet and waited for the Air Battle Manager aboard the AWACS to consult with the Air Boss. In the meantime, she enjoyed flying over the dark sea below. Sporadic glints of moonlight reflected off the waves, sending an unending stream of sparkles into the air.

Mother's next transmission to the Vermont-based F-16s patrolling to their north sent a chill down Buck's spine.

"Mountain flight, Mother. Turn left heading two-zero-zero, maintain altitude, and accelerate to intercept two low-flying, eastbound, unidentified aircraft squawking VFR, flying in two-mile extended-trail formation six-zero miles southwest of your position. Intercept and identify."

Limo keyed his tactical radio, and asked his flight lead, "Buck, what do you make of that? Two pair of aircraft flying in uncontrolled VFR airspace at night, both pair flying in the same unusual formation, and both heading toward New York City."

Buck paused and thought for a moment before keying her mic. "Limo, I think our night just got a whole lot less boring, and not in a good way."

***

Michelle Reagan looked at the Caller ID on her cell phone and pushed the green button to answer. "Hi, Ron. What's up?"

Special Agent Poland spoke rapidly. "Hey, good news. Management approved sending SWAT in to rescue Bella tonight."

"That's great!"

"They'll rally and gear up at the fire station. Can you ask the lieutenant or captain there if we can park in their back lot for a couple of hours until we wrap this up?"

"Of course," she said, and smiled to the others in the monitoring room. "Consider it done. What time should I expect them?"

"They're already on their way, so get ready if you want to go with us. I'm walking out of the JTTF office as we speak. One way or another, we'll get Bella away from Noor tonight, and if Wasif happens to be there, too, well... maybe I shouldn't go on the record to say what we'll do to him."

Chapter 28

Airborne over New Haven, Connecticut

Wasif Ali and Gabir Wahab flew a routine flight path from Pennsylvania to Connecticut and then made an uneventful training low-approach and go-around at New Haven's commercial airport. Gabir banked their Gulfstream G350 onto a southernly course and followed the air traffic controller's departure instructions to climb to thirty-five thousand feet. Their departure south over the Long Island Sound lined them up perfectly for the next phase of their plan.

Gabir flew the assigned heading and continued the climb to the assigned altitude while Wasif removed his electronics from a brown cardboard box. With suction cups, he affixed the four radar detectors to the windshield using a pre-measured string to mount them in a rectangle precisely two meters across and one meter vertically. He plugged each sensor's cable into the Raspberry Pi and that, in turn, into his laptop computer. He smiled at the familiar *bing-boing-boing-bing-bing* as the PC booted and the colorful Microsoft Windows logo flashed up on the screen.

"Is it working?" Gabir asked.

"Yes," Wasif answered, and tapped a few keys. A new window opened, and a grid appeared making the screen take on the appearance of a piece of graph paper. "Bank left twenty degrees, then go twenty degrees to the right and re-center on the assigned departure course."

Gabir slowly twisted the aircraft's yoke to the left and then to the right.

"Good," Wasif said as the plane leveled out again.

"What was that red cloud on the screen?"

"It shows that the US Air Force AWACS aircraft is somewhere south and east of our position. Stay on the assigned course for another seven minutes. That will get us off the departure controller's screen. Then, we'll turn east over Long Island."

Gabir ran his eyes over the navigation display and confirmed the G350 continued along the route dictated by the air traffic controller. "How far east of us is it now?"

"I don't know. This computer can only tell us the direction and general strength of the signal these radar detectors receive. It can't tell the distance. It's not that sophisticated."

"Okay, we'll know when we get close and then, if it pleases Allah, we will strike a blow for his kingdom against the imperialists."

"*Insha'Allah*, we will be successful tonight. If our brothers are on time, the Americans will see us coming and still not be able to stop us. The infidels will be able to do nothing other than watch their countrymen burn."

Chapter 29

FDNY Firehouse, New York City

Michelle Reagan leaned against the black, armored SWAT van parked behind the fire station and listened to FBI Supervisory Special Agent Matthew Decker brief the members of the two SWAT teams present for their planned rescue of Bella Cirrone.

Decker said, "Brian Jackson will lead Blue Team up the rear staircase and secure the landings at every floor. The door to the rear staircase is technically in the basement, so there'll be three landings. Brian, you'll continue up to the third floor, leaving two operators on each landing to secure our access in and out of the building. Blue Team will also send two operators up to secure the landing on the fourth floor, to cover our collective asses from above."

"Check," Jackson acknowledged.

"We're not expecting resistance," Decker said, "but be prepared for anything. This is both a hostage rescue and a terrorism investigation, so keep your heads on a swivel. Three Special Agent Bomb Technicians will wait downstairs with their gear in case we see something suspicious. Otherwise, we focus on rescuing a kidnapped US government employee. You have photos and physical descriptions of her in your briefing packets. Any questions?"

Replies of "no" and "nope" rippled through the assembled agents, all dressed in identical black tactical fatigues and body armor.

"Okay," Decker continued, "after Blue Team secures the stairwell, I'll lead Gold Team to the apartment door, and Gold's breacher will open the door with his battering ram. We'll detain anyone present inside the apartment, free the hostage, and then agents from case agent Ron Poland's squad will make any arrests he deems necessary. SWAT will continue to provide perimeter security while Poland's folks search the place and conduct interviews. Ron?"

"Right, Matt, thank you," Ron Poland said. "We appreciate your help on this. We don't know what to expect in the building, but when Matt and Brian went into the apartment a couple of weeks ago, they found and photographed a table full of electronic components. We think those are a critical part of the attack these subjects planned. If you see any electronics or boxes, try to avoid touching them. Of course, do whatever you have to do to protect yourselves and eliminate any threats, but we're still working to identify any other participants we don't know about yet. As always, the more evidence we can find and analyze, the better.

"By way of background, as far as the JTTF can tell, Wasif Ali al-Bakkar lives here with just his wife, Noor. There's no reason to believe there are any children present. We're monitoring an active listening device for activity inside the apartment, but it's been mostly quiet all day. If anything comes up while you're making your approach or entry, the agents in the monitoring room in the basement here at the fire station will let me know, and I'll relay the message immediately. Also" — he pointed to Michelle — "Michelle is our liaison from another government agency who'll be with me outside the apartment building. She has been part of the monitoring team since day one, is fluent in Arabic, and is the only one around here who is known to the hostage. Michelle will take control of the hostage once the rescue is complete. That's it. Thanks, Matt."

"All right, team," Decker said as he stood up to his full height and tugged on his black body armor, "this is what we practice for: high-risk entries and hostage rescues. Even the Hostage Rescue Team at Quantico hasn't made a real hostage rescue in years. Let's make HRT jealous!"

Two dozen SWAT agents bellowed whoops and hooahs across the small parking lot.

***

"Casino flight, Mother. VFR aircraft are still not responding to civilian air traffic control, and the aircraft are at risk of entering prohibited airspace. FAA is requesting your assistance to conduct a safety check of the pilots and determine if they might have lost cabin pressure or radios. Over."

Buck Hamilton acknowledged her orders and keyed her tactical radio mic. "Limo, you check out the trailing aircraft. I'll go up and check the lead."

"Copy," Limo Bentley replied.

Major Hamilton eased the throttle of her F-16 fighter forward and closed the five-mile distance in a minute. She settled her jet into position thirty feet off the left wing of the Gulfstream G350 and peered through the darkness into the business jet's cockpit. Faint red and white lights illuminated the charter jet's cockpit, and Buck made out the shadowy form of a single occupant sitting in the pilot's seat closest to her.

"Aircraft off my right wing, this is the United States Air Force on Guard. Acknowledge."

Her radio, tuned to "Guard" — the common emergency frequency monitored by all aircraft in flight — remained silent. As she stared into the other jet's cockpit, she thought she saw the pilot's head turn to look at her.

"VFR aircraft, if you are experiencing radio failure, change your transponder to squawk seven-six-zero-zero. Repeat, squawk seven-six-zero-zero. Over."

The commercial jet continued flying north in silence.

Buck heard Limo make an identical call to the trailing aircraft. His entreaty went unanswered as well.

Over the encrypted military network, Buck heard the AWACS' transmission confirming what she knew the case would be. "Casino flight, Mother. Negative transponder change by either aircraft."

Buck acknowledged Mother's transmission, and then tilted her F-16's wings back and forth, first to the left and then rapidly to the right. She repeated the maneuver three times. She keyed her mic to address the Gulfstream again. "VFR aircraft, if you hear my transmission, wag your wings in response."

The Gulfstream continued straight-and-level on its path northward.

Limo made the same request of the trailing aircraft and reported his lack of success to Buck.

"Mother, Casino 7," Buck called to the AWACS. "Negative results. Both pilots appear to be conscious but non-responsive to instructions."

"Copy, Casino. Stand by."

A minute ticked by as the Air National Guard jets flew abreast the stolen Gulfstreams.

"Casino flight, Mother. Be advised, Mountain flight is experiencing similar results with two identical aircraft. Air Boss authorizes you to use aggressive means to get the unidentified aircrafts' attention and divert both to Atlantic City International Airport."

"Mother, Casino. Copy use of aggressive, non-lethal force."

***

Gabir Wahab leveled his Gulfstream at thirty-five-thousand feet over Long Island and double-checked its heading on the cockpit's electronic compass.

Wasif Ali typed a command into his laptop computer, and said, "Turn right thirty degrees and maintain this altitude."

Gabir steered the aircraft into a gentle bank, and said, "I wonder how long it will take the air traffic controllers to call us for departing from our flight plan."

"It doesn't matter," Wasif said. "There is nothing they can do now. Go ahead and turn the transponder off."

Gabir made a show of flicking a switch on the console and smiled.

Wasif pointed to the small red splotch on the laptop's screen. "We are still far away from the Air Force aircraft, but have them in our sights now, brother. They are flying at a lower altitude than ours, so we'll pass right over them. Fly straight ahead, and we're guaranteed to find them — physics is physics. There can be no other outcome. We're on the right course. This red area on the screen will grow larger and turn blue when the signal strength grows. Once we fly over the top of them, it will change. Then I will take the controls and dive at the enemy to avenge my son's death and protect our brothers in their flights tonight."

***

Buck Hamilton banked her F-16 to the left and climbed one thousand feet. She keyed the mic for her tactical radio, and said, "Limo, put some space between yourself and your friend. I'm going to get my guy's attention."

"Copy. Falling back."

Buck nosed her fighter down and flew underneath the G350 she had been shadowing. She nudged her throttle forward and watched through her bubble canopy as the sleek lines of the business jet's belly slid over her head. She craned her neck and watched as the bigger jet passed behind her. With a flick of her right wrist, she pulled her jet into the line of flight of the Gulfstream. Turbulent jet wash buffeted the larger plane as it flew behind the agile fighter, but it didn't change course.

Major Hamilton repeated her earlier radio call for the Gulfstream to wag its wings in acknowledgement and change its transponder code.

The pilot of the G350 ignored her and continued to fly straight and level.

Buck studied the jet behind her in one of her two rear-view mirrors, cursed under her breath, and said to herself, "If you're not going to listen to reason, bub, things are going to get hot."

Buck Hamilton eased the F-16's throttle back slightly and raised her jet's nose to bleed off airspeed while maintaining altitude and position immediately in front of the Gulfstream. She repeated her radio call and listened for a response.

Nothing.

As her jet slowed in front of the G350, the Gulfstream grew larger until it filled the mirror attached to her arched canopy support.

"Okay, mister. You asked for it," she said, and thrust the jet's throttle forward until it stopped. She lifted the throttle over the detent and pushed it forward into afterburner. The jet lurched forward, pushing her firmly into the hard metal of her ACES II ejection seat. The thin cushion of her seat did little to make the solid-steel chair in which she'd flown over twelve-hundred hours in the past decade feel at all comfortable.

The inferno of the fighter jet's afterburner superheated the air behind it and accelerated the F-16 to nearly supersonic speed, thrusting it forward and away from the Gulfstream. A maelstrom of scorching air and jet fuel residue spewed from the Pratt & Whitney F100 engine in a glowing streak of turbulent red and orange waves which starkly contrasted the black curtain of the night's sky.

The raging air buffeted the Gulfstream, but the battering by the disrupted winter air soon smoothed.

Buck pulled the throttle back and banked her jet into a turn. Within thirty seconds, she leveled out, back alongside the unphased commercial jet. The G350 continued forward on autopilot, shadowed closely once again by the Air National Guard interceptor.

Major Hamilton repeated her radio call for the Gulfstream's pilot to acknowledge her. She received only silence in return.

"Mother, Casino 7. Negative results."

"Copy, Casino 7."

Buck thought back to her flight training and the time she'd spent in Nevada at the Air Force's Red Flag air combat exercise. She racked her brain for other creative ideas of how to communicate with—

A flash of white filled Buck's canopy and her jet shuddered violently. The ear-splitting sound of the impact of the G350 colliding into the F-16 preceded the high-pitched squeal of the F-16's automated alarms. The warning light to the left of the pilot's head's-up display flashed bright yellow, illuminating the words, "Master Caution. Push to Reset." To Buck's right, lights on the Caution Panel flashed brightly, indicating overheating electronics and a fault in the plane's only engine.

Her F-16 spun to the right, and the Gulfstream passed under her jet to the left. Buck cranked her right wrist to the left as hard as she could as she struggled to level out the jet and assess the severity of its damage. Her mind raced through the boldface emergency procedures she had long ago committed to memory and routinely practiced in the simulator back in Atlantic City.

She throttled back the engine to reduce its temperature and cranked the control stick with her right wrist as hard as she could to stop the jet's incessant roll. She had to stop the fighter from corkscrewing if she would have any chance of returning it to controlled, level flight.

Through the canopy above, a strobe effect caught her eye.

Yellow.

Black.

Yellow.

Black.

The yellow glow of the full moon repeatedly arced across her windscreen, chased relentlessly by the frigid black void of the icy Atlantic below.

A garbled radio call rumbled through her headset, but she couldn't make out the words. Buck's eye caught sight of the spinning artificial horizon in the center of her instrument panel. The spherical gauge spun as out of control as her jet felt. She lifted her head and scanned outside the aircraft to find a visual reference while repeatedly forcing the fly-by-wire stick in her right hand through its full range of motion, straining the tendons in her wrist to try to regain control of her spiraling aircraft.

She looked through the canopy to her right. Orange flames trailed from the ragged edge of what use to be her aircraft's wing.

Instinctively, she looked to the intact wing on her left, and back again at the remaining stub of the small fighter's burning right side. She eased the tension in her right wrist and flicked it to the left.

No response.

Buck glanced at the altimeter on the panel in front of her and watched it unwind from nine thousand feet to eight thousand. The needle continued its counterclockwise spin to seven as her aircraft plummeted toward the Atlantic Ocean.

Major Alexandra "Buck" Hamilton released the flight controls of her disabled jet, and the fleeting thought that she was about to cost US taxpayers eighty million dollars flitted through her mind. She reached between her thighs and gripped the yellow-painted ejection seat handle firmly with both hands. She sat back as far as she could and slammed her ankles back against the bottom of the seat. If her knees didn't clear the edge of the instrument panel when the rocket-propelled ejection seat activated, she could lose both of her legs from the patella on down.

Buck's training launched her into action. She mentally rattled off her memorized version of the emergency ejection instructions pilots refer to as boldface. "Back — straight. Ankles — back. Head — up. Ejection handle — pull, and kiss your ass goodbye." That last part, while not in the official flight manual, is well known to all military pilots.

Buck yanked up on the ejection handle as hard as her well-toned thirty-five-year-old arms could pull it. The explosive bolts holding the F-16's canopy in place detonated, sending the curved glass windscreen tumbling into the night. An icy blast of winter air smacked her in the face, punishing the skin not covered by her helmet or oxygen mask.

The CKU-5 Rocket Catapult powering her F-16's ACES II ejection seat violently thrust Major Alexandra Hamilton out of the aircraft and into the pitch-black night. Buck shivered and wondered how cold the Atlantic Ocean waiting below her would be. She was certain that this was not the best night of the year to choose for a midnight swim.

Chapter 30

JTTF Watch Operations Floor, New York City

FBI Supervisory Special Agent Nola Austin approached the desk of the JTTF analyst who'd waved her over, and asked, "What's up, Jeanne?"

"I thought you might want to see one of the law enforcement BOLO alerts that just came through from the Pennsylvania State Police. The FBI's Philadelphia Field Office is sending two agents out there to check it out, but let me know what you think. I'll put the alert up on the big board for you." The middle-aged woman pointed to one of the large video monitors in the front of the room, and said, "There you go."

The screen flickered, and Austin read the short alert. "Holy shit."

"Yeah," the analyst agreed, "that's what I thought, too. Two people shot dead and seven Gulfstream G350s stolen from an air-charter company. I know we've been focusing on your case as a threat to commercial aviation and scheduled flights, but what if the aircraft aren't airliners, but rather smaller, charter jets? They could still do some serious damage, don't you think?"

"Yeah, you're right," Nola said, and chewed on her bottom lip. "We've all been assuming the threat is to one of the major airlines, but neither the CIA undercover officer nor Fasil Mahmood gave us specific information. No reason not to pursue this, Jeanne. Good job. Call the FBI squad supervisor in the Philadelphia Field Office who oversees the agents headed out to the airport. Let them know what we're working, and that we need updates from them every fifteen minutes without fail."

"They're not going to like you very much," Jeanne replied with a wry smile.

Austin shook her head, and said, "Ask me tomorrow if I care."

Jeanne picked up her phone to dial, and Nola Austin walked briskly to the desk of the FAA's rep to get him to pull up all data he could find on the purloined Gulfstreams.

***

Two dark blue, angular vans with FBI SWAT emblazoned in white paint on all four sides led the way out of the firehouse parking lot. Their red-and-blue rooftop-mounted lights spun rapidly. Monotone sirens blared their undulating refrain as the armored vehicles turned south and sped along the streets of Manhattan for their five-block sprint to the apartment's rear entrance.

Ron Poland drove his unmarked Chevrolet Malibu behind the SWAT vans. Michelle rode in the passenger seat and shifted to her right to keep her left knee from being repeatedly bounced into the corner of the FBI radio mounted under the glovebox.

The agents on Ron Poland's squad followed close behind in their own vehicles.

As planned, two blocks from the fire station the drivers turned off their sirens. Two blocks later, the drivers extinguished their red and blue emergency lights to maintain the element of surprise on the team's final approach to the rear of the apartment building.

Poland looked at Michelle as they pulled into the alley behind the apartment building, and asked, "Is this your first raid?"

Michelle shook her head. "Not even close, but it is the first time I'm going on one and not armed to the teeth."

That surprised Poland. He looked at her and wondered what his passenger's real job was. Given the way she handled herself a week earlier in the NYPD holding cell, he guessed she had one of those CIA jobs one doesn't ask about.

At the apartment building's rear entrance, Matthew Decker led the gathering formation of SWAT agents up to the entrance and silently tapped his clenched fist on his helmet—the signal to Blue Team's breacher to open the door with his "master key."

The breacher angled the steel tip of his Halligan tool into the gap between the door handle and the metal door frame. To his right, another SWAT agent swung a sledgehammer at the back of the Halligan tool, forcing it between the door and doorjamb. With a strong push on the yard-long Halligan tool beloved by SWAT teams and fire departments alike, the heavy door swung out and ricocheted off its doorstop with a reverberating clang.

Brian Jackson entered the stairwell first. The flashlight mounted under the barrel of his M-4 rifle illuminated the dark enclave as he disappeared around the corner.

One by one, SWAT operators clad in black body armor bristling with radios, weapons and spare magazines of ammunition silently followed their teammates through the door. In less than thirty seconds, Jackson radioed to Matt Decker that his team had secured the stairwell without incident.

Decker waved his hand, and said, "Gold Team, on me." He entered the stairwell, followed closely by the stack of SWAT operators who would make the actual entry into Noor Ali's apartment.

At the third-floor landing, Decker paused and waited for Gold Team's agents to gather. "Ready?" he whispered to the third man in line.

The tall agent nodded and moved to the front of the line. A shorter, female SWAT operator followed closely behind. A member of Blue Team opened the door to the third floor and the two Gold Team members entered and turned left. They positioned themselves on either side of the hallway to serve as the rear guard for the entry team.

Matthew Decker and Brian Jackson surged through the doorway and turned right. They approached Ali's apartment door for the second time that month and waited for Gold Team's breacher to catch up with them. When he did, Decker repeated his helmet-tap and the breacher swung his three-foot-long battering ram against the door.

The door shuddered, and the ram bounced backward into the agent's hands.

"Again," Decker ordered.

The breacher pulled the ram back and up to gain the most momentum he could and grunted as he swung the thirty-five-pound cylinder. The ram's metal cap struck the door handle squarely and bent it awkwardly to the left. The metal frame flexed from the force of the impact, but held the door closed firmly.

"Shit. Again," Decker said.

***

The Air Force E-3C AWACS turned eastbound in its oval orbit above the north shore of Long Island.

First Lieutenant Denise Ziegler clicked her mouse twice to zoom her computer screen in on air traffic north of their position. "Air Boss," she said loudly, and raised her left hand to get his attention.

Major Bradley Kent finished talking to a controller in the next aisle and walked over to Station 6. "What's up, Denise?"

"Here, sir, look at this commercial aircraft. It deviated from the usual southbound departure from New Haven."

"Maybe they modified their flight plan in-flight, and the update hasn't made it from the FAA to our database yet."

"Yes, sir, could be, but they've turned their transponder off, and when we turned at the outer limit of our last orbit over western Long Island, they passed seven thousand feet over us and then began to turn. They're still turning in a slow circle to the north. It's just really weird."

Major Kent pointed to the screen. "Play back the last five minutes at ten times normal speed. Show me that aircraft's track."

Replays are a standard feature of every control station aboard the AWACS. Lieutenant Ziegler selected the playback command on her console and clicked the mouse over the "10x" option.

The major focused on the triangular icon of the Gulfstream on the screen. He tapped the toe of his black leather flight boot on the aircraft's carpeted floor as he watched the icon merge with the AWACS' own and then begin its circle. "Okay, that *is* odd. Designate it as contact 'George 1,' and keep your eye on it. Let me know in a couple of minutes if it's still acting hinkey."

"Yes, sir," she said, and clicked her mouse a few times. For the remainder of the mission, the AWACS' electronic systems would refer to the tagged aircraft flying its unusual course by a designator inspired by the famously curious monkey.

***

"Keep turning," Wasif Ali instructed Gabir Wahab. "We're close. We must have passed over the Air Force radar plane just a minute ago, if that. We're *close*."

Gabir tightened his grip on the aircraft's control yoke and kept the G350 in a steady bank to the right. As the plane continued its circular trajectory, lights of the Manhattan skyline replaced those of residential Long Island.

The large blue pulsating blob slid off the side of Wasif's laptop screen.

"Keep turning, brother. They're behind us, now."

Gabir adjusted the rudder trim on the Gulfstream to make the turn easier. Out of the corner of his eye, he saw the hazy blue oval slide back onto the computer's screen. He followed Wasif's instructions to slow the turn and eventually level out into straightforward flight.

Wasif grinned broadly. "They're in front of us somewhere and probably heading away from us. Look for their navigation lights. Our jet is newer and much faster, so once we find them, they cannot get away."

Gabir squinted through the windscreen and scanned the horizon for lights moving against the steady illumination of Long Island's neighborhoods.

***

"Beacon! Beacon! Beacon!" Captain Anthony Winters barked into his headset's microphone.

"Where?" Major Brad Kent asked. The Air Boss jogged a dozen feet down the AWACS' aisle, stopped to peer over Winters' shoulder at the screen, and immediately saw the blinking blue-force tracking icon showing the last-known location of a pilot who had ejected from an American military aircraft.

Tony Winters tapped the computer screen with one hand and keyed his microphone with the other. "Casino lead, Mother. Sitrep."

The Air Boss tapped the controller on the adjacent station on the shoulder. "Wilma, you're now on search and rescue duty. Contact the Coast Guard. Have them spin up a SAR helo to get our downed pilot out of the drink. It's cold down there tonight. Tell them to hurry."

"Yes, sir," she barked, and set to work.

"Tony, get an update from Casino flight. I want to know what happened."

"Sir, I've gotten no response from Casino lead."

"Replay the tape for me. I want to see what—"

A radio transmission interrupted Major Kent's instruction, but Captain Winters knew what the Air Boss wanted and typed the command into his console.

"Mother, Casino 8. I lost Casino 7. The explosion looks like a mid-air collision. I was trailing the rear aircraft, so I didn't see what happened up ahead."

Brigadier General Timothy Denton listened to the reports from his control station twenty feet forward of Kent and Winters. He stared intently at the Air Boss directing his team as they handled multiple simultaneous incidents—all in a day's work for an experienced crew of USAF air battle mangers.

"Casino 8, Mother," Winters broadcast calmly, "We have a beacon. Can you confirm a good chute?"

"Stand by, Mother. I'm circling, but it's dark. Stand by."

BG Denton clicked the button on his console to duplicate the replay being watched by the Air Boss and Captain Winters. The icon representing the Gulfstream flew in parallel with Buck Hamilton's F-16 until the G350 suddenly veered left and the icons merged.

"Replay it again," Kent instructed Winters. "Maximum zoom and slow it at the end to quarter-speed."

Three sets of eyes glued themselves to the icons representing the pair of aircraft as the screen's colored pixels moved silently in a tight formation. Even in slow motion, the Gulfstream's turn into the side of the F-16 happened in an instant.

"General—" Brad Kent said over the intercom.

"I saw it, major. What's the status of the second commercial jet?"

Tony Winters answered. "Unchanged, sir. Still headed north. Its flight path will take it west of JFK airport and over Brooklyn. It's still squawking VFR and has not asked for clearance to land at La Guardia, JFK or Newark. At its present speed and course, it will enter controlled airspace in seven minutes."

BG Denton pushed his arms forward against his control station and flexed the muscles in his legs. "Instruct Casino 8 to give the VFR aircraft one last chance to alter its course away from land."

Winters relayed the instructions to Limo Bentley.

"Mother, Casino 8," Bently replied. "Copy instructions and negative on the chute. It's too dark. If she fires a flare, I'll let you know what I see."

Bentley throttled up his F-16 and climbed. In ninety seconds, he took up a position a half-mile in front of the G350 and keyed his radio. "VFR aircraft, this is the US Air Force transmitting on Guard. You are ordered to divert to Atlantic City International Airport immediately. Turn right, maintain altitude, and come to a heading of one-eight-zero."

Limo tapped the fingers of his left hand gently on the F-16's throttle. He felt the ridges of the handgrip through his green, Nomex, flame-retardant glove and ran his thumb over the radio transmit button hoping to see in his rearview mirror the Gulfstream G350 turn as instructed.

When that did not happen, he cursed under his breath.

***

"There!" Wasif Ali shouted. The single word sounded to his ears like a victory shout as it echoed through the Gulfstream's small cabin.

"I see it," Gabir added. "About five thousand feet below us."

"Descend to one thousand feet above the Air Force aircraft so we can still see its blinking navigation lights highlighted against the dark ground."

"Yes, brother. We have them now!"

***

Outside Noor Ali's apartment, doors opened along the hallway. Heads popped into view as anxious residents strained their necks to see what the commotion at the end of the hallway was all about. FBI SWAT operators yelled for the residents to stay inside and close their doors for their own safety.

Decker keyed his radio and called to the FBI teams in the alley, below. "We're having trouble with the door. They must have a New York doorstop propping it closed. Our element of surprise is long gone. Blue Team, prepare for explosive breach and get up here."

Gold Team's breacher swung the battering ram again and, while the door remained shut, the metal frame bent further.

In the alley below, Michelle Reagan watched SWAT agents scramble to remove equipment from their vans. They pulled plastic explosive, detonation caps and spools of wire from the secured compartments and selected what they needed to blast open the apartment door.

Michelle's cell phone vibrated in her jacket pocket. She pulled it out and saw Nino Balducci's name on the Caller ID. "Hey, Nino, what's up?"

"Michelle, the agents monitoring the laser microphone say that Noor is yelling at Bella. Noor keeps saying it's all Bella's fault, but isn't specific about what. I imagine the banging we're hearing is the SWAT team trying to get in. Is something wrong?"

Michelle frowned. "Yeah, the SWAT team leader upstairs says that Noor must have a high-security doorstop holding her door shut. They're pretty common in big cities, and I'm kicking myself now for not having looked for it back when we were in the apartment. What else is going on inside? Is Bella saying anything?"

"No, she's just asking Noor what's going on. Bella's in the dark, since we didn't tell her anything in advance."

"Okay," Michelle said. "I'm going to go upstairs and tell the SWAT teams that both women are now in Bella's bedroom. That'll complicate things, but they need to know. Does the surveillance team see anything else on the thermal imager?"

"No," Nino confirmed, "nothing. Just the two women in Bella's bedroom."

"Okay, Nino, thanks. Call me back ASAP if you hear anything else that might be useful."

Michelle ended the call and walked toward the stairwell.

A SWAT operator securing the rear door moved in front of her, so she couldn't enter the building. Ron Poland interceded, and Michelle sprinted up the stairs. The SWAT agent radioed ahead to advise the rest of Blue Team that a civilian was coming upstairs and to let her through.

Michelle arrived at the door to Noor Ali's apartment just ahead of the agents carting their explosives upstairs.

"Again," Decker said to the breacher holding the battering ram, and looked over at Michelle. "Damn. Wasif must have expected this and prepared ahead, but we're almost through."

Michelle stepped against the wall to stay out of the arc of the breacher's repeated swings. The deformed metal doorframe curved at an unnatural angle and held firm but was giving in slowly. She pointed to the door, and asked Matt Decker, "Shotguns on the hinges?"

"Too dangerous with a hostage inside."

Michelle nodded. "The monitoring room called and said that Noor is now in Bella's bedroom. Noor is yelling at Bella about something or other and blaming all this on her."

As Michelle got the final word out of her mouth, Gold Team's breacher swung his heavy ram into the remains of the battered door handle. The metal doorframe gave way with a sharp *crack* and the door swung into the apartment. The steel New York doorstop—a four-foot-long metal rod which had been anchored into the apartment's floor at one end and the middle of the door at the other—flew into the apartment and skittered to a stop against the far wall.

Michelle flattened her back against the wall as a flurry of Gold Team's black-clad SWAT operators advanced methodically into the apartment.

A half-dozen calls of 'clear' were followed by a more ominous cry: "Contact!"

Michelle advanced into the apartment, turned left down the hallway she already knew, and stopped behind three SWAT operators. The men had taken up defensive positions outside Bella's bedroom.

Noor stood in the center of the room hiding behind Bella and holding a 9mm semi-automatic pistol in her right hand.

SWAT operators bellowed a cacophony of conflicting orders at Noor to not move, to drop the gun, to release Bella, and to put her hands up.

The short Iraqi woman who spoke almost no English waved the gun wildly at the intruding agents as tears streamed from her eyes.

Michelle might have thought the scene comical if she weren't so worried for Bella Cirrone's safety.

Michelle inched her way forward to get a better view of the scene unfolding inside the bedroom. She stopped behind Matt Decker on the left side of the doorway. In front of him, a SWAT operator from Gold Team knelt behind a curved armored shield with FBI painted in large block letters across its front. The operator looked through a transparent Plexiglas window and aimed his .45 caliber Smith & Wesson pistol around the side at Noor who used Bella as a human shield.

Brian Jackson stood on the right side of the doorway and pointed his M-4 rifle in Noor's direction. With Bella in the way, he didn't have a clear shot.

With three weapons pointed at Noor from the hallway, Michelle bristled at the realization that she held none of them. She had promised to protect Bella, and now a shiver ran down her spine from the fear that she might not be able to deliver on her commitment to protect the woman she risked her life to save in Iraq. The prospect of losing Bella on American soil twisted Michelle's gut.

Matt Decker and Brian Jackson continued to bark orders at Noor to no avail.

Michelle tapped Decker on the shoulder, and said, "Guys! Guys! Noor barely speaks English. You're overwhelming her."

The shouting died down, and Decker glanced back at Michelle.

She suggested, "Let me try. Okay?"

Matt Decker nodded. "Do it."

"Noor," Michelle said calmly in Arabic, "if you let Bella go, you won't be harmed. You'll get to walk out of here tonight instead of getting hurt badly."

Noor unleashed a tirade in Arabic at Michelle who stood silently and let the older woman vent. The more Michelle could get Noor to talk, the less likely anyone would get shot.

Decker kept his gaze on Noor and continued to look for an opening to take a clear shot at the terrorist's wife who now held the American hostage at gunpoint. He asked Michelle, "What did she say?"

Michelle paraphrased Noor's response. "Well, let's just say she's not a fan of truth, justice or the American way of life, and that we should all just leave her alone."

Jackson snorted. "Why am I not surprised?" He adjusted the aim of his rifle up and down, looking for a clean shot, but Bella's oversized white nightgown hung to the floor, preventing the SWAT team leader from seeing where Bella ended and Noor began.

"Noor," Michelle asked, "what do you want to happen now? If you had your way, what would happen?"

"I want you all to leave my home. This is *my* home!" the panicked woman yelled.

"Okay, Noor. Put the gun down, let Bella go, and we'll do that."

"No!" Noor roared. "You'll never leave. Wasif is gone, and I'll join him soon."

Michelle decided to go fishing. "No, Noor. Wasif's plan failed. You must have seen the news on TV. There was no attack. He's not in Paradise, so if you hurt anyone, you won't go there, either." She wasn't sure what Noor would believe, but figured it was worth a try.

"You lie! Americans are all liars! He is in Paradise, and I will take Bella there with me to join in his glorious arrival in front of Allah, Master of the Kingdom!"

"Noor," Michelle continued, "you're upset and scared. I can see the tears on your cheek. I want to help you, and I'm the only one who can." Michelle showed Noor that both of her hands were empty. "I'm not carrying a gun. I'm here to talk you through this. Do you understand?"

Noor looked from Michelle to the three SWAT operators in the doorway, and back to the CIA officer. "What do you want? Why don't you all just leave my home?"

"I want to leave, but I need to take Bella with me. You don't want to take her to Paradise. Do you really want to spend eternity with *her*? You don't want *her* to spend eternity with *your* husband—the man you love. He doesn't love Bella. He loves *you*. Give Bella away again, like you did in Iraq. Give her to me."

Tears ran down both of Noor's cheeks, and her hand tightened its grip on the gun she pointed at Bella. "I'm doing this *for* my husband!"

***

"Any response?" Brigadier General Denton asked over the AWACS' intercom.

"Negative, sir," Captain Winters replied. "We're monitoring all of the appropriate radio frequencies: Guard, local VFR, and approach control to all major airports in the area. We've not gotten any transmissions from any of the three remaining VFR aircraft that Casino or Mountain flights are shadowing. No radio acknowledgments of our transmissions at all. Also, no acknowledgments from instructions to wag their wings, either."

Denton took a deep breath and thought for a moment. "Brad, one of those aircraft is flying north while the other pair is flying east. Where do their tracks converge? What I mean is, where will those jets' flight paths intersect if they stay on their present courses?"

"Winters," Major Kent ordered, "plot it out."

Tony Winters selected the three icons on his screen and clicked a few commands.

While waiting for Winters to finish, Kent tapped the controller to his right on the shoulder, and asked, "Wilma, what's the status of Casino 7?"

The controller answered immediately and pointed to her screen. "Sir, an MH-65 Dolphin lifted off from Staten Island Coast Guard Station a minute ago. I designated the helicopter as Rescue 1. The Coast Guard is also diverting a cutter on patrol, the USCG Shrike out of Sandy Hook, New Jersey." She looked up at the Air Boss. "Sir, if Casino 7 is out there, they'll find her."

"Good," Kent said, and tapped the top of the metal console as if knocking on wood for good luck. "Let me know when they've located our pilot."

"Midtown Manhattan, sir," Tony Winters said, still looking at his screen. "If the VFR aircraft all continue on their present courses, they'll converge somewhere just south of Central Park in ten minutes, thirty seconds."

Major Kent and BG Denton looked at their watches simultaneously. The wristwatches all members of the crew synchronized, or "hacked," during their pre-mission briefing showed 11:45 p.m. The officers looked at each other over the top of the dozen controllers' stations separating them, and their eyes narrowed almost simultaneously.

Denton spoke first. "Just before midnight in Manhattan?"

Kent adjusted the microphone on his headset. "Times Square is my guess. Where the ball drops and about a bazillion drunk people are getting ready to celebrate."

"Damn," General Denton said. "It'll be live on every TV network and half the world will be watching. It's the perfect time and place for a terrorist attack. Major, connect me to Casino and Mountain flights simultaneously."

"Yes, sir," Kent replied, and smacked Tony Winters on the left arm. "Tony, patch Castle Wind and me in to both fights."

Winters tapped four commands into his keyboard and gave the Air Boss a thumb's up.

Denton keyed his microphone, and said, "Casino and Mountain flights, Mother. This is Castle Wind. I have determined that all three remaining VFR aircraft currently present an imminent danger to civilians on the ground in New York City. You are ordered to engage and destroy all three aircraft. I repeat. Engage and destroy."

Kent keyed his mic, and said, "Casino and Mountain flights, Mother. This is the Air Boss. I confirm Castle Wind's authority and orders to use deadly force over American soil. Weapons are free. Engage."

Chapter 31

JTTF Watch Center, New York

SSA Nola Austin hung up the phone, ending her call with the FBI agent leading the investigation of the jets stolen from Allentown, Pennsylvania.

She handed a neatly printed list to the analyst at the next desk, and said, "Jeanne, post this list of the stolen aircrafts' tail numbers to the big board, and email a copy to the JTTF's 'All Agencies' list."

Austin walked over to the Federal Aviation Administration's rep, and asked, "Are you able to put the flight paths of those tail numbers up on the big board?"

"Sure, Nola. Give me a minute," he said, and he logged into the FAA's database. "I'll pull the flight plans from our system and then put both the planned and actual flight paths up there using the commercial Flight Aware system."

"Whatever does the job is fine with me."

Caroline van der Pol walked up behind the FAA rep's chair and watched with rapt attention as he worked.

"*Hmm,*" he said, and looked up at Nola. "Only one of those aircraft filed a flight plan. A few minutes ago, it was over the north shore of Long Island after doing a training approach at New Haven earlier. But it must have turned its transponder off. That can't be good."

A voice from two rows back and a few seats over spoke up. "Hey, Nola," the DOD rep to the JTTF said, "the Air Force is tracking one of those tail numbers from the AWACS orbiting over New York for New Year's—"

Austin didn't wait for him to finish. "Call them and tell them that jet's stolen, and they need to do whatever they can to get it on the ground ASAP."

"Okay, well, I can't just telephone the airplane itself, but I'll send a Flash message to the Eastern Air Defense Sector upstate in Griffiss. The EADS can relay messages to operational units, as necessary."

"Good. Do it," Austin urged.

Caroline walked down the aisle and watched over the DOD rep's shoulder as he typed furiously. He slammed his fingers down on the Enter key, and said, "Done."

Caroline leaned down, and asked quietly, "What's an *ay-whacks*?"

"It's an old Boeing 707 jet with a ridiculously large radar dish on its roof," the DOD rep confirmed. "It flies around to find enemy aircraft and direct our fighters to intercept. Most NATO countries have a couple. We also sell them to Japan, Saudi Arabia, and, well, pretty much everyone nowadays. Its radar can see hundreds of miles in every direction. Pretty cool, actually."

Caroline looked over to Nola Austin, and said, "Wasif's electronics included radar detectors. Do you think he's using those to fly his jets and evade the AWACS, or maybe to find out where the AWACS itself is flying?"

The DOD rep shook his head. "There's no way to avoid an AWACS. I mean, with stealth technology, maybe, but it's bathing the entire Tri-State area with powerful radar beams continuously. There's no way for a commercial Gulfstream G350 to *not* be detected."

"Well," Caroline offered, "if not to escape detection, then maybe they want to find it. Thanks to Bella, we know Wasif Ali was an Iraqi fighter pilot who lost his only son to the US Air Force. We also know he has a connection to ISIS and is out for revenge, but what kind? If he wanted to crash a plane into a skyscraper, he probably wouldn't have flown from Pennsylvania all the way up to Connecticut and then back down to New York. What if he wants to get revenge specifically against the US Air Force somehow?"

Austin drummed her index fingers on the top of a computer monitor. "Could be. We've got a retired fighter pilot in a stolen aircraft not much bigger than a fighter. We know he built some kind of customized electronic lash up that includes radar detectors. Maybe he wants revenge for American attacks against ISIS to support their cause, I don't know, but he definitely wants revenge for the death of his son at the hands of the US Air Force. And now," she pointed to the G350's flight path shown on a large monitor in the front of the room, "we've got a stolen jet flying circles over Long Island, maybe trying to find the AWACS with radar detectors and some home-brew computer programming. How crazy is this shit?"

The DOD rep agreed. "It's nuts. No one can get close to an AWACS. They'll see them coming a hundred miles away, and they have fighter escorts to protect them."

Caroline asked, "They have fighters with them over Long Island?"

"No," the DOD rep said, "of course not. They don't need protection when they're flying over friendly territor —"

Three pairs of eyes went wide at the same time.

"Oh shit," the DOD rep said, and started typing furiously. "I'm going to send a follow-up message about that possibility to the EADS so they can alert the AWACS. You know... just to be safe."

Chapter 32

Noor Ali's Apartment, New York City

"Noor," Michelle Reagan said, "I can tell how much you love him, and any woman would be lucky to have a husband love you as much as Wasif does. I know that. But that's no reason to hurt Bella. She means nothing to you."

"No!" Noor screamed.

Michelle waited until Noor calmed down, and asked, "Well, then, how about if I buy her from you? Is that what you want? I have a hundred dollars in my purse downstairs. I can go get it and pay you. Will that work?"

Bella squinted at Michelle and tilted her head at the suggestion but remained silent.

Noor looked at Michelle as if she were seriously considering the CIA officer's offer.

Matt Decker spoke first. "What's going on, now?"

"I'm working on a way to get Bella out safely," Michelle responded. She turned to Noor, and asked, "Noor, how about it?"

Noor remained silent. Michelle wondered if Noor understood just how much — or how little — one hundred dollars would actually buy in the US. Not that Noor would ever get to spend the money in jail, anyway.

"Noor," Michelle asked, "do we have a deal?"

Noor's reaction surprised Michelle — the woman laughed.

Michelle cursed herself under her breath. *Shit, what did I do wrong?*

Noor's reaction concerned Matt Decker. "What just happened?"

"I'm not sure," Michelle answered, "but I'm confident she's not going to let Bella go."

"Noor," Michelle said, but the woman continued to laugh and shake Bella.

"Bella," Michelle said in English, "do you remember what I did to you when you ran from the medical clinic in Iraq? How we ended up when I wouldn't let you go?"

Bella locked eyes with Michelle, and asked, "You mean...." Bella dropped her gaze to the floor. She looked up at Michelle and dropped her eyes again.

"Affirmative," Michelle said, hoping Noor's English vocabulary was too limited to understand their exchange.

Noor looked at Michelle and repeated her rant against all things American.

"Matt," Michelle said, "when I tap you on the shoulder, count in your head the number of seconds there are letters in your agency's acronym." Michelle raised her left hand above her head, keeping it to the side of the doorframe and out of Noor's line of sight, but where Bella could still see it. Michelle held up three fingers for her fellow CIA officer to see.

Bella blinked twice, and Michelle interpreted that as confirmation she saw the signal.

Noor continued her tirade in Arabic, and Michelle let her continue without interruption.

Michelle tapped her right hand on the back of Matt Decker's shoulder.

The FBI agent felt the tap through his Kevlar body armor and silently counted down from three as Michelle lowered one finger at a time.

***

First Lieutenant Denise Ziegler hollered into her headset the phrase no one aboard an AWACS ever wanted to hear outside of a training simulation. "Gremlin! Gremlin! Gremlin!"

Air Boss Major Brad Kent looked up from his perch over Tony Winters' control station and locked eyes with Ziegler a dozen feet away. Instantly, he recognized the panic in the young officer's eyes. Kent jerked the headset plug out of the intercom jack, sprinted to the forward end of the aircraft, and dropped roughly into the seat at his own station next to BG Denton.

Kent jammed his headset's plug into the circular socket on his console and called up a copy of Ziegler's control station's display onto his own. The track she had designated as George 1 trailed the AWACS by five miles. The graphical bar on the front of the icon showed its velocity at fifty knots greater than the AWACS' own speed. At that velocity, the pursuing jet would overtake the E-3C in six minutes.

Kent fast-forwarded through the past five minutes of radar coverage on his screen. The recording showed George 1 executed a circular turn as if searching for something. Then, the G350 homed in on the Air Force E-3C as the AWACS made its own turn eastward on its latest orbit over Long Island.

"Pilot, Air Boss," Brad Kent said with urgency over the intercom. "Probable Gremlin. Repeat, probable *Gremlin*. Recommend immediate evasive maneuvers. Turn right heading one-seven-zero and accelerate to maximum safe speed."

"What the hell is it, major?" the pilot yelped.

"The flight plan that aircraft filed says it's a Gulfstream G350 commercial business jet. Our database says their top speed is fifty to seventy knots faster than ours. Expect them to be unarmed, but we've already seen Casino 7 taken out by a mid-air collision. If this turns out to be a real threat, expect them to go Kamikaze on our asses."

"Turning now. Give me updates every thirty seconds."

The Air Battle Managers in the AWACS felt the Boeing 707 lurch to the right. The force of the turn pushed each deep into their seats. Without needing to be told, every crew member snapped the straps of their seat belts and shoulder harnesses securely into the buckle and pulled the lap belt as tight as it would go.

***

Captain Peter "Limo" Bentley slid his F-16 into position two miles astern the Gulfstream G350 he'd been trying in earnest to convince to alter course. The time for talking had passed, and now he had orders to shoot it out of the sky.

Bentley pushed the Master Arm switch on his F-16's console forward with his left thumb. Within a second, his heads-up display, the HUD, updated and presented the status of each missile hanging from the wings of his F-16. The display showed all four AIM-9X air-to-air missiles successfully responded to the command to arm. He rotated the selector switch to position three, choosing a missile under his right wing to fire first.

Limo squeezed his right index finger, depressing the trigger on the control stick halfway. A warble in his headset turned to a steady tone as the heatseeking warhead on the missile reported the successful acquisition of its distant target. He hesitated, and said to himself, "Yeah, Buck, you were right. The night definitely did not change in a good way."

With a motion he had only ever practiced in simulations, he drew his index finger back all the way and, for the first time, felt the airframe shudder ever-so-slightly as the AIM-9X missile launched off its rail.

The missile's solid rocket motor thrust its twenty-pound explosive payload forward creating a small artificial sun in the night's sky.

Limo watched the missile accelerate to supersonic speed and disappear from view.

The fire-and-forget missile detonated eight feet behind the left engine of the Gulfstream G350 creating a sunburst in the night sky as the fuel tank in the commercial jet's belly exploded in a bright red and orange conflagration.

The sleek G350 disintegrated in midair as it tumbled and burned brightly in the bitter night air. A fiery rain of aluminum aircraft parts cleaved from the Gulfstream's wings and fuselage and fell harmlessly into the Atlantic Ocean twenty miles off the coast of Ocean Township, New Jersey.

Chapter 33

Atlantic Ocean, off the Jersey Shore

The *whup-whup-whup* of the distant helicopter's rotors broke the stillness of the ocean air. Buck Hamilton looked up at the helo's blinking navigation lights in the distance and fired her flare gun straight up over her head.

The Coast Guard MH-65C Dolphin's pilot followed the navigation display on the direction-finding system on his French-designed and American-built helicopter as it tracked the emergency locator beacon attached to the downed Air Force pilot's parachute harness. He looked up as his co-pilot in the left-hand seat pointed out the red flare rising from the blackness below.

The helo's rotors showered Buck Hamilton with salty sea spray as it came to a hover twenty feet above and a dozen yards to her left. The fighter pilot waved from her single-person survival raft at the USCG rescue swimmer sitting in the open doorway of the orange-and-white whirlybird.

The rescue swimmer in a bright orange, full-body wetsuit held his mask and snorkel in place as he jumped into the frigid Atlantic. He swam to the small raft bobbing in the choppy surf and signaled the helo to lower its lift belt. Once attached, the helo lifted both the shivering pilot and comforting rescuer into the relative warmth of the helicopter's belly for the twenty-minute flight to the Jersey Shore University Medical Center in Neptune, New Jersey.

***

"We're closing in on them, Wasif," Gahir said with glee. "They're too slow."

"They can't get away. They see us and turned away to the south, but we'll catch up with them soon."

Wasif Ali leaned back in the comfortable leather seat of the Gulfstream's cockpit and handed the laptop computer to Gabir. "Hold this facing me so I can see it. I'll take the plane's controls now. You've done a wonderful job getting us to this place. Now it's my turn to fly and exact revenge on the heathens for the murder of my son."

"With pleasure, brother."

***

The two F-16s patrolling the skies west of New York City followed a few miles behind the second pair of Gulfstream G350s. Lt. Col. "Gunner" Kelly in Mountain 3 led Mountain 4 in an arc behind the rear-most jet. "Railroad," he called out over the tactical radio to Captain Steve Zeller, "I'll take the rear jet and bank away to the left. You take out the lead jet, okay?"

"*Uhh*, sir," Railroad replied, "I heard Castle Wind aboard Mother and understand our orders, but the jets have to crash *somewhere*. This is a populated area. Someone's likely to get hurt."

"Steve," the senior officer said, "tell me now if you're going to take the shot or not. We have our orders, and the closer the jets get to the Big Apple, the more people on the ground are at risk."

Gunner pushed his F-16's Master Arm switch into the forward position and selected missile number two.

"Yes, sir, I'll do it."

"Good, Steve. That's the right answer." Gunner pulled the trigger on his control stick. A flame shot from beneath his left wing as an AIM-9X Sidewinder raced forward. "Fox two. Fox two," the lieutenant colonel called out over the radio advising that he'd fired his missile, and banked his aircraft to the left to give Mountain 4 a clear shot at the lead jet.

An orange fireball erupted in the distance, and a Gulfstream G350 fell in pieces over Morris County, New Jersey.

"You're clear, Railroad. Take the missile shot and give me a fuel readout."

"Copy, Gunner."

Within twenty seconds the lead Gulfstream exploded in midair. The wreckage streamed across woodlands behind a high school and started a three-alarm forest fire that would take firefighters until dawn to extinguish.

Gunner Kelly keyed his radio, and said, "Mother, Mountain 3. Confirm two kills. Repeat, two bandits down."

"Mountain 3, Mother. Copy. Radar confirms."

"Gunner," Railroad reported, "my fuel status is twenty percent. Close to bingo, but enough to get back to Vermont. What about you?"

"Same here," he said, "and it's getting close to my bedtime. At my age, I need all the beauty rest I can get."

***

Bella Cirrone looked intently at Michelle Reagan and took a deep breath. As Michelle's third and last finger curled into her fist, Bella swung her right arm out, pushing Noor's weapon hand away. The CIA officer let her legs go slack and dropped to the wooden floor.

Shots rang out simultaneously from multiple guns, and brass casings ricocheted off the hallway walls around Michelle's head. She slammed her palms over her ears to deaden the sounds of the gunshots.

The SWAT operator holding the ballistic shield surged forward toward Noor. Decker and Jackson followed immediately behind.

Noor arced backward. Blood spurted from four bullet holes in her upper chest and face as she fell. As she hit the ground, another *crack* of a gunshot rang out through the apartment. Wood splinters exploded from the door frame to Michelle's right.

Instinctively, Michelle ducked as needle-like shards fell into her hair. She flicked them out with her hand and watched three SWAT operators roll Noor's lifeless body face-down and cuff her hands behind her back.

The high-pitched yelp of a woman crying in pain filled the air.

Michelle glanced at Bella who had dropped next to her thin mattress and watched with eyes wide the commotion going on just a half-dozen feet away.

Bella tried to lean up into a sitting position but immediately fell backward onto her mattress. In a pained voice, she exclaimed, "*Owww*! Michelle, help me. I think I've been shot!"

***

Air Battle Manager Tony Winters relayed the Air Boss's urgent instructions to the lone F-16 flying south of New York City. "Casino 8, Mother. We're under attack and need immediate assistance. Turn to heading zero-three-five and make best possible—*repeat* best possible—speed. Bandit is designated George 1. Stand by for authority to fire on the civilian aircraft."

BG Denton and the Air Boss confirmed for Limo Bentley once more their direction and authority to destroy a civilian aircraft—this time, the Gulfstream pursuing the AWACS over Long Island.

Limo acknowledged the radio call and pushed his F-16's throttle all the way forward and lifted it over the detent. The force of the afterburner's surge pushed him back into the thin cushion of his fighter's seat as his jet accelerated past the speed of sound. He angled the Fighting Falcon into a gentle climb and watched the altimeter tick upward. He relied on the AWACS' powerful radar and its controllers' expertise to watch over him and ensure his safe separation from civilian traffic coming to or leaving from the region's many airports in the minutes before the east coast rang in the new year.

Air Boss Major Brad Kent keyed the mic on his headset and spoke to the AWACS' pilot. "The pursuing aircraft is close. *Really* damned close. I recommend you abort the mission and get us on the ground ASAP."

"I can't exactly land this bird on a highway, major."

"No," Kent agreed, "but here's one option. Republic Airport is a small commercial airfield to our south with a runway long enough for a jet this big. Turn right heading one-niner-zero and you can line up to land on runway zero-one. It's short, though. You'll have to stomp hard on the brakes after landing. But right now, overheating brakes may be the least of our problems. On the plus side, my system says the airport closes at 11 p.m. every day, so there shouldn't be any competing traffic. Unfortunately, there won't be any approach control, either."

The pilot grunted, banked the large jet, and leveled out on the designated south-southwesterly heading. His co-pilot rifled through aeronautical charts on his iPad to find the details for an instrument-guided approach into Republic Airport. With the data in hand, he punched the frequency for the civilian airfield's VOR/DME radio-navigation beacon into the AWACS' navigation computer. A closed airport may be just what they needed—an out of the way spot to land in which no one else would get hurt if everything went to hell in a handbasket.

The co-pilot looked at the pilot, and asked, "How close is the other jet?"

Instinctively, the pilot looked out the side window but couldn't see anything other than the dim, distant lights of the southern Connecticut shoreline. "*Close*. How far are we from Republic?"

The pained look on the co-pilot's face told the story. "*Far.*"

Chapter 34

Airborne over New Jersey

Flying their F-16s northeast toward their home base in Vermont, Mountain flight lead pilot "Gunner" Kelly looked over his right shoulder and confirmed that Railroad Zeller flew in formation off his right wing. The voice of the Air Battle Manager calling from the AWACS sounded rushed.

"Mountain flight, Mother. Turn to heading zero-four-five. Intercept and identify two VFR aircraft flying southbound in a two-mile trail formation at a distance of four-eight miles from your position."

Gunner acknowledged the AWACS' instructions and keyed the tactical frequency he shared only with Railroad. "Again? Shit."

"You said it, boss. Lead on. I'll stay on your wing."

Gunner Kelly led the flight in a turn to the new heading and called out to Mountain 4. "Railroad, dial your radar out to sixty miles and look at the traffic at five thousand feet."

Railroad twisted the dial to change the range of his AN/APG-68 fire-control radar. The pulse-Doppler radar showed forty blips ahead of him as aircraft lined up to leave or land Newark or LaGuardia airports. Two blips in particular caught his eye. "I see them, Gunner. Two bogies at five-thousand feet above sea level heading south. Mother was right. They're in the same two-mile trail formation as the pair we just shot down. What do you think?"

"Given the way things have gone tonight for us up here and Casino flight down south, it can't be good. The bogies are off to our north, so it's sorta on our way home, anyway."

***

"You've *got* to be shitting me," Brad Kent said to himself as he read the Flash messages from the EADS on his monitor. "*Now* they tell us?"

"Ten minutes advance notice would have been nice," BG Denton said.

"Sorry, sir, I wasn't aiming that air strike at you."

The general chuckled and keyed his intercom mic. "Pilot, Castle Wind. Intel from the EADS in Griffiss advises that the aircraft pursuing us is a jet stolen from Pennsylvania tonight and is likely equipped with a radar detection system. Expect a Kamikaze-style attack. That's probably what happened to Casino 7 earlier. Do anything you need to do to get us on the ground safely, captain. No limits."

"Sir," the disembodied voice of the pilot said over the intercom, "if they're using our radar against us, I recommend turning it off."

Air Boss Brad Kent said, "If we do that, we're flying blind."

Denton asked, "Captain, how long until we're on the ground at Republic?"

"Three minutes."

BG Denton asked the Air Boss next to him, "How long until George 1 catches up with us?"

Kent held up two fingers and keyed the mic on his headset. "Pilot, Air Boss. We can't outrun the Gremlin and aren't going to make it to the airfield before they catch us. We don't have an aft-facing window, so if we turn the radar off, we're blind. I recommend we keep it on and see if Casino 8 can get here in time to take a long-distance air-to-air missile shot. Plan B will be for you to make a last-minute turn and hope the Gremlin misses us so they have to come around for another pass. If so, that'll give Casino 8 another minute or two to close in for the kill."

The pilot's reply was short and to the point. "And if not, major?"

Brad Kent couldn't think of a reply. Instead, he called his controller. "Winters, what's the ETA for Casino 8?"

"Ninety seconds, sir."

BG Denton responded immediately. "Lieutenant, instruct Casino 8 to take the first-available shot at George 1."

Winters relayed General Denton's orders.

Limo Bentley acknowledged the radio call and dialed his radar display to a forty-mile range. At a distance of twenty-five miles, the two icons almost overlapped on his screen. Below him, and stretching off to the southeast, aircraft lined up at five-mile intervals to land at JFK. Their bright lights gave the formation its familiar 'string of pearls' pattern. To his left, the bright lights of Long Beach, New York, clearly delineated the shoreline as his F-16 approached land at Mach 1.2—twenty percent faster than the speed of sound.

Upon reaching a distance of twenty-two miles from the AWACS and its pursuer, Bentley depressed the trigger halfway and held it. The missile's prolonged warble oscillated in his headset. "Come on, baby, lock onto the bad guy. Lock on...."

The warble continued uninterrupted. The AWACS' Identify Friend or Foe — IFF — transponder prevented the F-16's missile from locking on to another USAF aircraft, but there's no way for the pilot to tell the heat-seeking missile to simply 'shoot the other one.'

"Damn it," Limo spat, and keyed his mic. "Mother, Casino 8. Negative missile lock. The Sidewinder can't differentiate between the two aircraft from this distance. Your heat signatures are overlapping. I need to close the distance further."

"Casino 8, Mother. Do you have radar missiles?"

"Negative, Mother. That would be too easy. Give me two minutes to close the distance and get behind George 1."

"Sir," Tony Winters advised the fighter pilot, "with all due respect, we may not have two more minutes."

***

"Pilot, Air Boss," Major Kent said. "The Gremlin is six-thousand feet directly behind us and closing at just less than one mile per minute."

"We won't make the airfield in time, major. I'm open to suggestions. I can see the Long Island Expressway below us, but there are so many vehicles on it, we'd crash at a hundred-fifty miles an hour and take too many civilians up in flames with us."

Brad Kent took a deep breath and said, "I have one suggestion, but it's a last-straw kind of maneuver."

"Lay it on me, major," the captain said from the flight deck.

"When I give the word, you bank hard right and make a nosedive below five-thousand feet. The Gulfstream should overshoot us, at least by a little. Then, you turn to heading two-two-five until we can turn right to land at Republic on runway one-four."

"Copy, Air Boss. Right turn and dive on your mark."

Kent looked at BG Denton who was cinching his seatbelt as tightly as he could pull the aging canvas straps. The Air Boss clicked the zoom icon on his screen, but the display was already set to the maximum resolution. He keyed his mic, and said, "Pilot, Air Boss. Four... Three... Two... One... Mark!"

***

"They turned!" Gabir Wahab shouted in surprise.

"*Rrrh*," Wasif Ali grunted as the Gulfstream passed through empty air over the top of his prey. He turned the control yoke sharply to the right and pushed it forward to follow the Air Force jet into a head-long dive toward the ground. The G350 shook as it struggled to make the high-speed turn Wasif demanded of it. "Hold the computer up so I can see it as I make the turn."

Gabir struggled to angle the screen toward Wasif as the force of the turn pushed him against the bulkhead to his right.

"Smart move," Wasif said to himself as he stared intently through the windscreen to reacquire the AWACS. "That's the kind of maneuver *I* would have made in his shoes. We've lost some distance, but we'll catch up. They still can't outrun us, so they're going to make another turn like that. Now, we'll be ready for them when they do."

"Do you think they'll turn to the left or the right again next time?"

Wasif thought for a moment, and said, "To the left. They've been heading south for a while, now. They must be leading us toward their fighters." He eased the control yoke to the right and centered the AWACS' silhouette in the left-hand portion of the windscreen. "There. Now, when they turn, I'll see them clearly and react quicker. It'll cut our distance down even more by making a tighter turn."

***

Limo Bentley aboard Casino 8 dialed his F-16's radar down to a twenty-mile range. The blips representing the AWACS and Gulfstream jets merged and the Sidewinder's warble continued in his headset. The heat-seeking missile could not lock onto the Gulfstream. He released the trigger and keyed his microphone. "Mother, Casino 8. Thirty or forty more seconds, and I'll be close enough!"

***

Wasif Ali watched the large AWACS bank sharply to its left and he reacted with the speed of a fighter pilot. "There!"

Gabir sat up straight and strained to see the Boeing jet through the Gulfstream's windshield. The blue blob on the laptop computer disappeared, and he shook the PC as if that would bring it back.

Wasif glanced at his co-pilot, and said, "That's okay. They've turned their radar off. They're too low, now, to keep it active. At low altitudes, radars receive too much random ground clutter to be useful."

Gabir let out his breath in relief. "I was afraid I broke it or something."

"No, brother. This is the end game." He leveled the wings of the G350 and continued his descent right behind the AWACS. He pointed through the windscreen, and said, "Look, they're trying to land at that airport. They've trapped themselves. They have no way to escape, now. They're too low to make another sharp turn and too large and heavy to climb faster than us. We have them now!"

***

"We're blind," Air Boss Brad Kent informed the AWACS' pilot. "The radar cut off when we dropped below the minimum operating altitude. It's all in your hands now."

The pilot nodded silently — not that Major Kent could see him — and furiously worked the AWACS' controls but didn't have a spare finger to use to key his mic. To his co-pilot, he said, "Lower flaps to ten percent."

"That's all?"

"Yeah, that's it. I hate to bleed off even the ten knots that'll cost us, but we have to. We can't afford to slow down too much with the Gremlin still on our ass, but we still need to come to a stop before the end of the runway. It's a balancing act." He checked the airspeed indicator, and said, "Lower the landing gear."

With his left hand, the co-pilot pushed the lever to lower the landing gear and jiggled it to ensure it remained firmly seated in the "down" position. He watched the indicator lights on the console for what seemed like an eternity. When the green light illuminated, he blurted out, "Landing gear down and locked."

"Good. How long did you say the runway is?"

"Sixty-eight hundred feet."

"We're going to need all of it tonight."

The pilot keyed his radio and broadcast on Republic Airport's approach frequency. "Any traffic in the vicinity of Republic Airport. This is US Air Force emergency aircraft on short final approach broadcasting in the blind. All traffic is advised to clear the approach airspace and runway one-four. This will be a full stop."

On the road in front of Republic Airport, cars lit the blacktop sporadically with ghostly headlights illuminating the two-lane road. The bright lights along Republic's Runway 14 extended into the distance, providing a path for the AWACS to follow directly to the airfield. The pilot gripped the control yoke firmly and wiggled his toes inside his flight boots. He pressed his boots against the stiff aluminum pedals that control the aircraft's complex combination of tail rudder, front-landing-gear steering mechanism, and rear-landing-gear wheel brakes.

As the airport's fence disappeared under the aircraft, the pilot pulled the four throttles on the AWACS' center console all the way back. His emergency power-down cut all thrust from the engines a thousand feet earlier in a landing than he'd ever done before, even in a simulator where pilots practice every crazy scenario their instructors can dream up. Except this one.

The Boeing jet's main landing gear dropped onto the runway with a thud and the tires squealed in complaint. The aircraft shook, and dust fell from between the rows of fuses fitted into myriad panels over the co-pilot's head. The pilot held the nose of the aircraft off the runway as the jet slowed below one-hundred-sixty miles per hour. As the aircraft bled off speed, he eased the control yoke forward and the nose gear dropped firmly to the runway. With the aircraft's weight on the nose gear, the pedals beneath the pilot and co-pilot transitioned from controlling the plane's rudder to steering the nose gear, allowing the landing gear's brakes to slow the speeding jet.

"Four-thousand feet," the co-pilot said loudly, advising the pilot how much paved runway remained in front of them.

"Now!" the pilot called.

The co-pilot pulled the throttles into the reverse-thrust position.

Both officers held the control yoke tightly and pushed forcefully on the toe pedals. The aircraft's wheel brakes activated, and the combined forces pushed both pilots forward, firmly into their shoulder straps.

"Three thousand."

The pilots maintained their focus on steering the speeding jet along Runway 14's centerline.

"Two thousand," the co-pilot advised anxiously.

The pilot glanced at the airspeed indicator and saw the needle drop below ninety miles per hour.

"*One* thousand," the co-pilot said.

"Get ready," the pilot responded as the airspeed indicator drop to eighty. He peered intently into the distance at the rapidly approaching end of the runway. A short paved overrun extended from the runway to the fence where the runway ended and a row of trees separated the airport from a local road.

"Left or right?" the co-pilot asked.

"Left," the pilot said immediately, and peered intently into the distance. "Speed?"

"Sixty knots. Fifty."

"Brake harder," the pilot instructed.

"Forty."

Both men pushed their toes as far forward as the pedals allowed.

"Thirty!"

"On my mark," the pilot ordered. "Three... Two... One... Mark!"

With military precision, both pilots simultaneously thrust the left pedals to the floor, lifted their heels, and pushed their toes into the tops of the pedals. Their complex dance put maximum pressure on the landing gear's brakes and simultaneously put the aircraft into a violent left turn onto a taxiway.

The AWACS slewed to its left and swerved off the mile-long runway onto the hundred-foot-wide paved connection meant to briefly hold aircraft awaiting clearance for takeoff. The Boeing 707's nose gear skidded left, leaving a black streak on the white concrete taxiway. The main landing gear under the left wing reverberated as its shock absorbers tried their best to dissipate the stress of the turn forced upon it by the pilots evacuating the runway as quickly as humanly — and mechanically — possible.

As the aircraft spun to the left and cleared the runway, its right landing gear swung wide and onto the grass adjacent to the taxiway. The rubber tires, blistering from the high-speed landing and forceful braking, scraped away the thin covering of grass and dug deeply into the dirt beneath. The insurmountable drag of the gear-turned-plow marauding through the turf dug the wheels in firmly and caused the right gear to act as a pivot. The momentum of the big jet spun the plane clockwise — opposite the pilots' commands.

The crew aboard the AWACS strained against their shoulder straps as the aircraft lurched first to the left, and then reversed itself violently to the right before shaking to a sudden halt. Coffee mugs flew from cup holders. The impact of Denise Ziegler's water bottle against the bulkhead cracked the plastic and sprayed spring water across the window.

The Boeing jet stopped half on the taxiway and half mired in mud. The jet's left wing flapped dangerously close to the ground as the fuel inside swirled violently inside its tank.

The pilot looked around the cockpit as the aluminum skin of his half-century-old aircraft creaked and complained about the abuse he'd forced it to endure.

Bright white light filled the AWACS' cockpit as a line of silvery sparks spewed across the blackness of Republic Airport's Runway 14. The AWACS' flight crew sat captivated, watching through the windscreen as the left wing of Wasif Ali's Gulfstream dragged along the runway, trailing behind it a thin river of flames. In front of their eyes, the G350 exploded into an orange-and-red inferno, tumbling off the end of the runway at sixty miles an hour. The stolen jet had tilted to the left as its determined pilot tried to match the AWACS' last-second turn off the runway, but the Gulfstream traveled too fast and Wasif reacted too late. The wreckage cartwheeled past the runway's threshold and came to rest in a line of pine trees.

"Holy shit," the co-pilot said as he removed his headset.

"Da-*amn*," the pilot agreed. "That would have been us."

The co-pilot pointed to the fire beginning to engulf the woodlands, and said, "The airport's already closed. We should probably call someone about that."

The pilot pulled his iPhone out of the left breast pocket of his flight suit, turned airplane mode off, and dialed 9-1-1.

The county dispatcher answered on the second ring. "Emergency Services Operator. What's the nature of your emergency?"

"Operator," the pilot said shaking his head, "you are *not* going to believe this."

Chapter 35

Noor Ali's Apartment, New York City

Michelle watched as a red splotch grew across the right sleeve of Bella's nightgown. She rushed into the room and dropped to her knees in front of the woman writhing in pain. Michelle slid her hands up the length of Bella's arm, stopping at the hole in the center of the expanding red stain. She spread the fabric with her fingers, inserted both of her index fingers into the hole a bullet ripped into the nightdress, and tore the cloth forcefully.

The fabric split with the sound of a zipper being opened. Michelle used the loose fabric to wipe away the oozing blood on Bella's upper arm and studied the oblong wound. She ran her hands completely around Bella's arm and felt up and down for any other injuries. Michelle ripped the rest of the cotton sleeve away from Bella's nightgown and folded it three times to use as a field dressing.

Bella began to lift herself up with her left arm, and Michelle gently pushed the wounded woman's shoulder down to keep her flat on the mattress.

"Stay down until I get this tied off. Good news, though, Bella, it's barely a scrape. No problem, girlfriend."

Bella looked at the blood flowing from the open wound three inches below her shoulder. Her eyes rolled back in her head, and she went limp in Michelle's arms.

Michelle pressed the folded nightgown over the open wound and applied pressure to stanch the bleeding.

"Matt!" Michelle yelled. "Bella's hit. Noor must have shot her as she fell. It doesn't look bad to me, but we need a paramedic. She just passed out. Do you have any smelling salts?"

The SWAT supervisor pulled the Velcro tab on a small, black nylon bag attached to the left side of his body armor. He handed bandages, smelling salts and a packet of antiseptic to Michelle.

Brian Jackson radioed for a medic and advised everyone that the situation had been contained.

An FBI agent in the alley responded immediately to the call for medical support.

Ron Poland acknowledged Jackson's report, and asked to be informed when his team could begin its search and interviews.

Jackson responded, "You can have the search team come up any time you want, Ron." He looked at Noor's body at his feet, and continued, "Negative on the interview, though."

An FBI agent with a medical bag bounded through the doorway. On the floor, Bella coughed and groaned at the stench of ammonia wafting up her nostrils. She shooed away Michelle's hand which was waving smelling salts under the injured woman's nose.

The agent dropped to the floor next to Bella, and said, "I'm Doctor John Pine. Where was she hit?"

Michelle removed the improvised field dressing from Bella's upper arm and showed the wound to Pine. "I didn't find any entry or exit wounds. I think she was just grazed."

"Let me take a look." Pine pulled on a pair of latex gloves, examined Bella's entire arm, and ran his hands along her side. He asked his patient, "Does anything else hurt?"

Bella spoke groggily. "No, just my shoulder. I can't really move my arm too much. It burns."

"Okay," Pine said, "I'll clean you up, dress the wound and we'll transport you to a hospital to get you examined thoroughly. The bullet took out a small chunk of muscle, but if that's the extent of it, then I'd say you're one lucky lady."

Bella groaned as she rotated to get as comfortable as she could while Dr. Pine worked on her.

Michelle looked at Pine, and said, "I didn't know the FBI had medical doctors as agents."

Pine answered as he wiped Bella's arm with antiseptic and applied bandages. "There are only two of us. Me and a guy in Los Angeles. We work cases just like other agents and support the SWAT teams for certain high-risk operations."

"That's convenient," she said, and rubbed her hands.

Pine looked at her bloody hands, and asked, "Are you hurt? Your hands—"

"No, no," Michelle replied, "I'm fine. This is Bella's blood. I was outside the room when all the shooting happened. I'll clean up at the sink in the bathroom, and then I'll accompany Bella to the hospital. She doesn't have any family around here."

"Good idea," Pine answered. "I'll make sure she also gets a full FBI escort to lead the ambulance through New York City traffic like a hot knife through butter."

Michelle looked at Bella's leg and realized the cable chaining her to the radiator remained handcuffed to her ankle. She held up the cable for all to see. "Brian, do you have a handcuff key?"

"Oh, man, I forgot about that," Jackson said, and proceeded to separate a small silver handcuff key from the others on his keychain.

After the SWAT agent unlocked the shackle, Pine examined the bruises around Bella's ankle. "Wow, okay, we'll get that X-rayed at the hospital. There's some bruising, but it doesn't look infected." He patted Bella's healthy shoulder, and said, "Just lie there and relax."

Michelle looked at Bella, rubbed the back of her hand and said, "You do realize, don't you, that two rescues in two months is my limit. I have to charge extra if there's a third."

Bella laughed and stared blankly at the white paint peeling from the ceiling.

Two paramedics squeezed past the SWAT team and dropped their red equipment bags on the floor. Dr. Pine introduced himself, explained Bella's wound, and described how he bandaged her arm.

Michelle looked at the newcomers, and said, "Hey, Pete, Amanda."

"Hi, Michelle," the female paramedic replied. "Is this who you've been after all this time?"

Michelle pointed to Bella, and said, "Good guy." She stabbed her finger in the direction of Noor's corpse, and said, "Bad guy."

Bella Cirrone looked from Michelle to the paramedics and back again. "You know each other?"

Michelle smiled at the woman sitting on the floor as John Pine draped a sling around her neck and adjusted the Velcro straps. "Yeah, I've spent the past few weeks practically living in the basement of their fire station and eating two meals a day with them. That's where we set up the monitoring equipment and our, um, special way of communicating with you."

"Oh, okay. Got it. Cool."

"Well," the male paramedic said to Bella, "let's get you to the hospital and checked out there. Can you walk?"

Bella nodded and stood up with Dr. Pine's help.

"Good," Amanda said. "It's a walk-up apartment, and that'll save us having to take you down the stairs on a stretcher. I owe you one. Here, it's cold outside." The paramedic extracted a tightly folded blanked from her equipment bag, draped it around Bella's shoulders and led the wounded woman toward the door.

Michelle accompanied them and asked the paramedics, "Is it okay with you guys if I ride in the back with Bella?"

"Sure thing," Pete said. "And unless we get another call, we can give you a ride back to the station afterward."

"No, that's all right," Michelle said. "I'll stay with Bella at the hospital for a while and then catch a cab."

Bella looked at Michelle, and said, "There you go, taking me to another hospital. We seem to do things in twos, don't we?"

Michelle chuckled. "Everything but run away. You're not going to make me chase you again, are you?"

"Not this time," Bella said as she lay down on the gurney in the back of the ambulance. "Right now, my kneecaps are the only things *not* hurting. I'd like to keep it that way."

"Good choice," Michelle said, and gently rubbed Bella's healthy shoulder.

The paramedics looked at the women, then at each other, and shrugged.

***

Lt. Col. Jordan "Gunner" Kelly gritted his teeth and repeated the radio call from his F-16 Fighting Falcon for the eighth time. "Mother, Mountain flight."

"No one's home, Gunner," Captain Steven "Railroad" Zeller opined.

Gunner Kelly switched frequencies and called the Eastern Air Defense Sector controllers in Griffiss, New York. "EADS, Mountain flight. Radio check."

"Mountain flight, EADS. Read you loud and clear."

"EADS, Mountain. Mother gave us intercept instructions, and we're on station trailing the two suspicious jets southbound, but we've lost comms with the AWACS. We need confirmation from Castle Wind before we can fire. Please patch us through."

"Negative, Mountain flight. We've lost their automated data feed and have no comms with them, either."

"Well, EADS, that puts you in charge. What do you want us to do?"

"Mountain flight, *uhh*, standby," Senior Airman Clark Marshall at EADS operations desk said. The young airman looked up at the lieutenant standing over him, and simply asked, "Sir?"

The lieutenant scratched his neck nervously, and said, "If they radio in again, tell them to stand by." He walked back to his console, picked up the green telephone handset, and pushed the right-most speed-dial button labeled 'NORAD Ops Center.'

***

"Hey, Railroad, look to your right," Gunner Kelly radioed to his wingman in the other F-16. "There's West Point again. Can't seem to get away from Hudson High tonight, can we?"

Railroad Zeller peered at the familiar bend of the Hudson River he had joked about attacking earlier in the evening. After shooting down a civilian aircraft just minutes before, he found no humor in his earlier jest. "No, guess not. It's such a gray and dreary place on the ground, but from up here, those three half-circles in the base housing area are always lit up brightly and kinda look like Christmas ornaments."

"Mountain flight, EADS," came the radio transmission. "NORAD is trying to find Castle Rock. Stand by."

"Stand *by*?" Gunner Kelly asked over the tactical frequency.

"Castle Rock must be having another glass of eggnog out in Colorado Springs. It's still two hours until midnight out there," Zeller replied.

"Be nice, Railroad. You should be so lucky as to make it to such a lofty rank someday."

"Yes, sir. And speaking of promotions, Gunner, I can't wait to see what my officer evaluation report looks like this year. Maybe it'll really showcase my skills by saying something like 'he controls the aircraft well enough, but truly excels at shooting down unarmed civilian aircraft while flying straight and level through clear skies in good weather.'"

Gunner Kelly keyed his mic and paused. He released the button, and said to himself, "Yeah, Steve, you and me both."

Kelly pushed the radio selector for EADS' frequency, and said, "EADS, Mountain flight. Bogies are thirty miles north of New York City and following the river south. We have position and are awaiting Castle Rock's authority to fire. Please advise."

"Mountain flight, EADS. Copy. NORAD is evaluating the situation. Stand by."

Gunner Kelly grumbled to himself. "*Evaluating* the situation. Hmph." To the controller, he radioed, "EADS, Mountain flight. Be advised that at their current speed the bogies will be over a densely populated city in less than two minutes."

Railroad's radio call asked the question Jordan Kelly could not yet answer. "Gunner, what happens if we don't get orders from NORAD in time?"

"Sit tight, Railroad. Just like the bridge below us, we'll cross that one when we come to it."

Kelly keyed his radio again. "EADS, Mountain flight. We're crossing southbound over the Mario Cuomo Bridge now, and the bogies are twenty miles from New York City. We have less than one minute to act. What are your orders?"

***

The duty lieutenant looked down at Senior Airman Clark Marshall, and said, "Tell them the truth. We've not heard definitively from NORAD, yet. We have no new orders to give them. Tell them to continue to track and report every minute on the bogies' positions."

Airman Marshall repeated his LT's instructions to the two Vermont ANG F-16s of Mountain flight.

The lieutenant grimaced and picked up the green phone at his desk. He stabbed his index finger at the button for NORAD in frustration and prayed for better news this time.

***

"'Track the bogies?' I can't believe them," Gunner fumed to Railroad. "We're going to track them right into the Empire State Building or Freedom Tower or whatever their target is this time. This is *bullshit!*"

"What do we do, sir?" Railroad asked.

Gunner Kelly clenched his jaw until it hurt. The ache reminded him that this was real and not a training simulation. A memory flashed through his mind of the day he was commissioned a second lieutenant. His father, himself a fighter pilot from the Korea and Vietnam era, proudly pinned his son's butter bars on the epaulets of his dark blue Service Dress uniform. The oath of office the senior Kelly administered to his son that warm May morning in Colorado Springs decided for him a decade and a half in advance the actions "Machine Gun" Kelly would take that night—to defend his nation against all enemies, foreign and domestic.

Lt. Col. Kelly keyed his mic, and said, "Railroad, without AWACS coverage to ensure separation from civilian traffic, we're risking a mid-air collision with commercial aircraft inbound to land at LaGuardia. I need you to fall back five or so miles and climb to ten-thousand feet. Use your radar to call out any traffic that I need to avoid."

"Copy, Gunner. Climbing."

Gunner watched over his shoulder as the navigation lights of Railroad's F-16 disappeared in the distance behind him. In addition to defending the nation that night, Jordan Kelly knew he had to defend his wingman, as well. He'd dispatched Railroad to watch what was about to happen from a perch several thousand feet above. The younger pilot would have a literal bird's-eye view, but not be a party to Gunner's own actions.

With a flick of the Master Arm switch, Kelly armed the remaining three missiles under his wings and locked one on its left side onto the rear-most of the two remaining Gulfstream G350s. His radar screen showed the civilian jets approaching Yonkers as the warble in his ear turned to a steady tone, signaling that the missile locked onto its intended target.

With his left index finger, Gunner pulled the trigger on the control stick. The night sky in front of his fighter brightened as a Sidewinder bolted forward for its short trip between the aircraft.

Seconds later, the rear-most G350 erupted in flames and tumbled into the Hudson River in a blaze of burning jet fuel.

Railroad's voice erupted in Kelly's ears. "Gunner, what the *hell*? Did you get Castle Rock's authority?"

Gunner's formality took the young captain by surprise. "Mountain 4, this is Mountain 3, maintain your position. This is congested airspace. I need you watching my six and calling out traffic. That's an order, captain."

Zeller paused, then replied, "Yes, sir. No traffic at your altitude. Be advised of a slow mover at one-thousand feet altitude to your ten o'clock. Range six miles. Possible rotary wing."

Jordan Kelly dialed the weapon selector to the icon for one of the missiles under his right wing and acknowledged Railroad's advisory. Kelly depressed the trigger halfway, and the familiar warble in his headset told him the heatseeking warhead easily identified the Gulfstream G350 flying four miles ahead of him.

Into the dark night, he said, "You bastards got us once, but never again." He squeezed the trigger and watched the remaining stolen Gulfstream disintegrate in midair.

Its wreckage showered down along the river's waterline and the rocky shore of Fort Washington Park, adjacent to the George Washington Bridge.

Gunner pushed the throttle for the F-16's single engine forward, turned to the right, and climbed to rejoin his wingman.

"Okay, Railroad. We've done what we were sent up here tonight to do. I'm bingo fuel, so let's head back to Vermont. The powers that be have two-hundred-fifty miles to decide whether to give me a medal or a court martial. Either way, I'm done for the night. Let's go home."

Chapter 36

JTTF Watch Center, New York City

Cheers flooded the Joint Terrorism Task Force's Watch Center as reports from the Air Force's Eastern Air Defense Sector confirmed that all seven Gulfstreams stolen by Wasif Ali's team were destroyed by the Air National Guard fighters, and none had reached its intended target.

Behind the CIA's National Resource Division rep seated at his console, Caroline van der Pol jumped up and down, clapped her hands, and hugged the DOD analyst standing next to her.

Nola Austin rushed to the front of the room and waved her hands over her head. "Everyone! Everyone, listen up."

The room quieted down enough that she could be heard above the background rumblings.

Austin pointed to an agent in the back of the room. "The director's on the phone. Go ahead and put the call on the main speaker."

The overhead speakers crackled, and an agent in the back row said, "Go ahead, Madame Director. You're on speaker at the Watch Center."

"Happy New Year, everyone," the director of the FBI said. "I want to pass on my thanks for the marvelous job you all did tonight and over the past week. I just got off a long and tense video teleconference with the president and the Pentagon, and I also want to pass along the thanks of the White House. Without your investigative and intelligence expertise, this matter looks like it would have ended quite badly. You've done a marvelous job, all of you."

"Thank you, Madame Director," Austin said for the team.

"I can't wait to read the case summary. Please expedite it."

"Yes, ma'am," she replied, and the director ended the call.

Chapter 37

Mount Sinai Union Square Hospital, New York City

An Emergency Department nurse entered Bella Cirrone's room, and Michelle Reagan leaned toward the CIA officer sitting upright on the hospital bed.

To Bella, Michelle said, "I need to go make a phone call. Are you going to be all right alone or do you want me to stay?"

Bella chuckled. "No, I'll be fine."

"Okay, I'll be just down the hall, so yell if you need anything." Michelle stepped out of the small exam room and phoned Caroline van der Pol at the JTTF.

"Hey, it's Michelle. We're at the hospital, and Bella's okay. The exam just started, so this may take a while."

"Oh, I'm so glad to hear she's not hurt," the counterintelligence officer said. "I talked to Nino. He and the FBI agents in the monitoring room listened to everything going on in the apartment. When he told me they heard gunshots, I got so worried. The agents there are wondering if they should close up shop."

"Yeah, might as well," Michelle said, and bit down on her lip. "And I heard from Ron Poland about the Air Force shooting down the stolen jets. That's terrific!"

"Yeah, everyone here at the JTTF is going to be busy with the aftermath for the next month, but you and I don't have to stick around for that."

"Personally, I can't wait to get home. Speaking of that, tell Nino he can have Katie come retrieve her gear from the rooftop at her convenience. One other thing... I have to attend the JTTF debriefing tonight since I took part in the evening's festivities in the apartment, as you heard. So, because of that, can you come over here and stay with our girl for a while? I don't want her to be alone anymore."

"Yes, definitely. Also, I called Langley as soon as things calmed down in the apartment. They're glad Bella's all right."

Michelle thought she could hear Caroline's voice quiver slightly when she said, "My boss, Phil Thompson, is coming back up tomorrow morning. Also, Mrs. Bhoti wants to talk to us by VTC back at the National Resources Division office at 7 a.m. I'll tell you more about that when I get to the hospital."

"I guess I won't be getting much sleep tonight, but that's fine. I'll be there tomorrow morning with bells on and sleep on the train ride home afterward."

Caroline's voice was drowned out briefly by a car's horn blaring in the background. "—just about to hop in a cab. Should be there in fifteen or twenty minutes. I'll call Nino and tell him to come, too."

"Great," Michelle said, and tapped her phone's red icon to disconnect the call. She walked back into the examination room as the nurse was sealing up the rape kit and left the room.

"Bella," Michelle asked, "do you remember Caroline van der Pol from the Farm? She's coming over to stay with you for a while. I have to go talk to the FBI about tonight's rescue and see if they found anything in the apartment. Is there anything else you can tell me? Anything you learned but haven't mentioned?"

"No," Bella said, slowly shaking her head, "nothing."

Michelle scooted her chair to the edge of Bella's narrow bed and spoke softly. "If there's anything you know that you don't want others to find out came from you, tell *me*. I'll say I got it from some other source, or I heard Noor say it quietly in Arabic, or something like that. I've put my life on the line for you twice, now. At first, after getting you safely to the Army hospital in Iraq, I wanted nothing more than to wash my hands of you and let them take care of you so you could get back to your old life. A lot has happened since then. Now, I feel like I still need to get you back on the right path, but I'm afraid there's not much more I'm going to be allowed to do from here on. So, if there's *anything* at all you can tell me—"

"*No*, Michelle, really, there's nothing else. I didn't know what he was up to. You heard everything that went on in the room, right?"

Michelle nodded. "Yeah, but some things were said softly, and the radiator hissed a lot, so maybe we missed something."

"No, I really *don't* know. If I did, I'd be the first to tell you. That's why I volunteered to stay behind—to find that out. I'm just sorry I couldn't be of more help."

Michelle squeezed Bella's healthy shoulder. "You've been a *phenomenal* help. It turns out that we did prevent Wasif's attack, and

Caroline will tell you more about that later. I'm convinced that if it weren't for you, we would never have known anything about it until it was too late. You've been through more than anyone had a right to ask of you, and you deserve more than just the medal I imagine you'll get. Just remember, if any other thoughts come to you in the middle of the night, you can always call me. Any time of the day or night. Okay?"

"Thank you, Michelle. I can't thank you enough for all you've done for me. I...."

Michelle smiled and stroked Bella's shoulder as Nino Balducci and Caroline van der Pol pushed through the examination room door and walked in. Nino placed a small bouquet of flowers on the side table next to Bella.

"Nino!" Bella cried in surprise.

"Hey there, champ. How are you?"

"You brought me flowers? Oh, you shouldn't have. Where did you find them at this time of night?"

Nino hooked his thumb toward the door, and said, "I shouldn't give away all my tradecraft secrets, but I'll make an exception just this one time, because it's *you*. There's a vending machine in the lobby."

Bella giggled. "Well, they're beautiful. Thank you. It's *so* good to see you again. It's been so long. Reading your messages as they scrolled across the wall of my bedroom over the past week just isn't the same as seeing you in person."

"It's great to see you again, too, my dear. As I recall, the last time we were in the same city together, you went to the airport and left for two years without even saying goodbye."

Bella laughed, and said, "*Left*, yeah, right, chief. That's not what I'*d* call it, but you're as funny as always."

"Yeah, well," Nino said, "looks aren't everything."

Caroline eased up to the side of Bella's bed, picked up the injured woman's hand, and said, "I reserved a hotel room for you adjacent to mine. When you're discharged from the hospital, I'll take you there so you can shower and change. I purchased a T-shirt and pair of sweats for you to wear. We can go shopping for real clothes tomorrow."

Michelle pointed to Bella, and said, "Oh, yeah, I forgot to mention it, but the FBI took your suitcase from the Marriott as evidence. I'm not sure when you'll get that back."

Bella shrugged and winced in pain as she moved her wounded shoulder.

The door swung inward. A nurse entered, followed by a man in light green scrubs.

The middle-aged nurse reviewed the clipboard she held and looked at Bella. "All right, young lady, Tommy here is going to wheel you down to radiology so we can get a look at your ankle. On your admittance paperwork, it says that this is a Worker's Comp case, and that you work for the Federal Aviation Administration. Is that correct?"

Bella nodded, and said, "Yes."

The nurse looked around the room, and asked, "Do you all work for the FAA?"

Nino nodded, Caroline remained silent, and Michelle said, "On that note, I'm outta here. *Ciao*, Bella."

***

At 7 a.m. the next morning, Michelle Reagan, Nino Balducci and Caroline van der Pol sat alone in the National Resources Division's conference room until the VTC screen came to life. The screen blinked, and images of Dagmar Bhoti and Dr. Ellyn Stone came into sharp focus.

"Good morning," Bhoti said. "Thank you all for joining us at such an early hour. We seem to be making a habit of speaking at the oddest times of day and night. So, where do we stand with Bella?"

Caroline said, "Ma'am, I have two female NR officers keeping her company at the hotel right now. I spoke to Phil earlier, and we made our travel plans for today. I have the rental car already, and he's flying up as we speak. Once he arrives at the hotel, he and I will drive Bella straight back to Virginia. He has the address of the medical facility Dr. Stone specified. We'll have Bella admitted by late tomorrow afternoon."

"Good. How is she doing? She's been through more than I can imagine."

"She's doing well," Caroline answered, "all things considered. She ate a late dinner when we left the hospital and fell asleep quickly last night. The NR officers are there right now to ensure Bella doesn't wander off."

"Good. Thank you, Caroline. When Phil arrives, tell him to call me once you're out of New York City and then again when you cross the river into Virginia. If I'm not available when you call, just leave the messages with my secretary."

Caroline said she would.

Dagmar smiled, and said, "I want to thank both of you for your work on this case and congratulate each of you on doing such marvelous work and stopping the attack on New York. That was a phenomenal accomplishment and a real team effort. Well done! If there's anything else we at headquarters can do for you as you wrap this matter up, don't hesitate to ask."

Dagmar Bhoti ended the call, and the VTC screen went black.

Michelle glanced at Nino who sat silently, and then swiveled her chair to face Caroline. "So, where exactly *are* you taking Bella?"

"It's a residential treatment facility in Virginia," Caroline answered. "She'll get the medical and psychiatric care she needs to recover from the multiple traumas she suffered, both here in New York and back in Iraq."

"She deserves to get the best care possible, and I'd like to visit her. You know, so she has a friendly face to connect with. Where's the facility?"

"I'm sorry, Michelle, I can't tell you, but call me next week, and I'll fill you in as much as I can about her progress."

"So, in other words, you're taking her to a black site? Aren't *you* the one who said we don't do that anymore?"

Caroline's eyes opened wide. "It is *not* a black site, Michelle. Bella needs help."

"*Hmm,*" Michelle said, and pointed at the CI officer. "Let me get this straight. You're taking her to a facility that's off the grid, won't tell anyone she knows that she's there, you'll probably check her in her under a false name, are going to pump her full of psychoactive drugs, and then interrogate her about whether or not she's a spy or joined ISIS or something equally nasty during her two years of captivity. How can *that* course of action make it sound like anything *other* than an interrogation at a black site?"

Caroline shrugged, and said, "Because we're the good guys, and it's for her own good."

Michelle sighed and shook her head slowly. "Do you honestly think she turned?"

"I don't know what to think."

"Well, *I* think she's a hero. Without her, there'd be thousands of corpses littering the streets of New York City right now. I think she proved herself beyond question."

"Nino," Caroline asked, "what do *you* think?"

"The Bella Cirrone I knew two years ago in Baghdad was an excellent case officer with a bright future. I never had reason to think she could be coerced to work for the opposition. Feel free to talk to anyone who worked in Baghdad Station at the time. Or anyone else who's ever known her, for that matter, and I'm sure you'll hear much of the same."

"I will," van der Pol replied. "Who else should I speak to?"

"Well," Michelle added, "you won't get to interrogate Wasif or Noor."

"No," Caroline agreed solemnly.

"And Achmed and his wives are dead, too."

Caroline nodded, and said, "I gather we have you to thank for that."

Michelle thought briefly about what the CI officer meant by her comment and decided to let it go. "No real firsthand witnesses left, are there?"

Nino said, "No, and that being the case, it seems as though Bella's version of the story will be the one to become the official record."

Michelle nodded, and said, "That works just fine for me. Hero it is."

Chapter 38

Arlington, Virginia

Michelle stretched out to her full length on her living room sofa and yawned. She pushed her bare feet into a throw pillow, pinning it to the armrest with her toes. She feared it might take her a week to unwind from the uncomfortable seat in which she half-slept/half-squirmed throughout her nearly four-hour Amtrak ride home.

Six weeks of living on the road and doing laundry in one hotel or another left its mark on her. She debated whether she should wash her two suitcases full of clothes, throw them out without even unpacking or just burn them in her condo's courtyard. The friends she'd made in the FDNY might have helped her with the third option, but she feared their Arlington brethren might not be nearly as understanding.

Her cell phone vibrated on the coffee table. The Caller ID flashed her boss's name on the screen. She jabbed her finger on the green button, and said, "Hi, Michael. How've you been?"

"Fine, Michelle. Long time, no hear. Are you home yet?"

"Yeah, I got in about a half hour ago, but I haven't made it past the sofa. It's good to be home. What's up? Checking up on me?"

"No, not specifically. I have a new mission coming up for you, but you don't have to brief until next week. Alex took two weeks of leave and went to Spain to visit his grandparents. He won't get back until Saturday, anyway. You should take the rest of the week off and rest up. I just wanted to hear your voice and ask you to join us in the office on Monday morning."

The condo's front door opened, and the alarm gave three soft beeps. Dr. Steven Krauss walked in and dropped his tan attaché case on the hallway floor. He stumbled over the pair of suitcases splayed across the hallway floor as he hurried to the living room to greet Michelle.

Michelle pointed to the cell phone in her hand, and said, "Okay, Michael. I'll see you on Monday."

She ended the call and placed the phone back onto the coffee table. She jumped up and hugged Krauss firmly. "*Oooh*, I've missed you."

"You, too," he said, and squeezed Michelle tightly around her waist. "So, you saved the world, eh?"

"No, no," Michelle said, and leaned her entire body into the welcoming hug. "I was just one of the team. This time we had quite the cast of thousands involved in the terrorism task force. There were a couple of CIA officers, a bazillion FBI agents, a handful of Air Force pilots, who knows how many NYPD detectives, and even the fire department got involved. Everyone and their brother seemed to get in on the action at one point or another."

Steve led Michelle to the sofa, and they sat down. He said, "And you got to run an agent, you said on the phone. One of our undercover officers?"

"Well, sort of. A case officer named Nino served as her formal handler. I just helped wherever I could. I learned a lot from him."

Steve looked at her sideways, and asked, "Nino *Balducci*?"

"Uh huh. You know him?"

"Everyone knows him. He's been around forever. He's famous throughout the Agency, or at least as famous as someone can be and still maintain his cover. He's been assigned to most — maybe all — of the stations in Europe at one time or another."

"Well," Michelle said, "he's good. I'll give him that."

"And now you get a week off? Finally, some time to relax and unwind. You missed the holidays," Steve said as he stood up and walked across the room, "but I saved something for you."

From the dining room table, he lifted two stacked, wrapped boxes topped with a bright red bow and handed the gifts to Michelle.

"*Aww*, sweetie, you shouldn't have. I've been so caught up in work, I didn't have time to get you anything. But I have the rest of the week off, so I have plenty of time to go shopping."

"That's all right," Steve said. "Just having you back is the perfect gift."

"That's nice and all, but I'm still going to get you something special."

Michelle leaned over and kissed him. She backed away slowly, pulled the wrapping paper and bow from the top box, and smiled wildly as she opened her gift.

That night as they climbed into bed, Michelle pulled back their faded blue bedspread and got under the covers. She laid her hand on Steven's chest, settled her head onto her favorite spot on his shoulder, closed her eyes feeling peaceful and safe and smiled.

ABOUT THE AUTHOR

Scott Shinberg has served in leadership positions across the US Government and industry for over twenty-five years. He has worked in and with the US Air Force, the Department of Homeland Security, the Federal Bureau of Investigation, and most "Three-Letter Agencies." While in government service, he served as an Air Force Intelligence Operations Officer and a Special Agent with the FBI. He lives in Virginia with his wife and sons.

Website: www.ScottShinberg.com
Facebook: @ScottShinbergAuthor
Twitter: @Author_Scott

WHAT'S NEXT?

Don't miss the next thrilling installment of this series, which is perfect for fans of Tom Clancy, Robert Ludlum, Dean Koontz, Brad Meltzer, and Len Deighton.

SARGON THE THIRD
Michelle Reagan – Book 4
(Available Now)

A SHOT IN THE DARK
Michelle Reagan – Book 5
(Available Now)

KILL BOX
Michelle Reagan – Book 6
(Releases in Late 2022 or Early 2023)

To remain up to date for plans and schedules related to this book, and to all works by Scott Shinberg, please subscribe to his newsletter at:
www.ScottShinberg.com

MORE FROM SCOTT SHINBERG

Is *Confessions of Eden* drawn from today's headlines, or are the headlines drawn from what little is visible of Eden's footprints?

CONFESSIONS OF EDEN
Michelle Reagan – Book 1

Michelle Reagan—code name Eden—is the CIA Special Activities Division's newest covert action operator, an assassin, who struggles between wanting to succeed in her new profession for herself and her charismatic boss, and the moral quandaries of what she must do to innocent people who are simply in the wrong place at the wrong time. Although she faces seemingly intractable decisions as she executes her missions across the globe, the adversary most difficult to overcome may very well be her own conscience.

Through it all, only one man has ever called her an 'assassin' to her face. Someday, if she has her way, she'll marry him—if she lives that long.

WINNER: Pinnacle Book Achievement Award - Best Spy Thriller
WINNER: Literary Titan Book Awards - Gold Medal

"This novel is purpose-driven; it is written for those who enjoy action, but the strength of the characters is one of the irresistible elements of this well-crafted thriller. ... Fast-paced and filled with action, it is one of those books you feel compelled to read nonstop."
~ *Christian Sia, Readers' Favorite Book Reviews (5 STARS)*

"For fans of crime and espionage, *Confessions of Eden* comes across as a tour de force in entertainment."
~ *Romuald Dzemo, Readers' Favorite Book Reviews (5 STARS)*

MORE FROM EVOLVED PUBLISHING

We offer great books across multiple genres, featuring high-quality editing (which we believe is second-to-none) and fantastic covers.

As a hybrid small press, your support as loyal readers is so important to us, and we have strived, with tireless dedication and sheer determination, to deliver on the promise of our motto:
QUALITY IS PRIORITY #1!

Please check out all of our great books,
which you can find at this link:
www.EvolvedPub.com/Catalog/

Thank you!

CPSIA information can be obtained
at www.ICGtesting.com
Printed in the USA
LVHW050624260523
748013LV00005B/583

9 781622 537105